BUT NOT FORSAKEN

A CLINT WOLF NOVEL
(BOOK 3)

BY

BJ BOURG

WWW.BJBOURG.COM

TITLES BY BJ BOURG

LONDON CARTER MYSTERY SERIES

James 516

Proving Grounds

Silent Trigger

Bullet Drop

Elevation

Blood Rise

CLINT WOLF MYSTERY SERIES

But Not Forgotten

But Not Forgiven

But Not Forsaken

But Not Forever

But Not For Naught

But Not Forbidden

But Not Forlorn

But Not Formidable

BUT NOT FORSAKEN
A Clint Wolf Novel by BJ Bourg

Cover design by Christine Savoie of Bayou Cover Designs

PUBLISHED IN THE UNITED STATES OF AMERICA

CHAPTER 1

20 years earlier…

Monday, July 24
Chateau Parish, Louisiana

Jolene giggled as she crawled from the back of her white 1995 Escalade and dropped her bare feet to the ground. Although it was nearly ten o'clock in the evening, the dirt was still warm from the heat of the day.

"Get back in here," her boyfriend called, reaching for her arm, but missing.

Screeching, Jolene hurried around to the front of the SUV, where the headlights lit up the cane fields in front of them. She stopped in the direct glow of the lights and smiled coyly. Lifting her arms to the sky, she stood with her eyes closed, allowing the light to wash across her pale body. She made no attempt to cover her breasts or her genital area. "God, you make me feel so free!"

She screeched again when she heard her boyfriend running toward her. She opened her eyes just in time to see him wrap his arms around her nude body and gently tackle her to the ground. They fell into a patch of soft grass and her laughter was cut short by his strong mouth on hers. She moaned as they kissed. When their lips separated, she looked up into his troubled eyes. "What's wrong, honey?"

He frowned, rolled off of her, and sat on the ground to her right. "It's nothing."

Jolene recognized that look. "It is something. I can tell." She sat up and leaned her soft breasts against his hard back, her mouth brushing the back of his ear. "You promised to never keep anything from me."

He sighed. "I know. It's just that…"

She waited for him to finish, but he didn't. "What is it, sweetie?"

"I hate that you're married."

"I hate it, too." She wrapped her arms around him and kissed the back of his neck. "If I can help it, I won't be married for long."

He pulled her arms away and stood. "That's what you said two months ago."

"Well, these things take time. Divorces are never easy, you know." She pulled herself to her feet and returned to the back of the Escalade. While her boyfriend sulked, she began pulling on her clothes. "I have to get back home."

"The bastard's at a conference—why do you need to hurry home?" He scowled. "You're always running off, even when he's not around. Sometimes I think you've got a number two on the side."

Jolene clipped her black bra in place and turned to face him, pulling at her breasts to make them comfortable in the cups. "After all we've been through I can't believe you'd even suggest that. You know I love you."

He was thoughtful, but said nothing. Jolene stepped forward and hugged him, repeating that she loved him. He sighed. "I know. I'm sorry. But why do you have to leave? I thought we'd be able to spend all kinds of time together when he was gone."

"Knowing him, he'll call the house to make sure I'm home." She shrugged into her red camisole and slipped her sandals on. "And if I don't answer, he'll have someone drive by the house to check on me."

Her boyfriend's shoulders drooped, but he nodded his understanding. "Okay. Will I see you tomorrow?"

She smiled. "Of course, you will." After kissing him one last time, she jumped into the Escalade and waved as he entered his pickup truck. As was their custom, he followed her along the bumpy cane field road and then most of the way home to be sure she made it safely. He flashed his headlights when he reached the bridge that marked his turnoff, and she responded with two taps of the brake. She smiled as she watched him wave his arm out of the truck. It was nice to have someone want her so much. All her husband cared about was his career and his image. He wanted the perfect house, the perfect cars, the perfect wife, the perfect family. She grunted. It would be a cold summer day in Louisiana before she gave him a child.

When Jolene got home thirty minutes later, she hurried up the sidewalk and rushed through the front door, checking the telephone to see if her husband had called. She sighed when there were no missed calls. She'd spoken with him right before she left to meet her boyfriend and had told him she was going into the shower. That would've bought her at least an hour and a half—he knew how she loved long baths.

Jolene glanced at the clock on the wall. It was almost eleven now. Her husband probably thought she was in bed and wouldn't bother her again tonight.

Still feeling weak from the orgasm she'd had earlier, she kicked off her shoes and walked on shaky legs to her bedroom. The blue plush carpet felt good on the bottoms of her feet. The bedroom was dark except for a night light in a corner outlet. Squinting to see better, she grabbed a set of night clothes from the top drawer in her mahogany dresser and placed them on the counter in the master bathroom. After lighting two candles and turning on the faucet in the Jacuzzi tub, she unbuttoned her jeans and started to push them—

"What the hell was that?" Jolene froze in place, trying to place the noise. It sounded as though something had fallen and she thought it came from the kitchen, but she couldn't be sure. Buttoning her jeans back, she took a cautious step toward her bedroom door and listened. Nothing. The hallway light was off, too. *Should I turn it on?* She decided against it. She was no tactical expert, but she was smart enough to know a light would only give away her location. Moving on the balls of her feet, she slowly made her way toward the end of the hall. She stopped a few feet from where it opened into the kitchen and waited. Still nothing.

Her heart pounded in her chest. Not knowing what to expect, she peeked around the wall and stared wide-eyed. She sighed when she realized the kitchen was empty. The refrigerator blocked her view of the back door, so she stepped into the kitchen just to make sure the knob was locked. As she rounded the corner, she stepped on something sharp.

"Ouch!" She leaned on the counter and lifted her foot. There was a small shard of glass protruding from a spot on her heel and a single drop of blood spilled from it. Pulling the piece of glass from her foot, she glanced at the floor and her heart stopped beating for a moment—broken glass littered the floor.

Jolene's eyes shot toward the door and she gasped when she saw that the window pane closest to the knob was busted. But that was nothing compared to the sheer terror that shocked her to her core when she saw a gloved hand reach through the broken window and grab the doorknob.

She smothered a scream in her throat and bolted for the bedroom, panic enveloping her every fiber. She had almost made it to the master bathroom door when something smacked her in back of the head and she collapsed on the carpeted floor. Her head pounded, but she pulled herself to her hands and knees and started crawling like a woman possessed, her fingernails clawing at the carpet. Diving forward the last few feet, she cleared the bathroom door and rolled to her back to kick it shut. Just before it slammed shut, she saw a shadowy figure reaching for the knob.

Jolene screamed and scrambled to her feet. With shaky hands, she desperately tried to twist the lock on the knob, but it was no use. The figure turned it and crashed it open, sending her flying backward. She landed hard against the side of the tub, and one of the candles sizzled out as it plopped into the bath water.

Her attacker stepped through the doorway and grabbed her ankles in a vice-like grip. She twisted onto her stomach and clutched at the ledge of the tub, but the person jerked her away and dragged her on her belly toward the bedroom. Her camisole rolled up high on her stomach as the attacker dragged her across the carpeted floor. When they reached the center of the dark bedroom, the person flipped her onto her back and straddled her. Her attacker's weight made it difficult for her to breathe and the face was covered by a makeshift mask and there was a large knife in the person's hand. Light from the one remaining candle glinted eerily off the blade. Tears flowed freely down her face now and she was trembling uncontrollably.

"Why? Oh, God! Why are you doing this?" she cried, trying to push her camisole down. "Please don't hurt me!"

Her attacker was breathing heavy and stared down at her. Setting the knife down on the floor, her attacker wrapped both hands around her throat and slowly applied pressure, as though enjoying the moment.

"No!" Jolene screamed, pushing at the person's hands. "Don't! Please don't!"

The attacker continued to squeeze and she felt her eyes bulge in their sockets as pressure filled her face. She kicked and squirmed, clawing at the gloved hands as best she could. Suddenly, her attacker drew a fist back and slammed it into her breast. She cried out in pain, but continued struggling to stop the person from choking her. The attacker struck her again, this time in the stomach, knocking the wind from her lungs. She gasped for air, pawing weakly at the sleeve on the person's shirt. "No," she wailed, tears causing her eyes to blur. "Please don't hurt me!"

The attacker returned to choking her and, in one desperate attempt to save herself, she leaned forward and punched the person on the side of the head. She immediately regretted it, because her hand stung and it only seemed to anger the person. Releasing the hold on her throat, the attacker leaned up and dropped one knee on her chest, crushing her. The attacker then grabbed a handful of hair with one hand and wrenched her head against a leg, exposing the opposite side of her neck. Groaning in anger, the attacker snatched up the knife with the opposite hand and placed the sharp point against the outside of her larynx.

Jolene screamed as the attacker shoved the knife into her flesh and through to the other side of her neck. Her eyes widened in disbelief and shock as she began gargling and struggling for air. She was fading fast, but aware enough to know she was drowning in her own blood.

CHAPTER 2

Twenty years later…

Monday, October 26
Susan Wilson's House – Mechant Loup, Louisiana

Susan Wilson moved lightly on the balls of her feet, circling the red punching bag like a mountain lion ready to pounce. She was a sergeant with the Mechant Loup Police Department by day, but at night she moonlighted as a cage fighter. Given a choice, she would choose fighting over police work any day of the week, and that probably had a lot to do with the fact that her dad had been a professional boxer when he was alive.

As Susan moved, the wooden porch creaked under her weight, but it provided just the right amount of bounce and the surface was just rough enough against her feet to replicate the canvas of a fighting cage. Her pink mixed martial arts gloves were worn from years of training, but she refused to replace them because they felt like a natural part of her hands. She kept them held high, ready to block any blows from her imaginary opponent.

Her brown hair was braided into cornrows and tied off into twin pigtails behind her head. She knew it wasn't the most attractive hairstyle—her mom had informed her of that fact more than a dozen times over the years—but it was practical. The sun was setting to the east over the swamps and there was a hint of coolness on the evening breeze—a sign that autumn was around the corner. While she had a lot to worry about, a smile tugged at the corners of her mouth as the wind caressed her face. She felt wild and free, training in the open air of her front porch. *If I just focus on staying in this moment,* she thought, *I can make it last forever.*

Long, tanned legs flexed under her fight shorts as she moved to the left, and then to the right, eyeing the bag with bad intentions. Without warning, she suddenly sprang forward and executed a violent combination of kicks and right punches that made the bag bend and swing under the impact of the blows. The chain that held the bag from the ceiling rattled its protest, but droned to a low creak as she circled away, looking for another opening in her imaginary opponent.

She'd been training for an hour and had managed to avoid throwing strikes with her left hand—despite how tempting it was. It was second nature for her to follow a straight right punch with a left hook, but she wanted the wound on her chest to heal so she could get back in the cage sooner, rather than later. She wasn't sure if that's what the doctor meant by "taking it easy", but she thought it was a hell of a compromise, because lying around and doing nothing was not an option.

Susan was about to explode into another combination when her cell phone rang. She thought about ignoring it, but then figured it might be work-related, so she ripped off her right glove and snatched the phone from the yellow bench against the wall. She glanced at the number and saw that it was Melvin Saltzman, one of her fellow officers.

"If you're not calling to offer up your body to the sweet science of me kicking your ass, then it had better be an emergency," she said. "I was fifteen rounds into a twenty-round workout and you know how much I hate to be interrupted."

Melvin stammered on the other end and finally managed an apology.

Susan laughed. "I'm kidding. What's up?"

Melvin was quiet for a long moment. When he spoke, she could tell he was troubled. "I know it's been a week, and all, but this thing with William still has me freaked out."

Susan sighed and sat on the bench, tugging her other glove off in the process. "Yeah. Me, too."

"I never saw it coming."

"None of us did, Melvin...none of us."

"If he can go bad..."

When Melvin didn't speak again for several seconds, Susan asked if he was still there.

"I'm here." After another pause, Melvin finally said, "If he can go bad, what's to keep me from going bad?"

Susan laughed. "Trust me, there's nothing bad about you."

"No, I'm serious. Beaver seemed like a good cop, but then he went and did what he did, and now William. What if I'm next?"

"Look, we might not have known they were bad, but they did...in their heart of hearts, they knew they were bad."

That seemed to satisfy Melvin and he turned the subject to work. "Do you miss me on the day shift?"

He was working the night shift with Amy Cooke, filling the spot that had been vacated by William Tucker's arrest. "Not one bit."

"I bet Chief Wolf misses me."

"Nope, Clint was telling me just today that he's glad..."

The humming of a car engine drew Susan's attention to the street that led to her house. It was a Chateau Parish Sheriff's Office patrol cruiser and it was followed by a state police car. There were two deputies in the patrol cruiser and one trooper inside the state car. They turned onto her dirt driveway and drove right up to the house, the three officers staring intently at her as they approached.

Melvin was still talking in Susan's ear, but she couldn't make out what he was saying. She stood slowly to her feet as the deputies stepped out of the cruiser and strode toward her porch steps. The trooper remained seated in his car, which aroused her curiosity.

"Can I help you?" Susan asked, as dread started to fill her throat with bile. Was it her mom? Had she been in a car accident? If so, why wasn't the trooper getting out of his car?

Melvin stopped rambling and asked what was going on.

One of the deputies cleared his throat. "Sergeant Wilson...um...I don't know how to say this in an easy way, so I'll just cut to it. District Attorney Bill Hedd just called and informed our office that you've been indicted by the grand jury for second degree murder. He ordered us to take you into custody immediately."

Susan's jaw dropped. "What the *hell?*"

The other deputy removed a set of handcuffs from a pouch behind his belt and stepped forward. "I'm sorry, Sarge, but you'll need to come with us."

Susan's mind raced. "Melvin, call Clint right away." She knew he would know what to do.

"I'm on it!" Melvin hollered.

The first deputy pulled the phone from her hand and tucked it into his pocket while the second deputy grabbed her left wrist. For a brief moment, Susan thought how easy it would be to strip her hand from the deputy's grip and knock him unconscious, but she quickly dismissed the idea. This battle would have to be fought in court—with lawyers. As the deputies pushed her arms behind her back, she lifted one of her feet. "Can I at least put on some shoes?"

"We'll get a pair for you when we lock up your house."

Susan glanced at the trooper, who had stepped out of his car and was standing beside it. "Why is he here?" she asked.

"He was in the area and came along in case you'd give us trouble."

Susan was numb as the deputies ratcheted the cuffs around her wrists and led her to the back seat of the patrol car. This was not the way her career was supposed to end, and for a brief moment she felt an overwhelming sense of failure. *Keep your chin up,* she told herself. *You did nothing wrong!*

CHAPTER 3

As soon as Melvin had called and given me the news about Susan's arrest, I'd jumped into my Tahoe and headed for Bill Hedd's house, leaving my girlfriend, Chloe Rushing, and my German shepherd, Achilles, wondering what was going on. I was angry that Bill hadn't given me a courtesy call. As Mechant Loup's police chief and Susan's supervisor, I should've been made aware that one of my officers was about to be arrested.

I turned left on Main Street and raced across the Mechant Loup Bridge, dialing Isabel Compton's cell phone as I drove. Isabel was Hedd's first assistant district attorney and one of only two allies I had in the DA's office. Her phone rang twice before a man picked up.

"This is Clint Wolf calling for Mrs. Compton," I said. "I'm the police chief for—"

"I know who you are, Chief," the man said. "I'm Izzy's husband. Hold on just a minute—she'll be right with you."

I only had to wait a few seconds for Isabel to pick up. "Dear God, Clint, I just found out about Susan."

"What's going on? Have you found out why he's doing this?"

"I have no clue. I just got off the phone with Reggie and he's at a loss, too. He said he didn't even know it was going down until one of his buddies from the sheriff's office called him." There was a pause and then Isabel asked me what I was going to do.

"I don't know," was all I said, and then disconnected the call. I tossed my phone to the center console and placed both hands on the steering wheel, gripping it so hard my knuckles were white.

I was several miles north of Mechant Loup when my phone rang. I glanced at it and saw Chloe's name displayed on the screen. I didn't answer. I was too angry to talk and I needed time to figure out what I was going to say once I got to the district attorney's house. I didn't think anything would change his mind, but I had to try. And whatever I did, I knew I needed to be levelheaded, because Susan's future and her freedom hung in the balance.

When I finally arrived at his house in Western Chateau, I coasted up the long and curvy driveway—passing two large ponds and several ancient oaks on the way—and brought my Tahoe to a stop in front of the cobblestone steps that led to the giant brick home. Taking a deep breath, I jumped from the driver's seat and jogged up the steps. Within a minute of knocking, I heard heavy footsteps approaching from the other side of the door. They came to a stop and I figured Hedd was looking through the peephole. I tilted my head down, hoping he couldn't see me, but it was no use and he didn't care. He flung the door open and bellowed, "What in hell's name are you doing at my house?"

"Sir, I was hoping to have a word with you." I shoved my hands deep into the pockets of my jeans to let him know I wasn't there for trouble. "If it's okay with you, that is."

The hard lines in his face softened a little and he ran a hand through his Elvis Presley hairdo. "It's late. What do you want?"

"It's about Susan," I began, still not sure what to say. "I was hoping you'd reconsider your decision to charge her with murder. She was only doing her job and she saved my life. She was justified by law to use deadly force to protect—"

"If you're going to try and lecture me on the law, I'll end this conversation right now," Bill said, his thick jowls flapping as he spoke. "I don't need the sermon and I certainly don't need some cop telling me how to do my job."

"You're right." My eyes must've been bloodshot and I knew there was smoke coming out of my ears. "Can you please reconsider your decision to charge her with murder?"

"Sorry," he said, a smug look on his face, "but it wasn't my decision. The grand jury indicted her—not me. It's really out of my hands."

"But you could dismiss the charges if you wanted to."

"There you go again trying to tell me how to do my job." Bill grinned, but his eyes remained cold. "I tell you what...if you don't like the job I'm doing, why don't you run against me in the next election? Oh, wait a minute...you're not qualified to be DA." Bill stepped back into his house and reached for the door. "Now get off my property."

"Why are you doing this?"

He paused, leaning against the doorframe. "Because it's my job to put murderers away."

I pulled my hands from my pockets and clenched my fists, a move that didn't go unnoticed. Bill squinted. "You'd better think long and hard about your next move, son," he said. "Every wrong move you make is going to cost Susan more years behind bars."

It took everything in me to turn and walk away, but that's exactly what I did. I was so angry I thought my eyes would start bleeding, but I was thinking clear enough to head to the Chateau Parish Detention Center. I arrived just as the arresting deputies were preparing to remove Susan from the back seat of their cruiser. A state police car was parked behind them and a trooper was watching as they removed the seatbelt from around Susan.

I left my door open and bolted from my SUV, calling out to Susan as I hurried to their location. The trooper spun around when he heard me. One hand was on his weapon and the other hand was extended out in my direction.

"Sir, stop right there!" he commanded in a loud voice. "Back away slowly!"

I stopped, but didn't back up. I introduced myself and pointed to Susan. "That's my officer in the squad car. I intend to speak with her before they bring her inside."

The trooper moved forward in a menacing manner and stopped when he was a few feet from me. "You will not have any interaction with the prisoner. Is that understood?"

I glanced down. There was a SWAT pin attached to his uniform shirt, but I hardly noticed it because my eyes were fixated on his nametag. I recognized the name immediately—he was the state police SWAT cop who shot Achilles when they raided my house last Fourth of July. I'd thought long and hard about what I would do when our paths ever crossed, and most of those fantasies ended with him on the ground bleeding.

"You're the little prick who shot my dog!" I looked up from his nametag and fixed him with cold eyes. "I've been looking forward to the day I run into you."

In my peripheral vision, I saw the two deputies straighten and look in our direction. The trooper's face turned a shade whiter. "Chief, look, I…I swear it was an accident. He came out of nowhere and his bark…it…he sounded so big and I didn't know what was going on. I love dogs and I really—"

"You shot his dog?" one of the deputies asked incredulously.

The trooper stammered. "I…I didn't mean to."

"That's some bullshit," the other deputy said, waving me forward. I don't know if he really felt bad for me or if it was the diplomat in him merely trying to diffuse a problem, but he said, "For that, I'll give you two minutes with Sergeant Wilson, but I'll want to search you first. You know, just for our protection."

I nodded my understanding and then glared one last time at the trooper, who turned and hurried toward his car. I held out my hands while the deputy frisked me. When he was satisfied, I slid into the back seat of his squad car, next to Susan. It broke my heart to see her in the back of a patrol cruiser with her hands cuffed behind her back. She was wearing workout clothes and her feet were bare. "Are you okay?" I asked.

I knew she must've been upset—*had* to be—but she forced a smile. I realized she was probably doing that more for my benefit than her own. "My nose itches," she said, "but I'm fine otherwise."

I reached out to scratch her nose, but she cocked her head sideways and smirked. "That was a handcuff joke, Clint."

"How can you joke at a time like this?"

"What other options do I have? Cry? Get angry?" She shook her head. "I don't know what I did to Hedd, but I won't give him the satisfaction of seeing me sweat. I know that my actions were justified, and I'll never apologize for it or regret it. Hell, I'd do it again tomorrow."

My chest flooded with admiration as I stared into her dark brown eyes. I doubted I could be as courageous in a similar situation, and I hated that she was there because of me. "How can you be so calm?"

"Clint, I'm terrified on the inside, but I won't let that bastard know it and he'll never break me."

"Well, I'm getting you out of here."

Susan shot a glance at the two deputies who stood nearby watching us. "What're you going to do about them?"

I shook my head as a smile played across her mouth, pushing her dimple deep into her cheek. "I'm bonding you out and then hiring the best lawyer around. You're not going down for saving my life."

"Where will you get a million dollars?"

I gasped. "Your bond's a *million* dollars?"

"It is."

I sank back in my seat. Where in the hell was I going to come up with that much money? Like a fool, I'd put up my entire savings as reward money for a previous case, and it would take me at least a year to build it back up. Of course, that still wouldn't be enough to bond her out. As I sat there thinking, one of the deputies approached my door and waved for me to get out of the car. "We need to bring her inside, Chief."

I looked back at Susan and nodded. "I won't rest until I get you out of here."

She smiled. "I appreciate it, Clint, but I don't want you borrowing money for this. I'll have my day in court and the truth will come out then."

"That could be a year from now—you can't stay in jail for a year!"

"I don't have much choice, now do I?"

A thought suddenly came to me. "I might know a way—"

"Chief," the deputy said in a stern voice, "we need to go...*now*."

CHAPTER 4

It was late when I got home, but Chloe was wide awake. "I tried calling you a bunch of times," she said.

I sank to the sofa and rubbed Achilles' head as I recounted everything that had happened. Chloe gasped when I mentioned Susan's arrest. "Are you kidding? She was *arrested*?"

"Please don't report that. It'll get out eventually—it's unavoidable—but I don't want it coming from you."

She was thoughtful, but finally nodded. We talked for a few minutes longer and then got ready for bed. I poured myself a glass of vodka—she had mentioned before that it looked better than drinking from the bottle—and took a long drink before spreading a blanket on the floor beside the bed.

"What's with the blanket?" she wanted to know.

"I can't sleep on a bed while Susan's sleeping on a jail cot for simply saving my life."

I finished drinking my glass of vodka and stretched out on the hard floor, sighing as I did so. It had been a bad day and I wanted it to be over. I glanced over at Chloe, who stood looking down at me. There was a weird expression on her face. "What is it?" I asked. "Why are you looking at me like that?"

"Are you really sleeping on the floor?"

"Absolutely."

"For how long?"

"Until I can get her out of jail."

"But you said the bond was a million dollars."

I nodded. "It is."

"You're going to be on that floor for a long time."

"Not if I have my say." I nodded positively. "I have a plan to get the money."

One of Chloe's eyebrows arched upward. "Prostitution is still illegal in the South."

I grinned. "I wouldn't be able to raise enough to buy a movie ticket, much less twelve percent of a million."

"I don't know," Chloe said, eyeing me seductively. "I'd pay top dollar for—"

"Anyway," I interrupted, "the plantation home is in Michele's name. Since she purchased it while we were married, I'm the sole owner and can do whatever I want with it."

"But she didn't really purchase it."

I shrugged. "It doesn't matter—she was the legal owner and now I am."

"Even if you put it on the market, it could take months or years to sell—if ever. The economy's not in the best shape right now."

"I'm not putting it on the market. I'm going to offer it to Pauline Cain for a quarter mil. She can afford it and she's mentioned wanting to reclaim that property someday." I nodded, pleased with myself for coming up with the idea. Mrs. Cain would be getting the property back for half what her husband sold it for, and I'd have plenty of money to get Susan out of jail and hire a good lawyer.

"I sure hope you know what you're doing." Chloe shook her head and walked into the bathroom, turning off the bedroom light as she went.

I just lay there staring at the ceiling, waiting for the alcohol to take effect before allowing my eyes to drift shut. I didn't dare close them too early.

My lips were starting to feel numb when the bathroom door opened and Chloe's bare feet padded toward me. She stopped when she was above me and dropped to her knees, sidling up beside me.

I stirred and turned toward her. "What're you doing?"

"I sleep where you sleep," she said.

I smiled and felt myself drifting off.

CHAPTER 5

I got to the police department early the next morning and found Melvin and Amy sitting around the dispatcher's desk sulking. Lindsey, our daytime dispatcher, had just relieved Marsha and was sitting in her chair staring blankly at the floor. Amy tucked a lock of blonde hair behind her ear and looked over at me. "What do we need to do to get her out?"

I told them my plan and their eyes lit up.

"That's awful nice of you, Chief," Melvin said. "I was talking to Claire about getting a loan, but she said we're already noted out." He sighed. "I didn't realize having a kid could be so expensive."

I was about to leave when the front door opened and a small-framed woman walked inside. She was in her late fifties and I immediately recognized her as Susan's mother, Lisa Wilson. Her hair was dark like Susan's but streaked in white. Other than the hair and brown eyes, she was nothing like Susan. Her movements were unsure—timid, even—and she looked frail.

When Mrs. Wilson saw us in our police uniforms—the same uniform her daughter wore—she broke down crying. I rushed to her and wrapped her in my arms. As I held her, I assured her everything was going to be okay and that I would get Susan out of jail.

"It's my fault she's in there!" Mrs. Wilson wailed. "I did this to her."

I heard a collective gasp behind me as I hurried and ushered the crying woman into my office. I kicked the door shut behind me and showed her to one of the chairs in front of my desk. I slid the other chair close to her and sat facing her. I pushed some of the clutter on my desk aside and grabbed a tissue. I handed it to her and put a hand on her shoulder, trying to calm her down. After about ten minutes, she finally wiped her face and took a shaky breath. "I…I think I'm okay now," she said, nodding for emphasis.

"Take your time," I said, but didn't mean it. I was wondering what she had done to get Susan arrested and I wanted to know right away. "You don't have to talk until you're ready."

Sniffling, she nodded again. "I'm ready."

I sat there staring at her, waiting, but she didn't speak. She just stared through bloodshot eyes at the floor. "Ma'am, you said it's your fault Susan got arrested. What did you mean?"

She turned her blank eyes in my direction. "I should've never gone on that dating website. I knew God would judge me for committing the sin of lust."

Confused, I asked her to explain.

Through sniffles and more crying, she said she had gone onto a dating website and searched for single men in the area. She came across a man named "Billy" who mentioned in his profile that he was hesitant to put up a picture because of his job. She was hesitant to put up a picture as well, so she felt they had at least that in common.

"I sent him a simple message at first," she said after pausing to blow her nose. "I saw he was from Chateau Parish, so I wrote and told him I was from here, too. We exchanged messages for a few days and then he asked me for a picture."

"Did you send him one?"

"I asked him to send one first, and he did. That's when I realized who he was." She broke out sobbing again. "I figured it was safe, you know? He's the district attorney, for goodness sakes. I never dreamed it would turn into this."

I shook my head involuntarily, trying to clear it. I thought I heard her say the man was the district attorney, but I knew that couldn't be correct. "Wait—what'd you say?"

Blubbering, she said, "It was District Attorney Bill Hedd."

My curiosity was fully aroused now. Did she reject him and he took his revenge out on Susan? I knew some men were sensitive that way. Was he holding Susan's freedom hostage, hoping Mrs. Wilson would come begging for her release? I'd heard of stranger things. I reached out and squeezed her shoulder. "Go on, ma'am…what does this have to do with Susan?"

She threw up her hands. "I don't know!" Tears sprayed from her lips and streaked my face as she spoke. She mumbled an apology and I smiled my forgiveness, wiping them away with the shoulder of my uniform.

I had to wait another long minute before she explained that the 'relationship' progressed to an in-person date, and they met at a diner on the west side of Chateau. "He was quite the gentleman, and very well known. Everyone stopped to tell him hello and he would introduce me as his date." Mrs. Wilson smiled and shook her head. "I haven't felt beautiful in twenty years," she confessed. "I was completely swept off my feet. He offered to follow me home to make sure I was safe. I almost rejected the offer, but something told me it was okay, that he was a gentleman. When he walked me to my doorstep, I decided to invite him in for a cup of coffee."

The smile faded as she explained how he was milling around looking at pictures on the wall and making small talk while she brewed some Community coffee. He saw a picture of Susan in uniform and asked if she was her daughter. When Mrs. Wilson told him she was, he told her he knew of Susan and said she was a good cop. "That's when he saw the picture I have of Susan and her father. I tell you, he turned into a different man right there before my very eyes. His face was red and he asked if the man in the picture was Isaiah Wilson. When I told him it was, he went to cursing and saying things I'd never repeat. He got really angry. I was terrified. He even called me an awful name for being married to him."

She stopped to take a breath and it was then that I realized I had been holding mine. I exhaled and asked her what happened next.

"He stormed out," she said. "He just left without saying another word and I never saw him again. Well, until yesterday on the television when he gave that press conference announcing…" Mrs. Wilson buried her face in her hands and continued crying.

My mind raced as I rubbed her shoulder. So, the DA's beef wasn't with Susan—it was with Susan's dad. But what had Isaiah done to Bill to make him want to go after Susan?

"Mrs. Wilson, when was it that you and Mr. Hedd went on the date?"

Still crying, she managed to say, "Three months ago, on the Fourth of July."

Two days before my thirty-first birthday and almost exactly a year after Susan had saved my life. I pursed my lips. I always thought it strange that a district attorney would wait over a year after an officer-involved shooting to convene a grand jury. Now I knew why he waited. "What did your husband do to make Mr. Hedd so angry that he would go after his offspring?"

"I have no idea."

I asked a few more questions about mutual friendships or possible run-ins they might have had with each other, but she knew of nothing. I was thoughtful for a moment, and then asked, "Did Isaiah have any friends—anyone who can tell me anything at all about his relationship with Bill?"

"He's been gone from us so long I doubt any of his friends are still around, or that they would even remember anything."

"Please…it might help get Susan out of this trouble."

Mrs. Wilson frowned and the wrinkles on her forehead grew deeper. I was guessing she didn't want me delving into their past. Finally, she sighed and nodded. "Okay, if it'll help Susan. His best friend was Damian Conner, a guy from the boxing gym. Damian knew everything about Isaiah—even things I didn't know—and I often thought he was a bad influence."

When I asked what made her say he was a bad influence, she refused to elaborate, so I said, "Where can I find him?"

She shrugged. "Like I said, I'm not sure if he's still around, but he used to hang out at the boxing gym in northern Chateau. Someone over there might be able to tell you more."

I hesitated, wondering if I should ask the next question. I had thought about asking Susan many times, but could never bring myself to do it. I'd always figured she would tell me if she wanted me to know, but she never did, so I figured it was none of my business. This time I had to make it my business—just in case it was somehow connected to her imprisonment. "Ma'am, I hate to ask this, but how did your husband die?"

"He…he died in his locker room after a fight. January will make twenty-one years since he's passed." Mrs. Wilson rubbed her swollen eyes. "I wasn't even there with him when he died, but Susan was. She saw it all."

My mouth slowly dropped open. "Susan was there when her dad died?"

"Not with my blessing, she wasn't. Our biggest argument— outside of him keeping late hours—was him taking Susan to that awful gym. I didn't want her in that atmosphere, but Isaiah was as hardheaded as they come and he wouldn't take no for an answer." Mrs. Wilson explained that Isaiah would get Susan all excited about going to the gym and, when she would object, he would make her feel like the bad one.

I nodded my understanding. "Susan has mentioned before that she picked up fighting from her dad."

"Oh, she adored everything he did and wanted to be just like him." Mrs. Wilson wiped a tear and shook her head. "I should've fought harder to keep her away, but I didn't want to be a killjoy, you know? I just wanted my little girl to be happy, so I let her go with him time and again. Before I knew it, they were both spending more time at the gym than they did at home."

Mrs. Wilson took a break from talking and stared at the floor for a long moment while I envisioned a young Susan bouncing around a boxing gym, throwing punches and kicks at an imaginary opponent. I'd seen more than one of her cage fights and it was readily apparent she had her father's blood.

When Susan's mother cleared her throat, she explained how, on the night of Isaiah's death, Susan was alone with him in the locker room when he collapsed. "Susan blamed herself for his death," she explained. "She said if she would've known what to do, she could've saved him. I tried to explain to her over the years that she was only twelve and there's no way she could've known what to do."

I was horrified as I imagined Susan being alone with her dead father. I remembered how helpless and lost I felt when I was alone with Michele and Abigail when they were murdered, but I was a grown man and a seasoned homicide detective. Susan was a little girl.

"No child should have to go through such a horrible event at such an early age," Mrs. Wilson said. There was a hint of bitterness in her voice. "I blame Isaiah for the pain she had to endure."

"I'm sorry for bringing it up," I mumbled, feeling there might be more to her anger with Isaiah. The poor man was dead and she was talking about him like she hated him.

"It's okay," she said. "If it'll help bring Susan home, I'll answer any questions you might have."

I interpreted her comment as a green light to delve a little deeper into the apparent resentment she felt for Isaiah. "Is there a reason you weren't at his fight when he died?"

"How would you like to watch someone punching your wife in the face and beating her half to death?"

I just stared at her, not knowing how to answer the question without disclosing that my wife *was* dead. When I didn't say anything, she nodded and said, "I thought not. I didn't like it either and I refused to be a part of it."

She explained that Isaiah decided to start boxing to supplement his income at the shipyard. His coach said he was a natural and it wasn't long before he was lined up to fight an exhibition match against a local professional boxer from a rival club who was undefeated after six fights.

"He won that match and they decided to let him turn professional even though he didn't have an amateur career." She grunted. "I was so angry with him. What responsible father takes up boxing at that age and selfishly risks his life and the livelihood of his family? And for six hundred dollars! It's not like they were paying him hundreds of thousands of dollars." She shook her head. "No, he died for nothing...absolutely nothing."

I wanted to ask for more details surrounding his death, but decided it was best saved for another time, or another witness. "Thank you for coming—"

"And you know what's the worst thing of all?" she asked, spitting the words. "He taught Susan to fight and then just died on her, leaving her to think she had to somehow continue his legacy—to make him proud." Tears started rolling down her cheeks again. "I feel so guilty for not going to her fights, but I can't bear watching my baby girl getting hit. And now, every time she fights, I just sit there by the phone having a panic attack, scared to death that the same thing will happen to her. It's so unnerving."

"Did you ever tell her how you feel?" I asked.

She frowned, shaking her head through the tears. "She loves what she does...I can't ask her to give that up. I just want her to be happy, so I suffer quietly—all alone. If you have kids, you know how it is."

I nodded, not knowing what to say, and she just hung her head and kept crying. I began to feel uncomfortable and started to wonder if she would be able to drive herself home. I was about to step out and ask Amy for some guidance when my phone chirped to indicate I'd received a text message. The noise seemed to snap Mrs. Wilson out of the moment. She took a deep breath and stood to her feet, wiping her face with the wet tissue she'd been holding. I stood with her and offered her several more pieces. She accepted them and took her time wiping her eyes and face. When she was ready, she held out her hand. "Chief, please bring my baby girl home. She's all I have left in this world."

"Ma'am, I won't stop until her name is cleared—that I can assure you." I walked her to the front door of the police department and watched her walk down the sidewalk toward her car. When she was gone, I shut the door and turned back toward Amy and Melvin, fishing my phone from my pocket as I did so. I felt them staring at me and I knew they were curious about my conversation with Mrs. Wilson. Lindsey was sitting behind her desk with her nose stuck in a book, but I noticed her eyes weren't moving.

I was about to start telling them what she'd said, but froze when I looked at my phone. The message was from Jennifer Duval, who was my old detective partner from the City of La Mort, and it wasn't good. My stomach turned and my blood boiled as I read the message:

Clint, sorry to have to tell you this, but because of a speedy trial motion filed by the defense, a judge released the Parkers from jail late yesterday afternoon. The ADA handling the case was trying to hold them in jail for a couple more weeks, but was unable to. The jail should've notified you by now, but I just found out and thought you should know. So sorry! Please be careful!!!

CHAPTER 6

I wanted to throw my phone across the room, but I resisted the urge. The jail had not bothered to notify me, nor had the prosecutor. I considered calling them and giving them a piece of my mind, but I had to get Susan out of jail. I grunted at the reversal—three murderous thugs who deserved nothing less than the death penalty were now walking free, while a good cop who saved my life was sitting in a jail cell for simply doing her job—and shoved my phone back in my pocket.

I turned to Melvin and Amy, who were waiting as patiently as they could. Amy was chewing on her bottom lip and had her arms crossed in front of her chest. The top three buttons of her tan uniform shirt were unbuttoned and it was open at the neck, exposing more cleavage than most of the town's God-fearing women liked. "Well?" she asked. "What did Susan's mom do to get her locked up?"

I sighed and took a seat at the corner of Lindsey's desk, giving myself a moment to push the news about the Parker brothers out of my head. I also had to think up a strategy, an attack plan. If I mishandled this investigation, things could go south—*deep* south— in a hurry.

When I was ready, I recounted what Mrs. Wilson had told me. "We need to find out what happened between Susan's dad and the DA," I said. "If we can prove Bill has a personal vendetta against the Wilson family, we can get him removed from the case and maybe even have the grand jury findings overturned." I paused, looking Melvin in the eyes first and then Amy. "This investigation can get real ugly real fast. Bill's the most powerful man in the parish."

Melvin rubbed his freshly shaved head and whistled. "I never thought I'd be investigating the district attorney of Chateau Parish. This is some heavy shit."

I nodded. "It's not good, that's for sure, but we need to help

Susan. She did nothing wrong—and it's not just us saying so. His own first assistant and chief investigator believe Susan's innocent."

"But even they are too scared to say anything," Amy said.

I nodded. "You're right, and I can't ask y'all to go to war with me. At best, this is career suicide. At worst…hell, I don't even know how bad it can get."

"I'm in," said Amy. "Susan's as solid as they come and she'd do the same for us."

"You already know I'm in," Melvin said. "I'd die for Susan."

I nodded and pointed to Melvin. "Get on the computer and run everything you can on Bill Hedd and Susan's dad. His name is Isaiah Wilson. Check former addresses, business affiliates, licenses, assets, employment history—everything you can think of. I want to know if there are any connections between the two of them."

Melvin was writing as fast as his hand could move. When I finished talking, he nodded and hurried off to the far corner of the room where his desk was situated against the wall. Without looking up, he attacked his keyboard with the fury of a man on a mission.

I turned to Amy. "Are you familiar with a boxing gym in the north?"

"I know where it is."

"Good…go there and try to find this Damian Conner fellow and find out everything he knows about Isaiah and Bill. When you're done, let me know what you find out and then go get some rest for the night shift."

When she was gone, Lindsey looked up from the book she'd been pretending to read. "Is there anything I can do?"

"Keep an eye on the town."

I started to walk out the door, but Melvin stopped me. "What about you, Chief? What are you doing?"

I paused with my hand on the knob. "I'm going to beg Pauline Cain to buy back my plantation house."

"You want me coming out for the night shift tonight, too?"

I told him I did and then hurried to my Tahoe. I backed out of the sally port, buzzing the driver's window down as I pulled onto Main Street and headed south toward Kate Drive. The sun was bright, so I turned the visor to block it from my eyes. As I drove, I called Chloe. She'd already made it to the news station and she asked if everything was okay.

I hesitated, wondering if I should involve her. I'd asked for her assistance before—mostly to elicit the public's help in providing information—but this was different. I needed someone to go back twenty-one years and search the local newspapers to see if anything big had happened involving Isaiah and Bill.

"Clint, are you there?"

"I'm here." I took a deep breath and then told her what I needed. "Look, if you don't think it's appropriate, just forget I asked. I'll figure out another way to research the information."

Chloe didn't hesitate. "I've got an intern assigned to me who'll love going back through our archives to dig up some local dirt."

Relieved, I thanked her.

"Not so fast, mister—if there's a story in this, I'm running with it."

I knew better than to argue, and hung up as I turned onto Kate Drive. I hadn't been back to the Cain mansion since investigating her husband's murder, but everything looked the same. Palm trees and lampposts lined both sides of the street and the end of Kate Drive opened into a cul-de-sac with an enormous waterfall at the center. I stopped at the large double gate and smashed the call button. Before long, the speaker scratched and Pauline's voice came across, telling me to drive up to the house.

I waited for the gates to part and cruised up the cobblestone driveway to the front of the mansion, where I slipped out of my Tahoe. One of the heavy wooden doors opened to reveal Pauline standing there, dressed in dark blue leggings with a loose-fitting sleeveless shirt. She tucked a lock of jet-black hair behind one ear and smiled, lighting up her entire face. "It's good to see you again, Clint." She descended the flight of stone steps and held out her hand. "Why'd you wait so long to return?"

Her hand was soft in mine. I released it quickly and apologized for intruding.

"It's no intrusion. I was just trying some new workout video. Now that Hays is gone, I've got nothing but time on my hands and I figured what better way to spend it than getting back into a twenty-year-old body, am I right?" She laughed and waved for me to follow her inside. "You're always welcome here."

I glanced around, wondering if her assistant, Stephen Butler, was there. I posed the question, but she said she had to retire him, explaining it wasn't appropriate having a man living in the house now that she was a widow. "He was sad to go, but pleased to know he would never have to work another day in his life, that's for sure." She smiled again, clearly proud for having taken care of the man who had taken care of her family for so long. She led me into the living room, pointing for me to take a seat on the couch and calling out to someone named Valerie to bring two lemonades. "The lemons were picked this morning from the trees in the backyard. They're divine!"

I nodded and waited as she met a heavyset woman at the entrance to the kitchen and retrieved two glasses from her. She handed me one and sat directly beside me, searching my eyes. "So, what can I do for you?"

I placed the glass on the coffee table and twisted around to face her. I backtracked to last July and started explaining what had happened when Susan saved my life.

"The whole town knows about that," she said, interrupting me. "We all know Susan saved your life. She should get a medal, if you ask me."

I nodded my agreement and continued, explaining about the grand jury hearing and how she had been indicted for murder and arrested.

"When did this happen?" Pauline asked, her face turning red.

"Yesterday. It was all over the news."

"I get so frustrated by what's happening in the world that I'm tempted to get into politics myself." She lowered her head. "I can't believe this has happened to Susan. She's such a good person."

"That's kind of why I'm here."

Pauline looked up, her expression curious. "Why's that?"

I fidgeted in my seat and explained my proposition.

"I had thought about making an offer on the property to reclaim it once again, but I realized no one wants that barren piece of land or that dilapidated old plantation." Pauline waved her hand. "Sorry, but you're stuck with that property."

I tried not to show it, but I felt deflated. She was my one shot at freedom for Susan. There had been no Plan B, no backup. For some reason, I never considered she might say no. She had seemed upset when she'd learned last year that her husband purchased the property and then sold it without her knowledge, and I thought she'd jump at the chance to reclaim it. I stood to go, but Pauline put her hand on my arm. "What're you doing?"

"I shouldn't have bothered you, ma'am. I'm sorry for the—"

"Oh, nonsense," she said, pulling me back to the couch. "Sit and listen. I don't want the property anymore, but I do want to help Susan. Where are they holding her and what is her bond?"

After I told her, she stood and grabbed a large cell phone from the foyer table and started texting furiously. She was mouthing the words as she typed, but I could not make out what she was saying. When she was done texting, she reclaimed the seat beside me and placed the phone in her lap. "My lawyer," she explained. "He'll text me right back."

She was right. Within two minutes, her phone chirped and she held it so I could see. It was a message from her lawyer saying he would head to the detention center within the hour to post Susan's bail and he would meet with her the next morning to start working on her defense. The relief I felt was so overwhelming it left me breathless. "I...I don't know how to thank you, ma'am. This is the nicest thing anyone has ever done."

She smiled, and I recognized the same sense of pride I'd seen earlier. "Just make sure she shows up in court, or you'll owe me a million dollars worth of property."

I nodded and stood with her, wanting to head north to the detention center immediately. I had to be there when Susan was released. I thanked Pauline again and turned to walk out, but she grabbed my arm. "Not so fast, mister."

I stopped and faced her, waiting patiently to hear what she had on her mind. She had just dropped a million dollars on Susan, so the least I could do was hear her out.

"How are you and that girlfriend doing? What's her name, again? Is it Chloe?"

"Yes, ma'am, her name's Chloe. We're doing great." I thanked her for asking and answered a few more of her questions. After she was satisfied with my answers, she pushed me toward the door.

"Now go get Susan out of jail. That poor girl's a hero, not a criminal, and I don't want her to spend one minute longer than she needs to spend in there."

CHAPTER 7

Quarter to noon
Chateau Parish Detention Center

I watched from the waiting area as Susan signed the bonding slips along with Pauline's lawyer. When they were done, a loud buzzer sounded and the locking mechanism on the large metal door released and they pushed through to my side. Susan lurched forward and threw her arms around me; squeezing me so tight I thought she'd smother me. "Thank you so much," she whispered in my ear. "But how'd you do it?"

When she let me go, I stepped back and explained everything to her. Her mouth dropped open. "Pauline did that for me?" I nodded and watched as she brushed her hair behind her ears. It was only the second time I'd seen her hair down. "I don't know how I'll ever repay her."

"I don't think she's expecting it," I said, studying her face. "Did they mishandle you in there?"

She shook her head. "They were good to me. The warden said Sheriff Buck Turner called and told them to set me up in a private cell and make me comfortable."

I made a mental note to remember to add Sheriff Turner to my list of all-time favorite people. If I did Christmas cards, he would be on the top of the list and would receive the gold one.

Pauline's lawyer—a tall, thin man in a pinstriped suit—handed Susan a business card. "As I mentioned earlier, the name's Perry Goldsmith," he said. "Once you're settled in at home, call my secretary and set up a time when you can come into the office tomorrow. I need to open a case and I need to get as much information as I can from you so I can start filing some motions. This whole situation reeks and I want to get a handle on it as soon as possible."

We both thanked him and Susan and I stepped out into the afternoon sunshine. "You must be hungry," I said.

She nodded and asked if I was buying. "I left my wallet at home when I was hauled away in handcuffs."

I drove to M & P Grill and the tantalizing smell of fried shrimp greeted us when we pushed through the front door of the diner. Malory, who was the manager, hurried out the kitchen at the sound of the door slamming, but she stopped momentarily when she saw us. She regained her composure quickly and showed Susan and me to our corner table. Malory was usually very talkative—nosy even—when we came in, but there was an awkward silence as she walked us to the table. She dropped the menus in front of us and returned to the kitchen.

I glanced around the dining room. An elderly couple was sitting to our right and four construction workers sat at a table directly in front of us. The construction workers didn't pay us any mind, but the elderly lady was staring at us. She turned her head when I made eye contact with her and whispered something to her husband. He looked up and his gaze fell on Susan. He stared for a few seconds and then turned back to his wife, nodding and saying something I couldn't make out.

"They act like I have Ebola," Susan muttered, noticing the reaction from Malory and the elderly couple.

I frowned. "I'm so sorry this is happening to you."

"It is what it is." She glanced at the menu, and then tossed it aside. "I've only been locked up for one night but it felt like a month."

"Are you that hungry?"

She nodded. "I'm tempted to order two of everything—especially since you're paying."

"It's the least I can do." I scanned the menu, tempted to try something new, but when Malory walked up, I settled for the shrimp on bun. When she was gone, I leaned my elbows on the table and stared at Susan, wondering how to kick off the conversation I knew we had to have.

She was busy on her cell phone. "I can't believe how much has happened while I've been in the joint," she said, smiling at her own joke. Suddenly, her smile faded as she read something on the screen. When she was done reading, she looked up and her eyes were inquisitive. "Did you know about this?" She turned her phone and I saw the headline: *Suspected murder suspects released due to lack of evidence.*

I nodded and told her Jennifer had texted me with the news.

"How could the DA let them go?" Susan asked.

"They were wearing masks at the time of the murders, and I admitted I couldn't positively identify them." I frowned. "There was no DNA evidence, no fingerprints...nothing at all to put them at the scene. I don't like it, but I understand their decision."

"But you killed Thomas Parker at the scene and—according to everything I've read—he always runs with his brothers. You said the ringleader was missing his front left tooth, and Simon Parker is missing his front left tooth." Susan shook her head. "How's that not enough?"

I just shook my head. My only hope was that they would eventually slip up and say the wrong thing to the wrong person or get caught with the murder weapon so the prosecutor could have what he needed. *Of course, they could come here like they promised and I could find a reason to put them away...*

When I didn't say anything, Susan said, "Clint, I'm really sorry. I know this has to be devastating. I couldn't imagine—"

"Let's concentrate on the task at hand," I said. "I have the rest of my life to worry about the Parker brothers, but we only have a short time to figure out why Bill is gunning for you." I hesitantly went over the conversation I'd had with her mom, recounting every bit of it as accurately and completely as I remembered. Susan sat playing with the straw wrapper while I talked, and never took her eyes off of it. When I'd finished, she placed the wrapper down and looked up at me.

In a low voice, she explained how she'd blamed herself for her dad's death. "If I'd only known CPR I could've probably kept him alive long enough to get him to the hospital."

Malory walked up before I could respond and placed our food on the table in front of us. We thanked her, but she stood looking down at the table, wringing her hands in front of her apron.

"What is it?" I asked.

"I...we...all of us here know you're innocent, Susan," she said. "I don't really know what to say about it, but I just wanted you to know we're all behind you."

I thought I saw Susan's eyes tear up a little, but I couldn't be sure. She nodded and thanked Malory, who scurried off and disappeared through the kitchen door.

Without saying another word, Susan dove into her food, moaning her approval as she chewed. I hadn't taken my first bite when I received a call from Amy.

"Did you find Damian?" I asked.

Susan's mouth stopped chewing and she stared, her cheeks puffed out and her eyebrows furrowed. She clearly recognized the name of her father's best friend. I nodded to let her know we had more to talk about.

"I didn't find him," Amy said, "but I know where he can be found."

"Where's that?"

Amy explained that the old boxing coach didn't know anything about Isaiah's dealings with the DA, but he was certain Conner could tell us anything we needed to know. "The only problem is he lives in the Smoky Mountains," Amy said. "The old man didn't know where, but he said Damian moved away shortly after Isaiah died." Amy had run a name inquiry and found an address for Isaiah's friend in Ridgeview, Tennessee. "I have a phone number if you want it."

Amy gave me the number and we hung up. Susan had swallowed her food and—not even waiting for me to put the phone down—asked, "You think Uncle D knows why Bill hates my dad?"

"I'm hoping he does," I said. "If he doesn't, I don't know who else would."

Susan sat chewing on her lower lip. Her brown eyes were troubled. When I asked what was wrong, she said, "I have this image of my dad in my mind. The kind of man I believe he was." She lowered her head and stared at her hands as she spoke. "I imagine him to be a lot like you. Well, you're a lot like the man I imagined him to be. I was really young when he died and I didn't really know a lot about him, so I've had to fill in the holes of his pedigree with character traits I imagined him to possess. Basically, I've had to create an image of who I believed him to be." She looked up and frowned. "I don't want to be wrong."

"I'm sure you're not."

"If a man hates you so much that he'll go after your offspring, you must've done something terrible. If my dad did something so awful that it would change how I feel about him..." Susan's voice trailed off and she just shook her head.

I nodded my understanding and stepped out into the parking lot to make the phone call. The wind was blowing and it felt cooler than earlier. I loved the summer, so the idea of winter being around the corner did not make me happy. I moved close to the building to get in the shade and dialed the number Amy had given me.

A man picked up on the fourth ring and he seemed out of breath.

"Conner's Boxing Academy," he said in a mountain twang. "How can we help you?"

"I'm looking for Damian Conner."

"You found him," he said.

I explained who I was and told him I needed to speak with him about Isaiah. I quickly apologized for his loss. "I understand from Mrs. Wilson that y'all were inseparable and I know how terrible it is to lose someone so close to you."

He was silent for a long moment and all I could hear was his heavy breathing and some pitter-patter in the background. Finally, he asked, "Who'd you say you were?"

I identified myself again and explained that I needed to find out if he knew anything about Isaiah's relationship with Bill Hedd. The line immediately went dead. I checked my phone to confirm the call had ended, and it had. Thinking the connection might be spotty up in the mountains, I dialed the number again. This time he picked up on the first ring. "Mister, I don't know who the hell you are, but you'd better never call this number again."

The line went dead again and I stood in the shadows staring down at my phone. Either the memory of losing his friend was still too much to bear after all these years, or I hit on a nerve. I hurried back inside and fished some money out of my wallet. Tossing it on the table, I waved to Susan that we needed to leave.

"Where are we going?" she asked, taking a last sip from her drink.

"You're going home to get some rest," I said. "I'm going to Ridgeview."

CHAPTER 8

Wednesday, October 28

It was a little after midnight when Amy Cooke backed her cruiser into her favorite hiding spot along the south-bound shoulder of Main Street. It was a narrow passageway between a large mound of dirt and the metal guardrail approaching the Mechant Loup Bridge, and it was just wide enough to fit one car. It was also a secure location, because the large mound of dirt, which marked the starting point of the Bayou Tail Levee, covered her three o'clock position, Bayou Tail had her six, and the railing secured her nine.

From her vantage point, she could see speeders long before they could see her. She averaged a dozen, or more, tickets a week from that spot alone—and she had three other such spots around town. She smiled to herself. Chief Wolf had told her on more than one occasion that he would have to build a new room in the police department just to house the records from all the tickets she wrote.

Amy buzzed the window down—letting in the cool night air—and leaned back in her seat. Propping her left elbow on the window frame, she rested her head in her hand and smiled as the smell of swamp gas rolled in on the wind. It was an acquired scent, for sure. Tourists often covered their noses and complained about the rancid odor when first being exposed to it, but she loved the smell. It meant she was home.

Her eyes were heavy. The gentle breeze, along with the familiar sounds and smells of the marsh, were having a hypnotic effect and she found herself dozing off. She hadn't gotten much sleep earlier in the day after arriving home from meeting with Isaiah's boxing coach. Her boyfriend, Trevor, was in from offshore and had come over to visit. She told him several times she had to work tonight, but it didn't seem to faze him, as he kept talking about his new truck and the boat he wanted to buy next. Finally, she'd marched to the door and opened it, telling him to leave before she threw him out. His feelings were hurt, but she knew he'd get over it.

Amy's eyes slid shut and her head slipped off her hand, causing her to jerk awake. She stared wildly about, but everything was secure. Mosquitoes swarmed the inside of her car and several buzzed by her ear, but she ignored them. She had sprayed a thin layer of 100% Deet over her clothes and exposed skin before leaving the office, so she was well protected. The breeze had subsided and it was growing warmer in the car. She pulled at the front of her polyester uniform shirt to let some air in and looked up as headlights approached from the south. It was a car and it was cruising five miles under the speed limit, seemingly in no hurry. Red light glowed from the back of the vehicle as the driver applied the brakes. The car slowed to a crawl as it passed Cig's Gas Station, making her think it would stop, but it didn't. Instead, it continued north.

As the car approached the bridge, Amy saw it was a white Crown Victoria. It looked like a stripped out police cruiser that had been purchased at auction. It had push bumpers and a spotlight mounted on the driver's side. She tried to get a look at the driver, but the side windows were tinted and there were no streetlights to illuminate the inside of the car, so she couldn't see anything.

Amy settled back into her seat and waited, hoping a speeder would come along and give her something to do. She checked her phone to see if Chief Wolf had called or texted. He had left several hours earlier for Tennessee to try and meet up with Isaiah's former best friend. Amy had begged to tag along, but he said they were already too shorthanded with Susan on suspension, so she offered to go in his place. He had actually considered it, but then decided it was something he needed to—

The bridge rattled to her left as a car drove over it. Amy turned and watched the same Crown Victoria drive by, this time traveling the speed limit. The red taillights splashed brightly as it came to a stop a quarter of a mile down the road. The car pulled onto the right shoulder of the road and then made a u-turn on Main Street and headed back to her location. Curious, she cranked up the engine and waited—her right hand on the gearshift and her left hand on the steering wheel. The Crown Victoria slowed as it approached the bridge and then suddenly came to a stop in the middle of the highway.

"What the hell are you doing?" Amy asked out loud.

From her open window, Amy could hear the driver rev the

engine. She glanced around to see if there were any other cars or people in the area. Nothing. *Can they see me? Are they trying to get my attention?*

After a few seconds, the car began moving slowly forward and then turned in Amy's direction, blinding her with its headlights. She tensed up, wondering if she should get out of her spot. Before she could make up her mind, the engine on the car roared and it lurched forward, heading straight for her.

Amy jerked her pistol from the holster on her gun belt and aimed it through the front windshield. Just as she was about to pull the trigger, the car came to a skidding stop in the gravel several feet in front of Amy's cruiser and sat there, the driver massaging the accelerator as though taunting her.

Amy's heart pounded in her chest. Keeping her pistol leveled at the car, she reached down with her left hand and flipped on her own headlights. Still unable to see the occupants, she switched on her bright lights, but it was no use. Their elevated position gave them the advantage. Not only was she trapped in her spot, but she was blind. Fear wrapped its icy fingers around her heart and squeezed until she felt she couldn't breathe.

The Crown Victoria shook violently and a plume of smoke spilled from the exhaust as the driver smashed the accelerator and held it down. Her hand shaking, Amy keyed up her police radio, yelling to be heard over the roaring engine, "Melvin, where are you? I need backup near the bridge on Main!"

The noise suddenly stopped as the driver released the accelerator and a deathly calm fell over the scene. Amy sat breathless, waiting, wondering what would happen next. She leaned toward her left and kept her pistol trained on the car. There were no sounds other than the steady humming of both car engines.

"Amy, what's going on?"

Amy jumped in her skin when Melvin's voice blared through the speaker, and the barrel of her pistol smashed into the windshield. "Shit!" Frazzled, she snatched up her mic. "A suspicious vehicle has me boxed in near the bridge. I need backup ASAP."

"Do you have a description?"

Amy opened her mouth to speak, but stopped when the headlights on the Crown Vic went dark. She blinked to get back some of her night vision and squinted to see inside the vehicle. She was able to make out two shadowy figures in the front seat, but couldn't tell anything more.

"Amy, what do they look like?" Melvin asked, his voice laced with concern. She could hear his siren blaring in the background and she knew he would be there soon.

"Stand-by," she said, leaning forward to try and get a better view of the two passengers. It was no use—her headlights were at the wrong angle and it was too dark. Taking a deep breath, she eased her car door open and placed one foot on the ground. There was no movement from the car, so she stepped out, keeping her pistol pointed forward. As she stood there wondering if she should step out from behind the protection of the car door, the interior lights on the Crown Victoria came on and she gasped when she realized both figures were wearing dark ski masks. The driver smiled when he recognized the look of fear on her face and, even from that distance, she could see he was missing his front left tooth.

CHAPTER 9

Mountain Bear Inn, Ridgeview, TN

It was almost one in the morning when I turned into the parking lot of one of the few hotels in Ridgeview. I stepped out of my Tahoe and stretched, happy to stand up after driving for ten hours. After bringing Susan home earlier and getting Damian's address from Amy, I'd stopped at my house to feed Achilles and pack some things for the trip. Chloe hadn't been home, but I'd called to let her know where I was going and asked her to look after my dog. She sounded upset on the other end.

"You mean I won't even get to see you before you leave?" she had asked.

"Time is my enemy," I'd explained. "I need to know why Bill hates Isaiah and I have to find out like yesterday."

After complaining a little about the short notice, she had finally offered to get more involved—to do some digging around town—but I told her I was sure Conner held the key to everything and I needed to speak with him in a hurry. She said her intern hadn't turned up anything of substance, but she was still searching old film. We said our goodbyes and I'd headed out of town. Mayor Dexter Boudreaux had sanctioned the trip without hesitation. He agreed it was our only lead and our best chance of freeing Susan. Right at that moment—700 miles from home and breathing in the cool mountain air—I wasn't so sure and I was hoping I hadn't steered my boss wrong.

The blinking sign in front of the hotel said there were vacancies, but when I looked through the window I couldn't see anyone behind the counter. I shrugged and tested the door, expecting it to be locked. It wasn't, so I pushed through and found myself in a clean lobby that smelled of disinfectant and air freshener.

Before I could close the door, I heard shuffling feet and a middle-aged man appeared from the darkness behind the counter. He was shoving eye glasses in place over a crooked nose and it appeared I had disturbed his sleep. "How can I help you?" he asked.

I told him I needed a room for the night and I didn't care what kind. Without saying much, he pulled out a ledger and started setting me up. He charged me eighty bucks and handed me a key. "It's around the side, near the ice machine."

I thanked him and found the room with no problem. After unloading my stuff, I kicked off my boots and pulled a bottle of vodka from my bag before settling on the bed. I stared at the bottle for a long moment before twisting off the top. Losing Abigail and Michele had changed my life forever. It seemed as though I was stuck in a perpetual nightmare. No amount of time or distance could ease the pain I felt and I couldn't close my eyes without seeing Abigail's lifeless face. I would often wish for a day when I didn't need the booze to sleep, but it had become such a part of my life now that I didn't think I could go on without it—even if I could sleep without having the nightmares.

I removed the cap and took a long drink, sighing as the warm liquid moved down my throat and burned my chest. My phone rang and I fished it from my pocket. I put it to my ear and said hi to Chloe without looking at the display screen.

"Did you make it?" she asked.

I told her I was there and gave her the name of the hotel I checked into. "It's not bad for a small town," I said. "They actually have electricity and running water."

Chloe laughed and we made small talk while I pulled from my bottle. My eyes were starting to get heavy and I told her I needed to get some sleep. She didn't answer immediately and I asked if everything was okay.

"I'm…it's just that I'm a little worried," she said.

I frowned. "About what?"

"You."

When I asked why, she told me she was afraid the Parker brothers would be coming after me. "You did kill their brother and I heard they sent a message through a stranger saying they were coming for you—and now they're out."

"Who told you about that?"

"I have my sources."

While she did have sources for work, I was surprised she'd found out about the threat. I had intentionally withheld that bit of information from her because I knew it would only make her worry, and I didn't need her worrying about me more than she already did. "Well, you don't need to worry about me—you should be worried about them. God help them if they make the mistake of coming into Mechant Loup."

Chloe didn't say anything and things got quiet for several moments. I'd finished the bottle and it was dangling from my hand. My eyes were growing heavy and they started to slide shut when her voice cut through the dullness. "Well, I guess I'd better let you get some sleep. I love you, Clint."

"I love you, too, Chloe," I mumbled. She hung up and I turned my phone on silent before letting it fall to the floor.

CHAPTER 10

Mechant Loup, LA

Amy immediately retreated toward the back of her cruiser, but the subjects in the Crown Vic didn't move. She dropped low and made her way to the passenger's side of her squad car, stopping near the back bumper to peek over her car, ready to shoot it out with the two strangers if necessary. Off in the distance, she could hear sirens and she knew Melvin was closing in on her location.

As Amy watched, she saw the driver turn toward the man beside him. She couldn't tell if he said anything because the mask was covering his mouth, but the man nodded and pointed over his shoulder. Suddenly, the headlights on the Crown Victoria came on again—blinding Amy—and the engine roared to life as the car shot in reverse. She hurried to the driver's side of her car just in time to see the vehicle whip around and speed off on Main Street, disappearing around a curve in the road.

Amy punched the shift in gear and smashed the accelerator. Her tires spun on the loose terrain and gravel popped against the undercarriage as the Charger strained to give chase. When her rear tires hit the pavement, they screeched loudly and she shot forward with such force that her head hit the seat rest behind her. Within seconds she was closing in on the suspect's vehicle. Her lights flashed brightly and her siren blared, but they had no effect on the suspects. Snatching up her police radio, she keyed it up to tell Melvin she was in hot pursuit, giving him her direction of travel. Melvin asked her to repeat her traffic several times and she tried, but he didn't seem to understand what she was saying over the siren and wind gushing in through her open window.

Amy could no longer hear Melvin's siren above her own. She glanced down several streets as she drove—hoping to see his flashing lights—but it was no use. He was nowhere to be seen. She dropped her radio to reach for the window button, but the suspect vehicle suddenly swerved around a slow-moving car and she yelped, clutching the steering wheel with both hands. The suspects had sped up and were now traveling over a hundred miles per hour—too fast to be distracted. She was thankful the chase was not occurring during school traffic, but Main Street was no place for a police chase at any hour, and she was one wrong move away from certain death.

Within a minute, Mechant Hotel and Mechant Groceries blurred by and they left the lights of town in their rearview mirror. Amy's heart pounded in her chest. Where were they leading her? What were their intentions? Should she back off and wait for Melvin? At that very moment, all he knew was that she was in pursuit in the area of the bridge and he didn't know her direction of travel. For all he knew, they could be heading north.

Just as she decided to slow down and call in her location over the police radio, she saw headlights in her rearview mirror. Relief flooded over her as she realized Melvin had caught up to her. The odds were even now! She was about to accelerate again, but the brake lights on the Crown Victoria lit up the road in front of her and the car slowed abruptly. She applied her brakes and matched the car's speed, which was now moving about twenty miles per hour. Melvin was still approaching at a high rate of speed and she thought about radioing for him to slow down, but she caught her breath when she realized something was missing—blue police lights!

Amy's reaction time was superb, but it was not fast enough to move completely out of danger. She had jerked her steering wheel to the right, shooting to the shoulder of the highway, but the speeding car crashed violently into her rear bumper and spun her Charger around in the roadway. Her head jerked from side to side as the car spun out of control and airbags exploded. The seatbelt locked her into the driver's seat, but she lost her grip on the steering wheel when the Charger came to an abrupt halt after hitting a tree on the southbound shoulder of the road. Dazed and confused, she choked on the powder from the airbags and strained to see through the smoke.

The lights on her cruiser were no longer flashing, but her siren still wailed. The noise pierced her eardrums, but she didn't have time to turn it off—she had to get out of there and find out who hit her and why. With hands that shook, she released the lock on her seatbelt and grabbed for the door handle. She tugged on it, but nothing happened. Grabbing the top of the door frame, she pulled herself up from her seat and started to squeeze out of the window. Before she could get outside, rough hands grabbed her by the arms and hair and ripped her from the opening. She heard several gunshots and her siren faded to a low murmur.

"What the hell are y'all doing?" she hollered, kicking out with both legs. It was dark and things were happening too fast for her to see what was going on, but she knew there were at least two people grabbing on her—and they were large and strong. Without warning, they flung her violently to the blacktop. She landed on her back and her head smacked the hard surface with a thump. Dazed and in pain, instinct kicked in and she tried to take in as much of her surroundings as possible. In the pale light from the moon and stars she saw two figures standing over her. Based on their shapes and the grunting sounds they made, she figured they were men.

They'd already crashed into her with a vehicle and they hadn't apologized yet, so she knew she was in trouble. She didn't know what they had planned for her, but she knew she couldn't wait to find out. Taking a deep and silent breath, she reached for her pistol with her right hand, moving as fast as she could. Just as her fingers wrapped around the grip, the first man lunged forward and planted a heavy boot on her wrist. She cried out in pain and twisted to her right, grabbing at the boot with her left hand in an attempt to free her wrist. The harder she tried to push the leg off, the harder the man scrunched his boot on her wrist. She felt a burning sensation as the rough blacktop ripped at her flesh. "Get off of me, you prick!" she said, punching at the leg in the boot. It felt like a tree trunk and hurt her knuckles, but she punched at it again.

Both men laughed and the second man leaned over her and jerked her head back by the hair. "You're a feisty little bitch, ain't you?" He laughed in her face and she gagged when she caught a whiff of his breath.

"Get your filthy hands off of me," she ordered, trying to see his eyes in the dark. She thought she might be able to shove a thumb through one of the eyeholes in the mask, but it was too risky. She was in a vulnerable position and didn't want to do anything that would provoke them into hurting her more than they had already. Melvin would be there soon, so all she had to do was remain healthy enough to stay in the fight once he arrived. Ignoring the pain in her wrist, she asked, "Who are you? What do you want with me?"

"Oh, we don't want you," Rancid Breath said. "We want Clint Wolf."

The blood in Amy's veins turned to ice as realization kicked her in the gut. These were the men who killed Clint's wife and daughter—they were the Parker brothers! Clint had warned them the Parker brothers might come looking for him, and he made it clear their fight was with him. He didn't want any of his officers getting caught up in his mess and he had ordered them to steer clear of the Parker brothers if they showed up in town. Although she was scared and her future was uncertain, Amy smiled in the darkness. *I guess I don't listen very well, do I?*

Rancid Breath saw her smiling and asked her what was so funny. "You think we're playing with you?" he asked. "You think this is a joke?"

Amy's hand was getting numb and she knew she had to get that boot off of her wrist soon. Clint had posted mug shots of the three Parker brothers and she remembered that Simon Parker was missing his front left tooth—just like the driver of the Crown Vic. They were wearing masks, so it was possible they preferred not to be identified.

Trying to throw them off of their game, she said, "Simon, why don't you let me up and we can talk about this. The department has insurance to cover the damage to the car and no one got hurt, so it looks like we're all good here."

The boot moved slightly and the man on the other end of it sucked in his breath. *Good—a reaction.*

She could hear sirens in the distance. Although they were faint, they seemed to be getting closer. It was only a matter of time before Melvin would think to check the road south of town.

"Come on, Simon, what do you say we put an end to this party?" Amy was terrified, but she didn't want them to know it. "Why don't you get your boot off of my wrist and I'll draw my gun and shoot you in the face—maybe knock out your other tooth."

Simon laughed. "This party will be over when I say it's over. Clint Wolf isn't in control anymore...we are. And he's going to pay for killing my little brother. He's going to pay with his blood and the blood of everyone close to him."

Amy could feel her pressure starting to rise. "You killed his innocent wife and daughter. How dare you cry about the justifiable homicide of your piece of shit criminal of a brother. I think it's you who's going to pay—"

"Shut your filthy mouth, pig!" Simon said, raising his voice and digging his boot deeper into Amy's wrist, bringing tears to her eyes. "You'd better watch what you say about my little brother. I've got no problem shooting you right here!"

Amy winced in pain, her mind racing. She knew she had to keep him talking so he wouldn't hear the sirens and catch on that backup was en route, but she didn't want to push his buttons too hard. She wasn't ready to die. "Look, we can work something out, I'm sure. If you just walk away, I'll forget this happened. I'll say it was a hit and run and no one will be the wiser."

"And what do I get?" Simon wanted to know, easing up on his boot just a little.

"You'll get to keep your freedom."

"I'm never going back to prison. They'll have to kill me first." Simon leaned so close to Amy she could detect the smell of stale cigarette smoke on his breath. "I tell you what, if you want to make a deal, I've got one for you."

Trying not to inhale Simon's stench, Amy asked him what he proposed.

"I hear Clint has a blonde lady friend." Simon paused and Amy could see him smile in the darkness. "If you tell me where I can find her, I'll let you go. I'll need your pistol, but you can just walk—"

"Simon!" Rancid Breath hollered. "I hear another cop car." He hurried to where Simon stood over Amy. "Do you think it's *him*?"

Amy knew he had to be talking about Clint. *So, they're trying to use me as bait to get to Clint,* she thought.

"Is the car coming this way?" Simon asked.

"It sounds like it's getting closer, so it must be."

"You get on one side of the road behind those trees and tell David to get on the other side behind the truck. If it comes down the road, shoot out the tires and disable the car. If it's Clint, don't kill him. His ass is mine. If it's anyone else, cut them in half."

Amy tried to remember everything Clint had told her about the Parker brothers. She knew there were four of them—Simon, Taylor, David, and Thomas—and Clint had killed Thomas during the armed robbery attempt and massacre of his family. Simon was the one whose boot was on her wrist and David was somewhere in the darkness, so Rancid Breath had to be Taylor.

Taylor started to walk away, but shot a thumb in Amy's direction first. "Don't go getting greedy with the blonde," he said. "After we kill that bastard Clint Wolf, I want my turn with her."

Once Taylor had strolled off, Simon leaned over and grabbed Amy's pistol, trying to pull it from the holster. Amy instinctively grabbed his thumb with her left hand and wrenched it back. Simon howled in pain and jerked his hand away. "You little bitch!"

Amy knew what would happen next. Simon was silhouetted against the moonlight and she saw his hand rear back to strike down at her. In that moment, she rolled onto her back and pushed off with her left foot. In one swift motion, she launched her right foot upward into the air and toward Simon's head. The heel of her boot landed flush on his face, catching him off guard. He grunted and stumbled backward. Amy seized the moment and rolled back to her right and shot a second kick toward Simon's knee. With a shriek, he toppled sideways and fell to the ground.

CHAPTER 11

Cradling her right wrist in her left hand, Amy bolted toward the northbound shoulder of the road, heading for the banks of Bayou Tail. The grass was tall along the shoulder of the road, but she could see the moonlight glinting off the water between the weeds. If only she could make it to the water she'd be home free.

Simon screamed in rage and a gunshot exploded behind her...and then another. Dirt exploded into the air to her immediate left and she cut to the right. Spurred on by fear and an intense desire to live, she crashed through the tall weeds and covered the short distance to the bayou side in record time. More shots exploded behind her and, without a bit of hesitation, she dove headlong into the murky, alligator-infested water.

"Get that bitch!" Simon screamed, snapping off more shots, but the sound of gunfire turned to muffled *pops* as Amy plunged deep into the water of Bayou Tail. Kicking her feet as fast as she could and taking long strokes with her arms, she turned left and headed north, trying to stay parallel to the shore. Her gun belt and clothes were weighing her down and she had to struggle to keep from sinking to the bottom of the bayou. Her throbbing wrist was making matters worse and she began to worry she wouldn't make it.

When she could no longer hold her breath, she fought to resurface and caught a mouthful of much needed air. Trying not to cause too much of a ripple, she treaded water and scanned the dark shoreline. The brothers had switched off all the headlights, so it was hard to get her bearings. She was about to dip back under the water when one of them spoke and gave away his position.

"Where is she?" It was definitely Simon and he was somewhere to her left. "Did we get her?"

"I don't see her," called a voice that was even with her position. It sounded like Rancid Breath, but she couldn't be sure. "We need to get set up. That cop is getting close. I think he's heading this way."

They were right; the siren did sound closer. Amy knew Melvin would eventually head south, if he wasn't already. She had to do something quick or he would drive right into an ambush. Taking a deep breath, she slipped under the water and swam north as hard as she could, angling toward the shoreline. It felt as though she were moving backward, but when she resurfaced two minutes later she saw the dark shadows of the weeds along the highway. In the dim glow from the moon, she was able to see what looked like a large willow tree that had fallen into the bayou along the shore. If she could put the willow between her and the Parker brothers, she would be safe.

Gasping for air, she dog paddled toward the north side of the fallen tree and said a silent prayer of thanks when she got close enough to grab onto one of the branches. Trying not to snap any of the branches or make the water ripple, she pulled herself along the edge of the tree until she reached shallow water. She tried to stand, but her boots sank in the soft mud and her head dipped below the surface. Black water poured into her mouth and she choked, trying to cough it out of her throat.

"Hey, did you hear that?" called one of the brothers. "I think she's over there."

Suddenly, a bright light shone across the water and began stabbing at the shadows. Holding onto a low-hanging branch, Amy allowed her body to sink into the murkiness, keeping only her lips above water. An occasional beam of light flashed through the branches, but she was confident they couldn't see her—the tree was too thick and they were at least forty yards on the other side of it.

Something splashed into the water along the opposite bank and she saw the light jerk in that direction. Someone fired shots at the noise—at least four of them—and she heard Simon scream at them to cease fire. "It's an alligator, you idiot!"

Amy gasped when she remembered the alligators. Careful not to make too much noise, but hurrying as fast as she could, she pulled herself hand-over-hand along the northern side of the tree. Although her arms screamed in fatigue from the long swim, she didn't stop until she was safely on dry ground. Exhausted, she dragged herself to the shoulder of the highway and collapsed. After taking a few deep breaths, she rolled to her back.

Amy's polyester shirt clung to her tight frame and she pulled on it as she lay there panting, her heart pounding in her ears. When she'd gathered up enough energy to move, she rolled to her hands and knees and began crawling north. Every now and then one of the brothers would yell that they saw her in the water, and that would be met with an occasional gunshot and lots of cursing. Based on the sound of their last shot, she knew they had not advanced toward her position.

She continued crawling until she was about fifty yards farther, where there was a slight bend in the highway. She was familiar with the road and knew she'd be able to see headlights approaching from about a mile away. She picked an enormous cypress tree as cover and backed into the dark shadows beside it, immersing herself in the thick weeds that grew naturally along the bank. Pickers clawed at her bare arms and left an after-burn, but she ignored it. The minor discomfort was nothing compared to what the Parker brothers would do to her.

Amy waited in the darkness, listening as Melvin's siren zigzagged across town. She hadn't worked with Melvin long, but she knew enough about him to know he would be frantic, driving like mad all around town searching for her. *When will you think to head south?*

The bayou water had washed away her bug repellent and she swatted at a flock of mosquitoes that buzzed around her head. Saying a silent prayer, she keyed up her radio, but the water had rendered it useless. Sighing, she flexed her wrist several times before trying to draw her pistol. If Melvin didn't find her in a hurry, the Parker brothers would, and she needed to be ready. After several attempts, and some help from her left hand, she was finally able to pull her pistol from the holster.

Amy squeezed the grip to test her strength and pain shot through her wrist. She transferred the pistol to her left hand and aimed it in the direction of the Parker brothers, waiting...watching.

After about five minutes, the siren in town seemed to multiply and it was getting closer. She looked to the north, squinting to see down the dark highway. She couldn't be sure, but she thought she saw bright flashes of blue against the night sky in the distance. As she watched, headlights came into view around the far curve in the road—lots of headlights and flashing lights. Melvin was coming and he had backup!

The Parker brothers were yelling at each other and Amy heard an engine roar to life. What were they planning? The reports from some of their earlier gunshots had sounded like an AR-15, so they were heavily armed. If Melvin and the other officers drove up on the Parker brothers, they would be trapped in the front seats of their cars and wouldn't stand a chance.

Amy bolted from her hiding spot and ran north along the shoulder of the highway, pushing her tired legs as hard as they would go. Her boots were heavy and her wet socks swished with each step, slowing her down. With every couple of steps she took, she glanced over her shoulder, expecting at any moment to be mowed down. She stayed close to the bank of Bayou Tail, where the shadows were thick, but Melvin was closing in fast and she'd have to get to the middle of the road soon. She wasn't sure how much of the highway the Parker brothers could see, but if they had a visual on this stretch, they'd definitely be able to see her figure silhouetted against the oncoming headlights and flashing blues. She just hoped they'd miss if they took a shot at her.

When the speeding squad cars were within three hundred yards, Amy left the safety of the shadows and hurried to the center of the road. She jumped up and down, waving her arms high in the air. There was no immediate response from the lead vehicle and a horrific thought suddenly occurred to her—what if they didn't see her in time? She could think of a dozen ways she'd rather die than being run down by a speeding cop car. She had worked her share of pedestrian accidents and they were never pretty.

Amy thought about firing a shot in the air, but then thought better about it, because it would certainly bring a response from the Parker brothers. Just when she thought she'd have to jump out of the roadway to save her own life, she heard tires screech and the headlights on the lead vehicle dipped sharply. The other cars followed suit and one of them swerved to the shoulder to avoid crashing into the rear end of the car in front of it.

The lead vehicle stopped within a few feet of Amy and she hurried toward the driver's side, getting out of the spotlight as quickly as she could.

"It's a trap," she yelled once she was beside the lead vehicle—a pickup truck. She saw the Mechant Loup emblem on the door and was relieved when Melvin dropped from the front seat.

Worry had slashed deep lines in Melvin's otherwise round face and he grabbed Amy by the shoulders, searching her for injuries. "Are you okay?" he asked.

Amy leaned a hand on his thick shoulder to steady herself, gasping for air, and pointing with the other hand. "It's the Parker brothers. They...they're over there and...and they've set up an ambush down the road."

Several other patrol officers joined her and Melvin near Melvin's truck, and she recognized some of them—they were deputies from the Chateau Parish Sheriff's Office. They all looked in the direction she pointed and instinctively put their hands on their weapons.

CHAPTER 12

Mountain Bear Inn, Ridgeview, TN

I opened my eyes. Something had stirred me from my sleep, but I wasn't sure what it was. My motel room was cloaked in darkness. There wasn't a sliver of light except for the clock on the nightstand and a dim glow from the floor to my right. I sat up, wincing when a dull pain stabbed at my temple. At Chloe's insistence, I'd scaled back to drinking half a bottle of vodka per night, but here I was, after only one night away from home, downing an entire bottle.

According to the clock, it was three in the morning. I'd only been sleeping for an hour or two, so why was I awake? I reached for my waistline and felt my pistol tucked into the front of my jeans. I pulled it out and set it on the bed beside me. The light on the floor had disappeared. I listened, but heard nothing in the tiny room. *What woke me up? And what had generated that light?*

The light suddenly appeared on the floor again and I realized it was my phone. I stood to my feet—a little too quickly—and swayed a bit, reaching for the bed to steady myself. I could hear my phone vibrating now. Still holding onto the bed, I leaned and picked it up to look at the screen. It was a call from Melvin. At this hour, it couldn't be good. I grunted and stretched my eyes open, trying to force myself awake. "This is Clint," I said, hoping I wasn't slurring my speech.

"Chief, thank God you answered!" Melvin sounded out of breath and his voice was laced with excitement. "We have a problem."

I fought through the fog in my brain and asked him what was going on. He explained that Amy had been involved in a high speed chase with one car when a second car intentionally crashed into her. She had been assaulted and shots had been fired. She fought back and was able to escape, but ended up in the bayou.

"Is she okay?" I asked. "Was she hurt?"

"Her wrist is banged up a little, but, other than that, she's fine."

"What about the people who did this?" I was pacing the floor in my motel, wanting to leave for Mechant Loup immediately. I cursed myself for drinking, knowing I'd have to wait to sober up before getting on the road. Even if I could leave now, it'd be a ten hour drive. "Did y'all get them?"

"It took me a while to find Amy, because she wasn't able to update her location on the radio," Melvin explained. "I had some deputies from the sheriff's office helping me look for her in town, when someone south of town called to say they heard shots fired across the bayou." Melvin paused to take a breath, and then continued. "We were hauling ass south when Amy flagged us down in the middle of the road. She was drenched from swimming the bayou, but she was okay, and she saved our lives, Chief. We were about to drive up on an ambush, but she risked her life to save ours."

"An ambush?" I stopped pacing.

"The men who attacked her heard the sirens and took up positions on both shoulders of the road. They wanted to kill us, Chief."

"Did y'all get them?" I asked again. "Are they in custody?"

"No, they got away." Melvin explained how Sheriff Turner had activated his SWAT team. "The deputies helped Amy and me block off the road until the SWAT team could get there. When they arrived with the armored SWAT vehicle, they approached the suspects' location and exchanged gunfire."

"Was anyone hurt?" I asked, wanting him to hurry and tell the story. The suspense was killing me. "How'd they get away?"

Melvin told me no one had been hit by the exchange of gunfire, and the suspects had fled south in a Crown Victoria that looked like an old police package vehicle. The SWAT team had pursued them and lost them when they ditched the car near a boat landing. "We heard an engine revving up in the distance, so we think they stole a boat and escaped into the swamps."

"Damn it!" My mind raced. I needed to get back to town so I could spearhead a search for the suspects. "Do we have any idea who they are? Was Amy able to identify them?"

There was a long pause from the other end of the line. All I could hear was Melvin's heavy breathing.

When he didn't answer right away, I asked my question again, knowing something was up. "Tell it like it's a Band-Aid, Melvin," I suggested. "Just rip the damn thing off."

"It was the Parker brothers," Melvin said quickly.

I caught my breath. *Damn, they didn't waste time coming after me.* My blood boiled and I slowly sank to the bed as I thought about those thugs putting their hands on Amy. Their beef was with me, not with the people who worked for me. What if there had been a mistake? What if Amy had misidentified them? "Is she sure it was the Parker brothers? I mean, in all the excitement, maybe she thought—"

"She's positive. Their leader was missing his front left tooth." Melvin took a breath and then said, "Chief, there's more."

When he didn't continue speaking, I said, "What is it, Melvin? Come on, man, spit it out."

He hesitated, and then said, "They want you dead. They were going to use Amy as bait to get to you. They were hoping it was you driving up to their ambush tonight."

"I wish it had been me," I mumbled. I knew they wanted me dead—that was to be expected. Hell, I wanted them dead. I started to say something, but then stopped. "Wait a minute, Melvin. There's more, isn't there? We all know they want me dead, so that's not news. What's going on? What more do you know?"

"Amy said they were asking about your blonde girlfriend. They…they want to kill her and everyone who's close to you."

"What the *hell*?" My heart was pounding against my chest like a kick pedal against a bass drum. I suddenly remembered Chloe was staying at my house. "Melvin, get someone out to my place as soon as you can! You need to get Chloe out of there! She's not safe at my house."

"She's at your house?" I heard Melvin yell some orders in the background. "Okay, Chief, I'm on it!"

As soon as we disconnected, I called Chloe. My hand trembled as the phone rang. What if I was too late? What if—

"What time is it, Clint?" Chloe sounded groggy. "Is something wrong?"

"You need to get out of my house right now!" I paced back and forth in my motel room as I explained how the Parker brothers were in town and they wanted to harm me and everyone close to me. "Take Achilles and go to your dad's house. Stay there until I get back. I don't want you going to work and—"

"Excuse me?" Chloe laughed. "Sorry, Clint, but I'm not going to shut my life down for a bunch of lowlifes. I've got a major story breaking tomorrow and I'm not going to let them interfere with it."

"These guys mean business. They attacked Amy and"—I didn't want to alarm her, but I didn't think I had a choice—"they were asking how they could find you. They want you dead, Chloe, so they can hurt me."

That seemed to get her attention and I thought I heard her gulp on the other end of the phone. "Do…did they know my name?"

"No, but they know I have a blonde girlfriend."

Silence from the other end. Finally, she took a deep breath and said, "Okay, so they know you have a blonde girlfriend, but they don't know it's me?"

"Right."

She was thoughtful and then told me she'd take Achilles and go to her dad's until I returned from Tennessee. "But I'm going to work tomorrow," she said. "This story could be the *one*. I've got to meet a source who—"

"Look, just pack your stuff and get Achilles ready to travel. Melvin should get there soon to escort you to your dad's."

"What about you? Are you coming home tonight?"

I was tempted to get on the road, but it was too dangerous. I didn't mind risking my own life, but I wouldn't risk the lives of other travelers. "It's not safe for me to get on the road."

"Oh…you've been drinking."

I stared down into the darkness where my feet should be. "Yeah. I was sleeping when they called."

"I wish you would try the pills again."

I ignored her comment and said, "Maybe it's best this way. If I'd be sober, I'd probably jump in my Tahoe and drive straight home without finishing the job here." I nodded to myself. "I need to finish this before I come home. Susan's counting on me."

CHAPTER 13

After being awakened by Melvin, I hadn't gotten another wink of sleep. Chloe had called an hour after we hung up to say she'd made it to her dad's house. I could hear Achilles barking in the background and had asked about him. She said he was enjoying her parents' back yard and peeing on everything. Right before we ended our conversation, I'd asked her to reconsider going to work.

"Clint, if we alter our lives because of the Parker brothers, they win," she had said. "Would you stay home if they threatened you? No, you wouldn't. Besides, this story will give my career a giant boost. It'll definitely make national news."

I couldn't argue too much, because she was right—I wouldn't alter my plans for some two-bit thugs. "It's just that I...you know what I've been through. I don't want to go through that again."

She'd finally promised she would meet with her contact and then go straight to her dad's house.

"Just be careful...please."

I'd spent the next two hours staring at the ceiling, watching the dark shadows slowly fade to light and worrying about Chloe.

When the alarm finally went off at six o'clock, I hurried through a shower, put on jeans and a pullover shirt, chugged two cups of coffee at the motel diner, and then headed for Conner's Boxing Academy.

The place was easy enough to find, as it was off the main highway and had a giant blue sign that read *Boxing*. I'd noticed a number of similar signs on some of the buildings in town, such as *Restaurant*, *Ice Cream*, and *Food*. My guess was they didn't want there to be any confusion.

I pulled into the paved parking lot and parked next to a red Jeep that was backed into the spot closest to the door. It was the only other vehicle in the lot. I called Melvin before stepping out of my Tahoe.

He was still at the office.

"Did you even go home last night?" I asked.

"No. I stayed here all night, keeping the place secure."

"Any sign of the Parker brothers?"

"No, and we've been searching all night and morning. The sheriff offered to have some of his SWAT officers conduct roving patrols around town, and I accepted his invitation. I hope you don't mind."

"It's what I would've done. I'm proud of you, Melvin, and I appreciate you stepping up. I'll be there as soon as I interview Susan's uncle."

I could almost feel him beaming through the phone. "Thanks, Chief." He paused, and then said, "Oh, and I hope you don't mind, but Susan's here."

"Susan? Why is she there?"

I heard her voice in the background telling him to give her the phone. After some rustling sounds, she came on the line. "I couldn't stay home. I heard what happened over my scanner and came right over. I know I'm technically on suspension with the arrest and all, but I won't sit idly by while my town is being attacked by a group of outlaws—worse yet, the same assholes who killed Michele and Abigail. I'm sorry, but there's nothing you can do to stop me from standing shoulder to shoulder with my family and protecting my home."

I frowned. Although she was being wrongfully accused by the same justice system she served, here she was, willing to risk her life for her community while expecting nothing in return. Most people would be bitter, but not her. "Thank you, Susan. I feel better knowing you're there. Keep the place safe."

"I will." She paused for a moment and then asked if I'd spoken to her uncle yet.

"I'm walking in the gym right now."

"Look, if you uncover some information that has the potential to change my feelings about my dad or hurt his reputation, please don't tell me. And don't use it."

I scrunched my brow. "What did you say?"

"You heard me."

"The whole purpose of me coming here is to find out why Bill hated your dad. Good, bad, or ugly, we need that information to get you out from under these bogus charges."

"I'm serious, Clint. If the information will do anything to tarnish my dad's name, don't use it."

When Susan made up her mind about something, I knew better

than to argue. First, I needed to find out what Damian knew. I'd figure out the rest later. "Thanks again for helping out," I said. "I owe you."

With that, I ended the call and approached the wooden walkway to the large building. It was two stories tall and there were two or three outbuildings scattered around the property. While it had a fresh coat of gray paint and a shiny green roof, there was a weathered look about it that told me it was much older than the paved parking lot. Back in the day, it had probably been an old grocery store or saloon with a hitching rail along the front.

The sign on the front glass read, *Come in*, so I turned the antique knob and opened the door. It dragged a bit and I had to pull it closed behind me. The lighting inside was dim and the air was musky and smelled of stale sweat and mold. An old boxing ring was nestled against the far right corner. A dozen or more heavy bags hung from the ceiling—most of them held together by yards of duct tape—and worn boxing gloves hung from pegs all around the gym. I smiled, feeling as though I'd stepped into a Rocky movie—the first one.

"What the hell are you doing here?" a voice boomed from behind me.

Startled, I spun around and found myself facing a man wearing gray sweat pants that had been cut off at the knees and a blue T-shirt that had stains across the front. There was a scar on the left side of his face and his left eyelid drooped to the point that it was almost closed. He didn't look like much, but one thing I'd learned in my profession is that you didn't judge fighters by their covers.

I stepped forward and stuck out my hand. "Mr. Conner?" I began. "I'm Clint Wolf from Mechant—"

"I know who the hell you are," the man said. He must've recognized the look of confusion on my face. "We spoke on the phone yesterday and today a stranger ends up in my gym. You figure it out." Without shaking my hand, he brushed by me and began tidying up the place. "It seems you drove a long way for nothing," he said. "I don't talk about my friends—living or passed."

I nodded. "I certainly understand where you're coming from, sir. I'm the same way. I wouldn't be here if it wasn't important."

"Of course it's important." Damian chuckled and shook his head. "Sorry, son, but your problems aren't my problems." He picked up a pair of boxing gloves and turned to face me. Pointing to the door, he said, "I've got work to do, so if that'll be all…"

I took a step closer to him. "This is your problem."

The gloves fell from his hands and he met my step with two of his own. In my peripheral vision, I could see his fists ball up, and there was fire in his eyes. "Is that so?" he asked, his voice so calm it was scary.

I met his gaze without wavering and nodded. "This is Isaiah's problem, so that makes it your problem."

His brow furrowed just a little, but he didn't say a word.

"It's Susan, his daughter. She's my dear friend and she's in trouble. She needs your help."

Damian's face softened and his hands relaxed. I thought I detected a cloud of mist in his eyes at the mention of his best friend's daughter. After studying my face for a long moment, he turned and headed toward the back of the gym. "Let's talk in my office."

CHAPTER 14

Damian's office was more cluttered than mine. He tilted a chair to dump its contents on the floor, and then shoved it in my direction. He then picked his way around the desk and sat in his chair. "Okay, son," he said, "you've got my attention. Now spill it."

I told him everything that had happened, leaving nothing out. I even told him about my conversation with Mrs. Wilson and how Susan would rather go to prison than bring her dad's good name into question. As I talked, his head never moved and his eyes never left mine. When I was done, he took a deep breath and spun in his swivel chair to face the wall behind him. He pointed to a picture hanging on the wall. "You see that?" he asked.

I looked up and studied the faded photograph. A boxer was casually leaning against one corner of a boxing ring with his arms draped over the top ropes. His black boxing shoes were crossed at the ankles and he was staring calmly across the ring. "Is that him? Is that Susan's dad?"

Damian nodded. "It is. Look at him—he hasn't even broken a sweat."

I looked closer. The man's face was lean and his muscles were chiseled, but not bulky. Had it not been for the red boxing gloves on his hands and his matching boxing shorts, I wouldn't have been able to tell he was in a fight. "Is he about to fight?" I asked.

"When that picture was taken, he'd just gotten through knocking out a number four contender with a single blow to the front of the face." Damian chuckled. "We all thought he'd killed the kid. Poor bastard dropped like he'd been shot in the brain stem. He recovered okay—took a while, but he lived through it." He shook his head. "He never did fight again, though, and that upset Isaiah a bit. He didn't mind knocking people out, but he hated it when they quit fighting. He didn't want to be a career killer, you know?"

I nodded, staring in awe at the similarities in Isaiah and Susan's facial features. "She looks so much like him," I said.

"That she does." He turned back toward me. "Lil' Suzy was his pride and joy. He'd do anything for her."

"I wish I could've met him."

"He's the kind of man that comes around once in your lifetime." Damian's eyes pierced through me. "Understand this…I would never say anything bad about my friend. Never tell his secrets, never betray him. If he killed someone, I'd go to jail before ratting on him. I'd take it to the grave, and you can take that to the bank."

My shoulders slumped. I knew he was telling the truth—could see it in his eyes. He had been my only hope, my one chance at saving Susan. If he wouldn't help me, who would? Who *could?* I sighed and sank deeper into my chair. I was tired and out of ideas. After a few moments, I started to stand, knowing I had to get back to town. There was no telling how far the Parker brothers would go to get to me, so the sooner I made myself available, the sooner this could end—and no one else would have to get hurt.

Before I made it to my feet, Damian placed his beefy arms on the desk and frowned. That softness returned to his eyes. I slowly returned to my chair and held my breath.

"I know Lil' Suzy wants to protect her dad's memory," he said, "but I have to do what Isaiah would want me to do. My loyalty was to him and I have to honor what I think his wishes would be. In this matter, I know he would help his little girl no matter what the consequences, so that's what I'm going to do."

My heartbeat quickened and I sat straight in my chair. "Wait…you'll talk to me?"

"I don't want to, but I have to," he said. "It's what Isaiah would want."

I reached in my pocket and pulled out a digital recorder. Setting it on the table between us, I nodded toward it and asked, "Do you mind?"

Damian sighed. "No, I guess not. I know you'll need to carry proof back to Louisiana."

I nodded and flipped the recorder on. I began by asking how he met Isaiah.

"I'd been boxing for about six years when he first walked in the gym." Damian pursed his lips, remembering. "I was wrapping my hands and about to start doing some bag work when he walked in. I think he got the attention of everybody in the gym, because he showed up wearing dirty jeans and a greasy T-shirt." Damian laughed. "That's how he fought, too. When we stepped in the ring—"

"Wait a minute…he fought the first day he walked in the gym?"

"My coach was a hard ass. *This is boxing*, he'd say, *not figure skating*. He made me tune up all the new comers on their first day. He knew I could press them just enough to find out what they were made of without hurting them."

I was thoughtful. "So, he was trying to find out who had the stomach for it?"

"Yeah, he always said you can't teach heart, and he wouldn't waste time on those who didn't have it."

"I take it Isaiah had heart?"

"*Had* heart? That boy was all heart. He came at me hard…right from the opening bell. I had to put some leather on him just trying to keep him off of me. I could tell right away he lacked any form of defense and he was easy to hit, but nothing I did slowed him down. Hell, he seemed willing to take four punches just to land one." Damian shook his head, chuckling as he continued. "I beat the hell out of him that first night—broke his nose in the first round—but he wouldn't quit coming. When the first round was over, Coach asked him if he'd had enough. He spat out a mouthful of blood and said he had me right where he wanted me."

Damian said they grew to be close friends after that night and became regular sparring partners. "He started bringing Lil' Suzie to the gym and we all fell in love with her. I'd work her on the mitts from time to time. She could throw a good punch for such a little kid."

He talked a lot about Isaiah's fights and gave blow-by-blow accounts of nearly all of them. I would've interrupted him, because none of it was relevant, but I was too intrigued. Finally, when he took a break from talking to grab a bottle of water from a small refrigerator in the corner of his office, I asked about something Mrs. Wilson had mentioned.

"So, Isaiah's wife told me she thought you were a bad influence. Any idea why she would say that?"

"I was a young man—younger than Isaiah—and single. I liked to party on the weekends to blow off steam from training all week long, and he was my best friend, so I wanted him to party with me." Damian hung his head. "I know I was to blame for a lot of his marital problems, and I'll regret that until the day I die. Lisa hated me. She told Isaiah more than once that he'd have to choose between me and her. It was usually when we were about to go out and I'd be waiting in my truck. She'd walk outside so Suzie couldn't hear the fussing and she'd give him an ultimatum. *It's your friend or your family*, she'd say. *Choose one!* I don't know why, but he always chose me."

"How'd she take it? Mrs. Wilson—what would she do?"

"She'd just stand there crying. I was always happy he chose to go out with me, but a small part of me felt guilty—well, until that first beer. After I'd get some alcohol in me I'd be fine. I remember looking back in my rearview mirror once and seeing her wipe her eyes dry and compose herself. I knew she was doing that so Suzie wouldn't know she was upset." He shook his head. "That image haunts me to this day. I never looked back again."

"Did Lisa ever leave Isaiah?"

"She loved Suzie more than she loved herself. She never left Isaiah because she didn't want to hurt Suzie, and she never said a bad word about him. My wife, she left my ass after a year and she told everybody in town I had some venereal disease I can't even pronounce. She filled my kids' heads with so much garbage that they still won't talk to me—even after all these years."

I thought I saw a shiny tear sliding down the side of his face at the mention of his kids, but I couldn't be sure. "So, what about Bill Hedd...do you know why he hated Isaiah?"

"I do," Damian said quietly. "Yes, sir, I know why he hated my friend."

When he remained quiet for at least thirty seconds, I nodded and said, "Why don't you go ahead and tell me what you know? For little Suzie's sake."

CHAPTER 15

9:45 PM
Ten miles north of Mechant Loup

When I ended my interview with Damian ten hours earlier, I'd ridden hard for Mechant Loup, his words burning a hole in my brain. Susan wouldn't like what I'd discovered and she wouldn't want me to use it, but it was the smoking gun I'd hoped for and I wasn't going to let her go to jail for something she didn't do. When I called Isabel and told her what I had learned, she suggested I get with Susan's attorney as soon as possible and have him set up a meeting with Bill.

"This might just do the trick," she'd said. "Bill would never let that information go public."

I glanced at my phone again, but I hadn't received another message from Chloe. I'd called her at least six times on the drive back, but she never answered. The first two times I called, her phone rang a dozen times before going to voicemail. Afterward, they would go immediately to voicemail. I sent her a text message at about six o'clock when I'd stopped for gas and she'd finally replied with a message that read, *In interview. Will text again later.*

The lights from town glowed bright beneath the dark sky up ahead and I wondered what was going on at the office, so I called.

"What are you doing at work?" I asked when Amy answered. "I thought you got hurt."

"My wrist is banged up a little, but I'm fine." She went on to tell me everything was quiet. "We've been hitting the south side of town hard, but there's no sign of the Parker brothers. I think we might've scared them away."

"I doubt it. They don't scare easy. Did y'all get arrest warrants for them?"

She told me they only obtained one for Simon. "The judge didn't think I could properly identify Taylor and David, so he refused to sign those. I got pissed, but Melvin said it was okay because they'd all be together anyway."

"He's right." I told her to be careful and hung up. Just ahead of me in the sky was a dim glow that marked the town of Mechant Loup. I inadvertently sped up—feeling a burning desire to find the Parker brothers—and was taking the final curve in the highway at seventy miles per hour. It wasn't a good idea in daylight, much less at nighttime. As I shot around the bend in the road, my attention was immediately drawn to the lift bridge that separated Mechant Loup from the rest of the world. Something seemed odd about it— different—but I couldn't put my finger on it. Maybe it was the long drive or my mind was preoccupied, but I didn't slow down until it was almost too late.

"What the—?" I smashed the brake pedal to the ground and was lurched forward—the seatbelt locking me in place—as the vehicle abruptly slowed to a stop just inches before crashing through the barrier arms of the open bridge. I took a moment to catch my breath and then stepped out into the cool night air, my knees weak. Relieved that I hadn't plowed through the arms and over the edge of the bridge, I watched as the lift span began its slow descent. The gears on the bridge squeaked and the chains rattled in protest as it closed. I shook my head in awe. I'd been in town for over a year and had never seen the bridge open to boat traffic. Hell, I didn't even know there was a bridge tender up in the cabin. *So much for my detective skills.*

I stepped forward and realized there were red lights on both barrier arms, but they were busted, which accounted for the reason I couldn't see them. They probably hadn't been turned on in years. I made a mental note to let the town's maintenance department know about it and then ducked under the arm.

I made my way to the edge of the deck and stared down into the blackness below. It was too dark to see clearly, but the moonlight sparkled off of waves lapping against the shore, apparently caused by a passing boat. There was a gurgling sound from somewhere below, and I couldn't help but wonder if the large alligator that had taken Dexter's arm was back in Bayou Tail. I shuddered, hoping never to encounter that beast again.

A gentle breeze blew in from the marsh and felt good against my face. A cold front must've blown through while I was gone. It felt like the seventies, which could almost be considered below freezing this far south.

"Where's the boat?" I asked aloud. I turned my head to the right and left, scanning up and down Bayou Tail, but didn't see anything. Shrugging, I returned to my vehicle and waited to cross over to the other side. My Tahoe rocked gently as the lift span made contact with the deck and settled roughly into place. Seconds later, the barrier arms made a jerky motion and began to lift upward. As soon as there was enough room for me to pass, I sped across the bridge and entered town.

When I reached Cig's Gas Station, I turned right on Grace Street and then hooked a left on Jezebel. I sighed when I pulled into my driveway and saw that my house was still standing. I wouldn't put it past Simon and company to burn my house down or destroy it in some other way. Of course, I figured they'd rather set it ablaze with me inside. I was not entirely opposed to the idea, because that would mean they'd have to come to me and I wouldn't have to go looking for them.

Although my place appeared undisturbed, I wasn't taking any chances. I drew my pistol and moved into the shadows as I made my way around the exterior of my house, searching for broken windows and checking the doors. There was no barking from inside, so Chloe had taken Achilles with her. This made me feel even better, because if anyone could protect her, it was him.

Once I'd confirmed that my house was secure, I holstered my pistol and entered through the back door. I began packing a duffel bag for a few days. I couldn't leave the police department unguarded. It was the heartbeat of the town and I had to keep it secure.

After I packed my clothes, I opened my gun safe and grabbed my AR-15 and a case of ammunition. Slinging the rifle over one shoulder and the box of ammo over the other, I strolled to my car and loaded them in the front driver's seat. As I was leaning into the car, something snapped behind me in the bushes. I whirled around, gripping my pistol with my right hand. Holding my breath, I tried to penetrate the darkness with my eyes, listening for the slightest hint of movement. Nothing.

Suddenly, the stillness of the night was shattered by the obnoxious chirping of my cell phone. I ducked low and reached for it with my left hand, switching it to *silent*. I held my breath and listened for more movement. Still nothing.

When I was certain all was clear, I straightened, holstering my pistol as I did. I glanced down at my phone and sighed when I saw a message from Chloe. She said she'd just gotten to her dad's house and was beat. *Call you in the am,* she wrote.

I scowled. *What about a phone call to tell me goodnight or to ask how my day went?* Disgusted with the impersonal nature of text messages and cursing the person who invented them, I tossed my phone into the Tahoe and returned inside my house to grab my duffel bag. I also snatched two bottles of vodka from under the counter and stashed them between my clothes.

I locked up my place and headed for the office. The radio traffic was light. It scratched to life as I was pulling into the sally port and I turned up the volume. One by one, Amy contacted three sheriff's deputies who were patrolling the town and asked if there were any signs of the Parker brothers. They each reported that everything was clear. I knew it wasn't a matter of *if* the brothers would resurface…it was *when* and *where*.

Slinging my bag over my shoulder and snatching my AR-15 from the seat next to me, I stepped out the Tahoe. I smashed the button to lower the garage door and then made my way through the processing area and into the patrol room. I was surprised to see Amy sitting at the dispatcher's station. There was a 12-gauge shotgun on the desk in front of her and her left hand went for it when I opened the door.

She relaxed when she saw it was me. She waved and it was then that I noticed a bandage around her right wrist. "Welcome back, Clint."

"Where's Marsha?" I asked. Marsha was my night shift dispatcher and she was as regular as the summertime heat in Louisiana.

"Susan sent her home," Amy explained. "We didn't know what to expect tonight and we didn't want to put her at risk."

I nodded and looked around. All of the office doors were shut and the shades were drawn in the front lobby. "Where's Melvin?"

She shot a thumb toward the conference room. "He crashed on the floor. He said he's going back out on the water early in the morning to try and track the Parkers down. He spent some time out there today, along with the sheriff's water patrol guys, but they didn't find anything."

"He's not going without me." I glanced at the door to Susan's office. "Is she in there?"

Amy nodded. "We're sleeping in shifts. She'll be up at midnight to stand guard while I sleep for a little bit. There's also a deputy sleeping in the break room and two SWAT officers hiding around the building. We're trying to keep this place guarded because Susan thinks they'll either attack us here, or call in bogus complaints and ambush us one by one."

I nodded my agreement. "They're cowards that way. When you go back out on patrol, I want that deputy riding shotgun. No more single cars until we've dealt with those bastards."

She nodded, but her eyes narrowed and her lips formed a thin line, as though she were angry.

I'd seen that look on my own face and knew immediately what was going on. "You're pissed at yourself for not taking them out last night."

"I feel like such a fool. I didn't even consider that it was a trap." She shook her head. "I should've started shooting right when they approached my car."

"You had no way of knowing what you were dealing with, so you did the right thing. For all you knew, it could've been some teenagers trying to taunt you on a dare." I shifted the duffel bag on my shoulder and headed for my office to get some sleep. "I was right in hiring you. You're a fighter."

I pushed through my office door and noticed the shades were closed and the drapes pulled tight. Someone had put a cot with a pillow in the corner. I kicked off my boots and shirt, and then sat in the dark pulling from one of the bottles of vodka, wondering how Achilles was handling being in a strange place. Since bringing him home as a puppy, he'd never slept in a different bed. If he was anything like me, he could sleep anywhere, but not everyone was like me.

The last thing I remembered wondering was what I would tell Susan when she asked about my conversation with Damian.

CHAPTER 16

Thursday, October 29
Mechant Loup Police Department

The sun was shining through a sliver of a crack between the drapes when I opened my eyes the next morning. My head pounded and my neck and back ached. It took me a minute to realize where I was. When I did, I quickly sat up and looked at the clock on the wall. Six-thirty. I'd called Susan's lawyer on my drive into town and told him I had some important information about Susan's case. He'd agreed to meet with me at noon—it was the earliest he could manage. That gave me a few hours to hunt down the Parker brothers.

I pulled on a T-shirt, grabbed my duffel bag, and walked out into the patrol area. Lindsey was sitting at her desk staring at the front door. Her head jerked around when my door opened.

"You okay?" I asked.

Her bottom lip quivered. "Do...do you really think we'll be attacked?"

Not one to lie about such things, I shrugged. "I can't say for sure. If you feel uncomfortable being here, you can go home until it's all over. I'll pay you for your missed days."

She shook her head. "I'm scared, but I'm not leaving. Y'all need me working the radio."

I smiled and hurried to the shower room located at the back of the police department and got ready for work. Once I was cleaned and dressed in my polyester uniform, I strapped on my gun belt and stared at myself in the mirror. I couldn't help but wonder if this would be the day I'd get to see Michele and Abigail again. I pulled out a picture of them that I kept in my wallet and frowned. I missed them so much. I knew I had to go on living, but I was ready to be with them. I'd often wondered what I'd say to them when that moment came. I would certainly apologize for trying to intercede in the robbery. I hung my head low and frowned, wishing time travel was real and I could go back and—

"Chief, come quick!" It was Lindsey and she was just outside the shower room. "There's been a murder."

I rushed out and followed Lindsey to her desk. Susan was standing there with Dexter, who cradled a rifle in his good arm. I avoided making eye contact with Susan, still unsure how I would handle the information I'd received from Damian.

Dexter nodded when I walked up. "I'm here to help defend the fort."

"You don't have to be here," I said. "Along with Sheriff Turner's people, we've got it covered."

"I'm the mayor here, Clint...it's my responsibility to help protect this town. Like all good captains, I'd go down with my ship."

I knew it would be pointless to argue, so I thanked him and said we could use his help. I turned to Lindsey and she handed me a piece of paper with an address and name scribbled on it. "The owner—some guy named Ed Brody—called it in. He found his manager, Megyn Sanders, dead behind the bar. He said it looks like a robbery."

I recognized the address. It was the Bayou View Pub on the southeast corner of town. "Where's Melvin?" I asked.

"He and Seth took the airboat and headed for Lake Berg," Lindsey said. "They're going check some abandoned camps, just in case the Parker brothers are holed up out there."

Seth was Melvin's friend from the sheriff's office and he worked the canine division. He was a solid officer with a background in SWAT, but there were three Parker brothers. "Just the two of them?" I silently cursed myself for sleeping too late and missing the ride.

Lindsey shook her head. "Three deputies from the sheriff's office water patrol division took a boat and went with them."

"Tell them to stay on the radio and—for the love of God—be careful." I looked at Susan and indicated toward the door with my head. "I want you riding shotgun on this case."

Susan hesitated. "Are you sure it's a good idea, considering I'm out on bond for murder?"

I took a deep breath and exhaled, shaking my head. "I'm not sure of anything right now, except that you're the best officer I have and I want you with me. I *need* you with me."

"What about guarding the office?"

Dexter hoisted his rifle into the air. "I've got this place covered. You kids run along and get a handle on that murder. Lord knows, the last thing we need right now is another murderer running around town."

That was enough to convince Susan, and she followed me to my Tahoe. We sped across town and arrived at the bar a few minutes later. The owner was sitting in a rocking chair on a large covered porch that extended the entire width of the building. His elbows were propped on his knees, and his face buried in his hands.

We sauntered up the concrete steps on one end of the porch and made our way to him, our boots echoing against the hollow wooden floor. It was only when we were standing over him that he looked up, his red face streaked with tears. He pushed back his white, thinning hair and sniffled loudly. "This is something that…this hasn't…I…I never thought this would happen here."

Susan put a hand on Ed's shoulder and knelt beside him. While she consoled him, I made my way to the front door, careful not to disturb any evidence that might be on the porch. There were two entrances located at the front of the building—a modern double-door made of glass and an antique-looking wooden door with nine individual panes of glass. The wooden door was open, so I approached and picked my way through it.

The flickering florescent lights overhead cast a dim glow about the place, and I had to wait a few seconds for my eyes to adjust. I'd been inside the establishment a few times since landing in Mechant Loup, so I knew the layout of the ancient building. The left side of the room opened into a large dance floor, with a DJ setup in one corner and a secondary bar in another corner. The main bar was to my right. It was constructed of rich mahogany and stretched nearly the length of the room. Nothing was out of place on my side of the bar. Each barstool was in its place, the top of the bar had been wiped clean, and every salt shaker and ashtray was in perfect position. To the untrained eye, it was just a normal day at the establishment. But I knew better.

As with most homicide scenes I'd worked, an aura of death clung to the air like an invisible fog. Bracing myself for what I would find, I carefully strode toward the end of the bar, searching the worn floor before taking each step. When I reached the far wall, I noticed two holes in the paneling. They were chest high and about four inches apart. They looked like bullet holes, so I checked the floor around me, searching for spent shell casings. There were none.

Next, I rounded the corner of the bar and located the victim, Megyn Sanders, lying on her right side next to a toppled barstool. She wore blue jeans, a faded red T-shirt, and women's sneakers. Her right arm was trapped under her body and her left hand was draped across her chest. Her mouth was open in apparent shock and her eyes were wide.

I pulled out my cell phone and activated the flashlight feature on it, aiming it at Megyn's head, which rested in a pool of coagulated blood. I immediately noticed a gunshot wound to her left temple. I scanned what parts of her body I could see and noticed more blood on her clothes. Upon closer inspection, I located two more bullet wounds. One was in her chest, above her left breast, and the other was to her left shoulder. I turned my attention back to the gunshot wound in her temple. Something about it was off. I leaned close and realized what it was...this was a contact wound. The star-shaped tattooing around the hole made that clear, but I needed to know if it occurred while she was standing or lying down. Due to the amount of blood that had spilled from her body, I knew the bullet had exited. I straightened and scanned the wall behind her and to her right, searching for more bullet holes. When I didn't find any, I turned back toward the victim.

As I stood staring down at the contact wound to her temple, my mind drifted back to when Ringleader was holding Abigail in his arms. My eyes were open, but I could see him shoving his pistol roughly into the side of her temple, making her cry even louder. I flinched when the gun went off inside my head. In my subconscious mind, I replayed the scene where Ringleader shot the life right out of my baby girl over and over, and I nearly vomited.

I shook my head to clear it and took a few deep breaths, trying to focus on the investigation. I turned my attention toward the side wall next to the door I had entered. Picking my way around Megyn's body, I moved to that side of the bar and noticed the wall was covered in old newspaper clippings and Polaroid photos from years past. Although it was cluttered, it was plain to see there were no bullet holes on that side of the building. I lowered my gaze to the register, which was against the wall. It was open. When I stepped closer I noticed the money slots were empty.

I scowled, looking from the empty register to the gunshot wound in Megyn's head. It was the same type of wound as Abigail's, in the same location, and during an armed robbery. The similarities were too obvious to ignore.

I keyed up the radio clipped to my uniform shirt and called Lindsey. "Call Melvin and tell him to come back to town. Simon and his brothers might already be back here. We need to check all the businesses in town to make sure there haven't been other robberies."

Susan walked up as I was finishing my message to Lindsey. "What's going on in here?" she asked.

After I told her what I'd found, she handed me a camera so I could photograph the body and evidence, and then she began surveying the scene for herself. She examined Megyn's body first and the cash register next. When she was done, she chewed on her lower lip. That usually meant she was either thinking really hard or she was about to say something I wouldn't like.

"What're you thinking?" I asked.

"I think we need to dig a bit deeper before we make the leap that Simon and his brothers did this."

I pointed to the body. "How often have you seen a murder victim with a contact wound? For me, it was only once—when that bastard Simon shot Abigail in the temple. I checked the wall behind her and there are no bullet holes to line up with that shot, so he must've bent over her as she lay dying, pushed the muzzle of his pistol to her temple, and pulled the trigger. And why? Just to make sure she was dead? That takes a special kind of evil—the kind Simon possesses." I then nodded toward the cash register. "And they specialize in armed robberies. That's how they make the majority of their money."

Susan nodded. "I hear what you're saying, but I think we should keep our options open. You know, just in case there's something else going on here."

"Like what? We haven't had an armed robbery in this town since I've been chief, and it's probably been a lot longer than that."

"That *is* true, but this doesn't necessarily have to be a robbery. It could've been a murder made to look like a robbery."

I couldn't argue the point. I picked my way back to the door and stood facing the interior of the bar. I held out my hand like I was holding a gun. "He came in shooting," I offered, "and his first two shots hit the far wall. That would've gotten Megyn's attention and she would've jumped up, knocking over her barstool. He then corrected his aim and fired two more shots, putting her down." I walked around the bar and stood over Megyn. "And then he cold-bloodedly shot her pointblank in the temple."

"So, you think he came in shooting?" Susan challenged.

I nodded.

"If it was a robbery, wouldn't he have demanded the money before killing her? What if he needed her to open a safe or tell him where to find the key to the register? It wouldn't make sense to barge in with guns blazing."

"You act like I was here and saw everything," I joked. "You're right—the robbery could've been staged or an afterthought. Let's get this scene wrapped up so we can interview Ed. Maybe there's something about Megyn's life that can help shed some light on what happened here, but my money's on the Parker brothers."

CHAPTER 17

While I processed the scene and Susan watched—careful not to touch anything because of her current status—Ed waited on the porch, smoking his way through an entire pack of cigarettes. Once everything was documented, I examined Megyn's body more closely and noticed she was cold to the touch and her body was stiff. She'd been dead over twelve hours, which put the murder in the evening hours, possibly before dark.

Once I'd measured and photographed her body, I carefully lifted her head to see under it. There—resting on the hardwood floor—was a copper-jacketed lead projectile. It had punched a hole through her head and lost most of its energy, making it no match for the solid oak planks. I picked it up in my gloved hand and held it close to my face, nodding. It was definitely a nine millimeter bullet.

I checked Megyn's back and found that the other two bullets hadn't exited her body. By my count, five rounds had been fired—three hit Megyn and two landed harmlessly in the wall. But where were the spent shell casings?

I posed the question to Susan, who had combed every inch of the floor. "Either the killer collected the spent casings or he used a revolver—provided *he* wasn't a *she*."

"Unless it was a nine millimeter revolver, the bastard picked up the casings."

After I'd finished processing what I could of her body at the scene, I called the coroner's office and requested their investigators respond to retrieve her body. While I waited for the investigators, I dusted the door handles, the register, and the area of the bar near Megyn's body. Most of the prints I recovered were partials or smudges, and they could've belonged to anyone—including Megyn. I then set about swabbing any area I thought the killer might've touched, hoping to recover some DNA evidence.

The last thing I did was retrieve tools from my Tahoe and cut a large square chunk from the far wall that encompassed both bullet holes. Once I'd removed the wooden paneling, I was able to locate two copper-jacketed lead projectiles in the wall, both of them nine millimeters like the first. One was entangled in the fiberglass insulation and the other had lodged in the sheetrock of the opposite wall. After packaging the bullets and securing them in the evidence bin behind my Tahoe, Susan and I returned inside to ensure we hadn't missed anything.

"Well, what do you think?" I asked Susan.

"It's clear someone came into the bar, fired several shots, dropping Megyn, and then took the money and shot her pointblank in the side of the head. Or shot her in the head and then took the money—that part isn't clear." Susan sighed. "Now we have to figure out who *done* it."

"I've got my thoughts," I said as we walked outside and each took a seat in rocking chairs on either side of Ed. After apologizing for what he had been through, I asked him what he found when he arrived.

Instead of answering my question, he just shook his head and said, "This isn't supposed to happen here. In all the years I've been in business, we've never been robbed. But to have one of my employees—who was like family—murdered? That's unthinkable!"

I was silent for a moment, allowing Ed to compose himself. His hand trembled as he brought a cigarette to his lips and pulled from it. A pile of crushed cigarette butts were on the floor of the porch at his feet. He blew out the smoke and hung his head. "Megyn's worked here for thirty years—even before I took over. She started out working her way through college, but then fell in love with the job and dropped out of school." He chuckled to himself, seemingly going back to a more pleasant time in his mind. "Her parents were so pissed off that they came down here and threatened to sue my brother-in-law."

"Your brother-in-law?"

Ed nodded his head. "My father-in-law built the bar himself forty years ago. He passed it on to Lance when he retired and Lance hired Megyn back then when he first took control of the bar. Megyn's parents blamed him for *ruining their daughter's future*, as they put it."

"You said Megyn's parents threatened to sue Lance—did they actually go through with it?" Susan asked.

"No, they settled down when they realized Lance was running a respectable business here. Of course, it didn't hurt when they realized how much money Megyn was making. She was tipped well, that one." Ed crushed out his cigarette and looked up at me. "When Lance went to jail, my father-in-law offered the bar to my wife but she didn't want anything to do with it. They wanted to keep it in the family, so they asked if I would run it. Like most men around here, I had begun working in the shipyard right out of high school. I'd spent a lot of hot afternoons sandblasting barges and cursing myself for not going to college. When they offered me the bar, I saw it as an opportunity to get out of the yard. I was ready for a change of pace."

"How long ago did you take over?" I asked.

"It's been about twenty years now." Ed shook his head. "I didn't know anything about running a bar, so Megyn took me under her wing and taught me everything I needed to know. She helped make the business great. I promoted her to manager and gave her a hefty raise. And she deserved it."

"Do you know of anyone who would want to hurt Megyn?" Susan asked. "Any enemies?"

"Hurt her? Hell no. Everybody loved her. As y'all know, we get some drunken idiots in here every now and then looking for a fight, but Megyn could talk any of them down. She just had a way with people."

I was thoughtful, and then asked the obvious question. "What about relationships? Does she have a husband or boyfriend? Or an ex lover out there who might be upset over losing her?"

"She's been divorced for fifteen years, and she wasn't dating anyone that I knew of."

I asked for the ex-husband's name, and Ed told me what it was, but said he didn't live around here anymore. "He's been gone for years," Ed explained. "Got remarried, moved to Mississippi or Alabama, and had a few kids with his new woman. My mom is still friends with his mom and she mentions what he's up to every now and then."

"What about ex-boyfriends?" I asked. "Or anyone she's been on dates with recently?"

Ed shook his head. "None that I know about."

I made a note of that. "So, what time did you get here this morning?"

"I'm not sure. I drove up a minute or two before I called 9-1-1. About six o'clock, I guess. As soon as I walked in and saw her on the floor I called y'all." Ed went on to explain how it was Megyn's job to close up every night and he would open up every morning. Right at closing time, which he said was two o'clock, Megyn's routine was to clean up the bar, remove the money from the register, and then lock it in the safe. Once Ed would arrive the following morning, he would empty the safe and make a deposit at the bank. "After I called 9-1-1 this morning," Ed said. "I noticed that the register was open, so I checked the safe. It was locked. I opened it and checked inside, but it was empty."

"Well, I can tell you Megyn's been dead anywhere from eight to twelve hours, so it was definitely before closing time."

"You mean she's been like that all night...alone on the floor dying?"

"If it's any consolation, she didn't suffer long." I decided to change the subject and handed Ed my notebook and pen. "We'll need a list of regular customers—names, addresses, and telephone numbers if you know—so we can interview them. We need to know if any strangers came into the bar within the last couple of weeks."

"Please understand—I work the day shift and I'm gone by three, so I wouldn't know all of our nightly customers." Ed frowned. "Megyn would be the one to answer that question, but she's not here anymore."

"Do y'all get many customers on Wednesdays?" Susan asked.

Ed shook his head. "We make most of our money on the weekends. Other than filling lunch orders, we're pretty slow during the work week. Things usually start picking up by Friday afternoon."

"Look," Susan began, "I don't want you to be offended by my next question, but I have to ask it." After a brief pause, Susan asked Ed for his whereabouts yesterday. "Please understand, we can't leave a stone unturned."

"I do understand." Ed took a breath and exhaled. "Let's see, I got to the bar around six yesterday morning and stayed here most of the day. I locked up at ten-thirty to deliver some pre-orders and was back by eleven. I served plate lunches here until one-thirty and then hung around until about three, which was when Megyn showed up."

"What'd you do between one-thirty and three?" Susan asked.

"The usual—caught up on my books, cleaned the kitchen, and swept the floors. When Megyn arrived I talked to her for a few minutes and then left."

"Where'd you go when you left?"

"I stopped at home to change into some old clothes and then drove out to my hunting lease. I go out there every day during hunting season."

"Did you kill anything?"

Ed shook his head. "I worked on one of my tree stands for about an hour and then just sat there watching the deer until sundown."

Susan studied Ed's face closely. "Can anyone verify that?"

"My wife was home when I stopped to change and she was there when I got back from the lease," Ed said. "She can verify that much. If need be, I'll take a lie detector test. I'll do whatever y'all need me to do. I just want y'all to catch the person who did this to her. Megyn was like family to me and I want the person responsible brought to justice."

Susan put a hand on his shoulder. "There's no need for a lie detector test, sir. We just need to know where everyone was and what they were doing so we can move this investigation along."

"I understand."

CHAPTER 18

"I don't know." I squinted in the sunlight, considering Susan's theory that someone had staged the scene to look like a robbery. "The Parker brothers just happened to roll into town yesterday morning and attack Amy, and then we get an armed robbery-homicide this morning—one that fits their MO like a pair of broken-in shoes. I'm telling you, Sue, my money is on them."

"It *is* highly coincidental." Susan acknowledged. Without saying more about it, she pulled out her phone and called the coroner's office to find out when the investigator would arrive.

While she did that, I walked in circles in the parking lot and called Chloe's phone. It went straight to voicemail. I grunted and shoved my phone in my pocket. *What in the hell's going on? Why won't you talk to me?* I began to worry if she was angry about something.

I didn't have long to think about it, because the coroner's investigator arrived shortly after Susan called and we helped him load Megyn's body into the van for transport. When he was gone, Susan and I wrapped up the scene investigation and were about to leave when an elderly man rode up on a bicycle. His clothes were tattered and his face stained from lack of bathing. He looked at my Tahoe and then at us.

"Not again!" he complained.

"What's that?" I asked.

"I came by here yesterday at seven and it was closed, so I came back at ten last night and it was still closed. Now, I come back the next day and it's still not open? Where in the hell is a man supposed to get a drink around here?"

"How do you know it was closed at seven yesterday?" Susan asked.

"I already told you—I came by here and I saw the sign that said it was closed."

I looked toward the front of the building. Sure enough, the red sign on the double-door to the left read, *Closed.* "Were there any cars in the parking lot when you came here at seven and then again at ten?"

The man pointed to Megyn's car. "Just that one, but it's always here when I come."

We asked him more questions, but the only thing he really cared about was getting some alcohol in his system. When we'd extracted all the information we could out of him, Susan and I returned to the police department. Melvin had just pulled up and was backing the airboat into the bay behind the building when we parked on the street. I waved in his direction and asked Susan to get with him about notifying our victim's next of kin. "Let him take the lead because of what's going on with you, but make sure he finds out if she had any friends or enemies. Tell him to get a warrant to search her house and property, and make sure he checks all of her electronic devices. I want to know if she was on any dating sites, if she's been involved in recent arguments on social media, if she'd received any—"

"So you don't think the Parkers killed her?"

"I do, but I want y'all to eliminate as many doubts as possible."

Susan cocked her head sideways and stared curiously at me. "And where are you going?"

"I have a meeting at noon."

"You're late."

I glanced at the time on my phone and nodded. "I sent a text earlier and he said he'd wait for me."

"Who's *he*?"

"Your lawyer, Perry Goldsmith."

Susan studied my face, scowling. "You haven't said a word about your conversation with Uncle D since you've been back. That means what he had to say was bad, doesn't it?"

I was wondering when she would ask about my trip to Tennessee. I nodded slowly.

"What did he tell you?"

I pondered her question, trying to choose my words carefully. When I took too long to answer, she lowered her head. "How bad is it?"

"It's not the best news, but I don't think it's as bad as you're imagining. I think it'll definitely help our case."

"If it'll ruin his reputation, I don't want you using it."

I stared off in the distance, watching Melvin and Seth unhitch the airboat. When I looked back at Susan, her jaw was set. "I'm serious, Clint. I don't want my dad's name being destroyed."

"I don't think it'll come to that."

"It had better not." Without saying another word, she stepped out of my Tahoe and shut the door. I watched her walk toward Melvin and then I drove away.

I called again for Chloe as I traveled north to Perry's office, but it went straight to voicemail. I left another message asking her to call me as soon as she could, but a sense of dread began to settle in the pit of my stomach. I realized I didn't have her parents' number, so I called Lindsey and asked if she'd research it for me. "Just text it to me when you get it," I said, and thanked her before hanging up.

CHAPTER 19

Perry's secretary led me to a large conference room and showed me to a plush rolling chair at one end of a long table. "Mr. Goldsmith will be right with you," she said, and then scurried away.

When I was alone in the room, I checked my cell phone. Still nothing from Chloe. Unable to help myself, I called her number again, but it went straight to voicemail. *Maybe her phone's dead?* I decided to send her a text message asking her to call me as soon as possible, and I also let her know I was starting to worry about her. I was about to call Lindsey when Perry bustled in carrying a large file folder filled with legal documents and other papers. He dropped it on the table and settled into a chair next to mine.

"As you can see, I've been busy," he said. "I interviewed Sergeant Wilson yesterday and then—thanks to Sheriff Turner and Isabel at the DA's office—I was able to obtain every report that was generated in connection with the shooting last year." He stopped and shook his head. "Chief, there's not a single shred of evidence to support a murder indictment against Sergeant Wilson. I don't know what Bill Hedd's thinking. From everything I've read, she should be getting a medal." He took a breath and blew it out forcefully. Staring over the large file at me, he said, "My secretary says you have some information that might prove helpful."

I pulled the digital recorder from my shirt pocket and placed it on the table beside me. "This is the voice of Damian Conner, Susan's dad's best friend."

I flicked the recorder on and watched Perry's face carefully while the audio file played. His eyes grew wider and wider as he listened to Damian explain how Isaiah had been sleeping with Bill's wife for six months prior to his death. Bill hadn't found out about the relationship until after Isaiah died. When he confronted his wife, she claimed Isaiah raped her. "I never thought I'd say this about my friend,"

Damian had said, "but he was better off dead at that point, because if he would've still been alive, they would've arrested him on the word of that lying bitch."

The recording continued to play and Perry and I listened as Damian explained how Bill had sent a detective to the gym to question him about a rape allegation. Damian told the detective Bill's wife was lying and that she'd been carrying on with Isaiah behind Bill's back for months. Damian even showed the detective three Polaroid pictures of Isaiah and Bill's wife together at a crawfish boil that the trainers threw for all the boxers. The pictures had been primarily of other people at the party, but Isaiah and his mistress had been captured in the background. They were holding hands in one and she had her arm around him in the other two.

Satisfied, the detective had left, but a week later Damian was served with a DA subpoena ordering him to appear in Bill's office to answer questions. "When I got there, the DA himself met with me," Damian had said. "He told me I'd better never say a word about Isaiah having an affair with his wife or he'd bring me up on charges of helping with the rape. He called it something else—accessory something or other—but he made it clear he would destroy my friend's name and have me sent to prison for a long time. He told me the pictures I had—or used to have, because the detective never gave them back—only proved Isaiah was stalking his wife. He said his wife was of high moral character and would never willingly accept the advances of another man. He said he'd see me rot in prison before letting me defile her good name." Damian sighed audibly on the recording. "I would fight any man, anytime, and anywhere, but I know better than to fight the law. There're too many of you guys. So, I packed up what little I had and got my ass out of town in a hurry. I'd always wanted to move back home, and I figured that was as good a time as any to do it. I went to work for a logging company and kept boxing for about fifteen years, and then I opened this here place of my own."

I had asked Damian a few more questions, but the recording soon ended. When it was over, Perry's brows furrowed and he gave a cautious nod. "If what he's saying is true, our district attorney might've committed prosecutorial misconduct. Putting aside the witness intimidation and possible tampering of evidence that occurred back then, he knowingly and maliciously swayed a grand jury to indict an innocent officer to get back at her dead father for having an affair with his wife. This is a serious offense. I'm going to immediately file a complaint with—"

"Not so fast." I stood and paced back and forth beside the table. "Susan won't let us use anything that'll cast her dad in a negative light, and it doesn't get any worse than a rape accusation. She'd rather go to prison than ruin his reputation."

"Excuse me?" There was a bewildered look on Perry's face. "We're not talking about six months in the parish jail…she could go to prison for the rest of her life if she's found guilty. I mean, I doubt any jury would convict her based on Bill's trumped up charge, but there's still some risk associated with going to trial, and I wouldn't recommend it to anyone. I say we end this now by having Bill himself indicted."

I loved the sound of that and I wanted nothing more than to see this bully pay dearly for what he'd done to Susan, but I had to honor her wishes. Now, the trick was to use this information to force Bill to back off while keeping my promise to her.

"If you file a complaint against Bill," I explained, "the news will spread faster than a wildfire across the dry marsh, and everyone will know that his wife accused Isaiah of raping her. Even if we clearly demonstrate it was a false accusation, that's the kind of bell that can never be unrung. We can't do that to Susan and her mom. That dark cloud will follow them to their graves."

"Well, I can't let Sergeant Wilson stand trial for a crime she didn't commit, especially if I have the silver bullet that can stop this train dead in its tracks."

"I think we have another option." I slid the recorder toward Perry. "Why don't we meet with Bill and play the recording for him. If he's willing to threaten to bring false charges against a witness to keep his wife's name pure, I'm guessing he's willing to play ball with us to save his own ass."

"So, are you saying you want me to coerce the district attorney into dropping charges against Sergeant Wilson?"

"That's exactly what I'm saying."

A wicked smile played across Perry's mouth. "I never liked Bill Hedd anyway, so I'm going to enjoy this a little too much. Even if he refuses to drop the charges, the mere fact that his wife had a sexual relationship with Sergeant Wilson's father—consensual or otherwise—will disqualify him from being involved in any criminal proceeding against her, so we'll be able to have him removed from the case with no problems."

"When do we leave?"

"I'll have my secretary call and see if he's willing to see us right away. When I tell him what it's about, I'm sure he'll make time."

Perry stood and gathered up his files and the recorder. "You can tag along, but I think it's best if you stay out of the meeting. I'll have my partner come in to witness the conversation and you can wait out in the lobby until we're done."

I started to object, but realized he was right. Having me in the meeting would only antagonize Bill, and that's not what I wanted at that moment. "If he doesn't want to cooperate with us, we need to get the audio recording to Isabel Compton," I said. "She's the voice of reason at the district attorney's office, and she's been in our corner since the beginning. Now that we have this information, if anyone can convince him to back off, it'll be her."

CHAPTER 20

Twenty minute later I was following Perry and his partner to the district attorney's office. On my suggestion, Perry had spoken with Isabel first and provided her with the information. Within five minutes she'd called back to say Bill had cleared his schedule and would meet with Perry immediately.

"She told me she'd never seen him so flustered," Perry told me once he hung up with Isabel. We'd left immediately—Perry and his partner in his black Cadillac and me in my Tahoe.

I called Susan a few minutes into my drive.

"What happened?" Her voice was taut. "What did Mr. Goldsmith say?"

"We're going to meet with Bill right now. Perry's got a proposition for him, and I think he'll go for it. I'll call as soon as I know something."

"Clint, please don't use anything that'll disgrace my dad."

"Don't worry. Bill Hedd won't want this information getting out. Your dad's name is safe."

Susan was silent for a long moment, and I knew she was mulling it over. I interrupted her thoughts and asked if they had notified Megyn's next of kin.

"Yeah, we notified her mom and dad. It was bad, Clint. She was their only daughter. We had to get an ambulance for her mom."

"Did y'all search her place yet?"

"We're here now. So far, we haven't found anything suspicious. She's never been on dating websites, doesn't have any social web pages, and barely uses email."

"What does she do in her spare time?"

"Crossword puzzles and Sudoku...in print, too, not on the computer." Susan sighed. "The girl doesn't even text. Her phone can make calls and that's all."

"It's got to be Simon and his crew." I pursed my lips, wondering where they could be hiding out. Melvin had towed their vehicles when they attacked Amy, so they were either on foot or they'd acquired new wheels. I slowed my Tahoe as Perry tapped his brakes in front of me and turned into the district attorney's office. "We're there," I said. "Keep me posted, and I'll let you know what happens here."

I hung up and followed Perry and his partner into the lobby, where we didn't have to wait long for Isabel to meet us. She wore jeans and a flannel shirt and her hair was down. I was surprised how short she was, but realized she had on sneakers instead of the high heels she usually wore.

"No court for me today," she explained, holding the heavy wooden door for Perry and his partner to enter. Once they had made their way down the hall, she joined me in the lobby and sat in one of the chairs. She put her feet up on a small coffee table and sighed. "I don't want to be in that room when he hears what they've got to say."

I agreed and sank to one of the chairs opposite her and leaned back against the wall. It was then that I realized how tired I felt. Every muscle was tense. My heart was pounding. What if Hedd didn't play ball? What if he interpreted what we were doing as bribery and brought all of us before the grand jury? I shuddered at the thought. We were counting on him wanting to keep his wife's name pure, but what if he no longer cared about that? After all, she'd been dead for twenty years, or so, and he might've moved on.

"What do you think he'll do?" I asked.

Isabel frowned. "It's hard to tell with Bill."

I nodded and looked anxiously around the room. I wanted to be in that meeting. Susan's freedom was hanging in the balance and I needed to know she would be okay. Seconds ticked slowly by and turned into minutes. The longer we waited, the more nervous I got. It wasn't until thirty minutes had passed that an angry voice boomed from somewhere deep in the building, and I recognized it to be Bill.

"Get the hell out of my office and don't ever come back!"

Isabel and I jumped to our feet just in time to see the door burst open. Perry and his partner came hurrying out, both of them stifling smiles. I waved a quick goodbye to Isabel and followed them toward the door.

"What happened?" I wanted to know.

"Let's get outside," Perry said. "He wants us gone, so we'll leave. We don't want to give him a reason to file some bogus *remaining after being forbidden* charges against us."

I matched Perry's stride and followed them out into the sunshine. We all gathered in the parking lot near Perry's car. "Well," I said impatiently, "what the hell happened?"

"He was so angry he was blowing smoke," Perry said. "He didn't say a word the entire time the tape was playing, but his face grew redder and redder. I thought he was going to have a stroke. When it was done, he—"

Perry stopped speaking when my phone began ringing loudly from my pocket. I quickly checked to see if it was Chloe, but scowled when it wasn't.

"Do you need to take that?" Perry wanted to know.

I shook my head. "I don't recognize the number. Please continue…what happened next?"

My pulse rate quickened with excitement as he spoke. When he'd finished telling the story, he told me he was heading back to his office and that he'd be in court early the next morning. I waved goodbye and jumped into my Tahoe. I was on the phone with Susan before I pulled out of the parking lot. She said she was at the coroner's office with Melvin and they were attending Megyn's autopsy. It was just down the road, so I told her to meet me outside and that I'd be there in a few minutes.

When I arrived, she was standing in the shell parking lot near the gate, chewing on her lower lip. I stepped slowly from my Tahoe and approached her. Her face was a shade lighter than usual and I didn't want to leave her in suspense any longer.

"You're back, Sue. It's over."

Her eyes widened and her mouth dropped open. "Wait…what? Are you sure?"

I nodded. "Isabel's going into court bright and early tomorrow morning and dismissing all charges against you. Bill would be doing it himself, but Perry convinced him it would be in his best interest to cease his involvement in any proceeding involving you—"

Susan didn't wait for me to finish. She bolted forward and threw herself against me, wrapping her arms tightly around my neck. "Thank you so much," she whispered into my ear. "You did this…this is your work."

I felt something warm splash against my neck and I knew she was crying…but they were happy tears. I squeezed her back and we held each other until it felt awkward, and then she loosened her death grip on me. Embarrassed, she turned her head away and dabbed at her eyes with her hand. "Does this mean I can put my uniform back on?" she asked.

"It does, but do you mind waiting until the autopsy is done?"

This brought a chuckle from her and then she turned to head back into the building. "Are you coming in?"

"I am." As I started to follow her, my phone rang again. It was the same number from earlier. I picked it up. "Hello, this is Clint."

"Clint, your secretary said for me to call you." It was Chloe's dad and his voice was curious. "Is there something wrong?"

"Oh, no, I've just been trying to call Chloe's cell phone all day, but I keep getting her voicemail. I figured it was probably dead and that I could catch her on your house phone."

"Um, she's not here. We thought she was with you."

"Is there something wrong?" I heard Chloe's mother call from the background.

"What do you mean you thought she was with me?" I asked.

"Well, she sent her mother one of those text things last night to say she was going back to your place. She never came home, so we figured she was with you."

My heart dropped to my boots. "Are you sure she's not there? Can you check her room?"

"Clint, I would know if she was here or not. Once she left for work, she hasn't been—"

I ended the call and rushed toward my Tahoe, with Susan hollering after me wondering what was going on.

CHAPTER 21

I skidded to a stop in the gravel driveway of Chloe's dad's house and jumped out of my Tahoe. Andy and Viola Rushing were out in the front yard before I could reach the house. Tears rolled freely down Mrs. Rushing's cheeks and there were deep worry lines in Mr. Rushing's leathery face.

"Are you sure she didn't get home last night?" I asked, pushing past them and into the house. "She texted me around ten o'clock to say she'd made it home and was tired, and she said she'd call me in the morning."

They followed close behind me, with Mr. Rushing trying to convince me she hadn't come home. "I fell asleep on the sofa waiting for her, but I went to bed when she sent that message. I'm telling you, Clint, she said she was staying with you. Now, she told us earlier she had to stay here because those evil men were threatening harm and you were out of town, but then we figured you'd returned early since she decided to stay with you."

I pushed through the doorway of her childhood bedroom and glanced around. It looked eerily like a shrine. Other than the crumpled sheets on the bed, it appeared as though Chloe had left for school one day and her parents had come behind her and locked everything up without moving a single item. One thing was clear, she wasn't there.

I turned to walk out, but Mrs. Rushing stepped into my path. She was clutching at her throat and wailing. "Do...do you think they did something to her? The bad men...do you think they got to her? Oh, dear God, please tell me she's okay...*please!*"

My stomach burned with fear, but I didn't want to freak them out even more, so I masked it as best I could. "I'm sure she's fine. Maybe she got to my house after I left last night and just decided to stay there. I could've easily passed her on the highway and not known it was her. I'll check it out first thing when I leave from here."

"Then why not answer her phone?" she asked. "I must've called a dozen times since we hung up with you, but it's ringing straight to her voicemail. I've left a dozen messages, but she hasn't called back yet. That's unlike her. She never goes that long without answering her messages."

"Maybe her battery died and she didn't bring her charger," I suggested idly, my mind on other things. I needed to retrace her steps, beginning with yesterday morning. "What time did she leave for work yesterday?"

"She and Achilles got here late, so she slept in a little." Mr. Rushing rubbed his face and shook his head. "I'm guessing she left at about eight, eight-thirty."

"She did leave in a hurry," Mrs. Rushing said through her tears, "because she didn't make her bed."

I walked out the front door and around to their back yard, where Achilles was tearing up a water hose in the fenced enclosure. I winced. "Sorry about that."

Mr. Rushing just waved his hand. "Our last dog—a big yellow lab—did much worse."

When Achilles heard my voice, he yelped and bounded toward me, trying to jump over the six-foot cyclone fence. I let myself in through the gate and dropped to my knees beside him, ruffling his ears as he rolled onto his back and squirmed in delight. My mind was racing as I knelt there scratching my dog. I told him to stay and then stood to face Chloe's parents. "Mr. Rushing, is it okay if Achilles spends some time here while I figure out what's going on in town? I'll pay for all the damage he causes."

"That's not necessary." There were tears in the elder man's eyes. "Just please bring our daughter back home. She's all we have."

I nodded and left, heading for my house. I knew better than to hope that Chloe was there, but I felt deflated when I turned the corner and didn't see her car. I headed for the office next and found it buzzing with activity. Several deputies were milling around eating from plastic bowls and Mayor Boudreaux's wife was walking around refilling their drinks. The place smelled of chicken and sausage gumbo. Although I hadn't eaten lunch, I wasn't even tempted. I had to find Chloe first and foremost—I could eat after that was done.

Susan pushed through the crowd and tugged at my arm. Her eyes were troubled. "What's going on? Lindsey said something about Chloe being missing."

My jaw burned as reality settled in. "It's got to be Simon and his brothers. Somehow, they figured out who she was and...and they got to her. I need to find them, Sue—and fast."

Susan pursed her lips. "Melvin said they searched everywhere. They checked with everyone living along Bayou Tail and on Lake Berg, but no one's seen anything. They even rummaged through all the abandoned camps, but there's no sign of them or the stolen boat."

I nodded. "I need to go to—"

"Chief, is it true?" Melvin had rushed up and grabbed my arm. "Is Chloe missing?"

"I'm afraid so."

Amy walked up and handed me a bowl of food. "You need to eat so you can keep your strength up. We'll find her."

Knowing she was right, I took the bowl and forced the food down. While I ate, Susan updated me on the results of their investigation into Megyn's murder. "There were no surprises at the autopsy. She was shot three times, with the fatal wound being the one to the head. Her friends and family can think of no one who would want to hurt her. Like I told you before, her computer and phone turned up nothing." She paused and frowned. "I think you were right—this is a robbery and our prime suspects are the Parker brothers."

"Yeah, it's the only thing that makes sense." I looked up as Mayor Boudreaux approached and slapped Susan on the back.

"Congratulations, Susan! I heard the bogus charges are going to be dropped tomorrow."

She smiled. "Thanks, Dexter."

"I know a good lawyer if you want to sue that bastard for false arrest," he offered. "That was one hell of an injustice."

"No, I'm just happy to put it behind me," she said. "I've had enough drama for one year."

"I understand." The mayor then turned to me. "I'm going to take the missus back home. She's tired from cooking all morning and needs to get her rest. I'll get some rest, too, and come back for the night shift so you kids can get out there and find Chloe."

I thanked him and watched as he patiently helped his wife gather her purse and a bag. She wanted to take her dishes with her, but he told her he'd bring them home tomorrow. Taking her by the elbow, he then guided her toward the front door of the office.

"That'll be me and Claire a hundred years from now," Melvin said, smiling at the old couple. "You know they've never even dated anyone else? They were each other's first love."

"They're precious," Susan said. "I hope to someday find a love like that."

I only frowned as I watched Dexter open the door for Mrs. Boudreaux. I couldn't watch them without wondering about Chloe. Where was she? *How* was she? A sense of panic threatened to seize my breathing as a thought crept into my mind…was Chloe alive?

I hung my head as I focused on pushing the thought from my mind. I knew I couldn't go there in my mind or—

A distant *pop* and a nearby *splat* caused me to jerk my head upward. I gasped out loud when I saw Mrs. Boudreaux fall to her knees, clutching at her stomach. Blood oozed between her fingers and a look of shock fell across her face as she toppled onto the floor, groaning in pain. Another *pop* sounded and Dexter's lower jaw was ripped violently from his face. He collapsed in a heap on top of his wife and lay still.

"Dexter!" I drew my pistol and lunged forward as more gunshots erupted in the distance and bullets rained into the police department. I saw Mrs. Boudreaux's head flinch and she lay still, her eyes open and her mouth sagging. Screaming in anger, I continued toward the door. I had sixteen bullets in my pistol and I had every intention of sending each one of them in the direction of the Parker brothers. I was about to reach the doorway when something struck me violently in the ribs, knocking the wind from my lungs and sending a sharp pain through to my core. My knees buckled and I dropped to the floor, nearly losing my grip on my pistol. As I lay there struggling for air, my eyes locked on Dexter's lifeless and disfigured face.

CHAPTER 22

Bullets whizzed by overhead and splattered the back wall. I saw two deputies squatting in the corner returning fire through one of the lobby windows. I strained to breathe, but it felt like a sack of oysters was on top of me. Melvin entered my plane of view from the side and sprang toward the front door, kicking it in an attempt to shut it. The door smashed into Dexter's lifeless body and flung wide open again.

Gripping my pistol, I situated my hands under me and tried to push myself up to help him, but the weight held me down. It was only then that I realized Susan was on top of me. She had tackled me to the ground and once again probably saved me from certain death. She rolled off of me and scrambled toward the right side of the door where Melvin squatted. She flinched once as a bullet splintered the floor just inches from her face, but she made it to Melvin without being injured. The exterior walls were wrapped in brick and provided decent cover from the gunfire, but the open doorway was another matter. I could almost see the bullets spraying through the opening.

Staying clear of that funnel of death, I managed to reach the left side of the doorway and prepared myself to move the bodies. I grimaced as I looked down at Dexter and his wife. They were two people who had done nothing but work hard and help others their entire lives. They didn't deserve to go out like this. While I was upset and angry that they were gone, I remembered the way Mrs. Boudreaux had acted last year when Dexter disappeared in the swamps, and I knew neither of them would've wanted to go on living without the other. As horrible as it was, it felt appropriate that they would expire at the same time.

Seth appeared directly behind me and shoved my boot. "I'm here, Chief, I'll get the woman."

I nodded and grabbed Dexter's arm and dragged him off of his wife and out of the way of the door. Seth grabbed Mrs. Boudreaux and pulled her body beside Dexter's. In one smooth motion, Melvin lunged forward and delivered a kick to the door that sent it slamming shut. He sighed and started to wipe sweat from his brow, but bullets zipped through the door and splattered against the back wall, sending him ducking for cover.

Susan worked her way around three deputies who were huddled behind Lindsey's desk and she headed toward my office. Melvin and Seth disappeared into Susan's office and I heard them fire off some shots from the one window in her office.

I began to follow Susan to my office when I saw Lindsey crouched behind her desk with the deputies. Her hands were covering her head and she was crying out loud. Crawling to her, I grabbed her by the shoulder and pulled her toward me. "Get to the shower room," I yelled into her face. "You'll be safe. There're no windows and it's made of concrete."

She was shaking uncontrollably and refused to move. Shoving my pistol in its holster, I wrapped my arm around her back and began dragging her in the direction of the hallway. She finally pushed her knees under her body and scurried along until we were halfway down the hall. I let go of her back and told her to keep going.

The gun battle was increasing in intensity and I needed to get into it. I whipped around and rushed toward the patrol section, staying low as I ran. I'd last seen Susan enter my office, so I headed in that direction. I caught sight of the three deputies firing their handguns from behind Lindsey's desk. They would take turns popping up and aiming across the room and through the windows in the lobby, and then drop down behind cover. I grunted, wondering if they could even see anything from that position.

I crashed through my door on hands and knees, trying to stay lower than the windows in my office. Susan turned when she heard me bump against the doorframe. She was crouched near one of the windows, her pistol held firmly in her hands. Most of the bullets from the opposing gunfire impacted the exterior brick walls and disintegrated harmlessly against the hard surface, but an occasional bullet found its way through the window and whizzed by overhead.

"Where's your AR?" she asked.

I pointed to my cot. "Under there!"

As she went for the AR, I crawled behind my desk and pulled the shotgun from where it was leaning in the corner. I pressed the release switch and pulled the pump back slightly, checking to make sure a round was chambered. One was, so I made my way to the opposite side of the window where Susan was crouched. The window provided a view of the front of the building and I knew I should be able to get a bead on the shooters. Although I hadn't seen them, I knew it had to be the Parker brothers. Only they possessed the intestinal fortitude to declare war on an entire police department, and they were ruthless enough to kill an elderly woman and her husband for no good reason.

One of the window panes was shattered, but the curtains were still in place and the room was dark enough to hide us from the view of anyone outside. Susan—my AR-15 in her hands—pulled her feet under her butt and prepared to spring upward. She turned to look at me first and her eyes twinkled. "I guess we don't have to go looking for them," she said. "It seems like they've found us."

"That was a bad move on their part!" Gritting my teeth, I jumped to my feet and shoved the barrel of the shotgun through the shattered window. I had to squint to try and penetrate the long shadows growing across the street. I searched for hostiles, but saw none. I dropped back down and took a deep breath. "I don't see anyone."

I'd caught a glimpse of a pickup truck and some trees across from the office, but I couldn't be certain they were behind them. I didn't want to shoot if I couldn't identify my target. A citizen could've gotten caught in the crossfire and sought refuge in the trees. And what if they had Chloe with them? I shuddered at the thought and tried to push it from my mind. That would only distract me and cause me to hesitate at a crucial moment. Chloe's best chance of survival would be us taking out the Parker brothers as soon as possible.

Susan pointed overhead to let me know she was going up for a look and I nodded. Scooting back from the wall, she took a deep breath and lunged to her feet, the AR extended out in front of her. I stood up at the same time and scanned the area again.

"There," Susan said, "behind the truck!"

She squeezed off two quick shots and the rear tire blew out. I saw movement behind the truck and a large man bolted from behind it and ran toward another truck parked several feet in front of it. I swung the muzzle of my shotgun in his direction and pulled the trigger, but the buckshot pellets landed harmlessly against the front quarter panel of the first pickup.

Out of the corner of my eye, I saw the figure again. This time he was moving toward a clump of bushes to my left and he had something long in his hands. Before I could work the pump-action on the twelve-gauge and turn it in his direction, he snapped off a shot and a window pane above my head exploded. Shards of glass peppered the side of my face and I quickly dropped to the ground with Susan, who grabbed my chin and turned my head so she could look me over. "You're bleeding!"

"It's nothing—just a little glass." I took a moment to catch my breath and waited for the barrage of gunfire to cease. When there was a break in the action—possibly for them to reload—I jumped up and fired off a shot in the direction I'd last seen the movement. The figure was gone, but someone returned fire from the right and I dropped back out of sight.

Susan squatted beside me, her chest heaving with each breath. She grabbed her radio and switched to the sheriff's office channel and called for their dispatcher. After a few seconds, she called again, but there was no answer. She messed with the buttons and tapped the radio on the floor, then shook her head. "The radios are down."

I pursed my lips. The first thing they did was take out the radio tower behind the office. They'd planned this out and were fully committed to destroying us. "Use your cell phone," I suggested.

Susan nodded and pulled it from her shirt pocket, using her thumb to punch in a set of numbers. She put the phone to her ear and then pulled it away again. "It's dead."

"Your battery?"

"No, the line. It's dead."

"What?" My ears were ringing from the shots we'd fired inside the enclosed space and her voice sounded muffled, but I heard what she said. I jerked out my own phone and tried to make a call. She was right. "How is that possible?"

"You know the cell tower north of here?" she asked.

I nodded.

"That tower is the only cellular link between us and the outside world." She pursed her lips. "Everyone who lived through Hurricane Amanda ten years ago remembers full well how isolated we are down here. It took them weeks to get the tower back up and we were reduced to only using land lines—and most people don't even have hard line phones anymore."

Land line phones! I slid across the floor to my desk and snatched the receiver from the cradle and put it to my ear. Nothing. They'd even cut the lines to the building. A slow chill moved up my spine. If they'd thought of that, what else did they have in store for us?

"We've got to get out of here and flank them," Susan said. "We're pinned down."

I nodded. "There're only three of them, so they can't cover all four sides of the building."

"I think they're all in the front."

"I think you're right."

I'd detected three different firearm reports—one sounded like a shotgun, one like an AR-15, and the other like an SKS or AK-47. It sounded like the shots were being fired from somewhere in front of the building, which faced the east. The sally port opened to the east, so we'd have to head straight into the gunfire if we decided to drive out of the building. There were five smaller windows on the back side of the building and we might be able to squeeze out of one and mount an offensive against the Parkers. We certainly needed to get out of the office, because it was a death trap and we were a bunch of little rabbits waiting to be flushed out and killed. If they decided to set fire to the building, all they'd have to do was sit back and wait for us to come running out. They'd then be able to drop us one by one. We had to take the fight to them in a way that would take them by surprise.

I told Susan my plan to escape out the back, and we both hurried toward my office door. Just as we entered the patrol area, several more shots were fired from outside. Most of the bullets landed harmlessly on the exterior wall, but several found their way through the windows and door.

I told Amy to follow Susan and me, and we made our way to Susan's office. Amy and Susan waited near the door while I entered and spoke with Melvin and Seth, who were taking turns firing out of the window. "I can't see shit," Melvin said. "The sun's going down and that side of the building is in shadows."

"It's like they planned it," Seth said over his shoulder, jumping up and popping off three rounds from his pistol.

I told them Susan and I planned to make a break out the back window. "We're going to circle around and take these bastards out."

"The sun will be in your eyes," Melvin said. "If they've got people—"

A sickening *splat* of a bullet striking flesh and a strained voice hollering in pain somewhere behind me cut Melvin off.

CHAPTER 23

An evil grin split Simon Parker's face as he slipped back behind the large cypress tree. He'd gotten another one. It wasn't Clint Wolf, but it was wearing a uniform, so it would do for now. After changing the magazine on his AK-47, he crouched behind a line of shrubs and darted toward another tree south of his position. Once he reached the safety of the large tree trunk, he leaned the AK-47 against the tree and picked up the AR-15 that rested there. He peered around the tree and studied the police department. Other than a few shots now and then from the front of the building, all was quiet. He'd had a couple of close calls—like when that cop shot out the tire on the truck he'd been hiding behind—but, for the most part, he'd remained a ghost.

Days earlier, Simon had carefully scouted the building and drew up a diagram showing every point of ingress and egress—just like he'd been taught in prison. While most criminals used their time on the inside to write letters, whine about being innocent, and look for Jesus in every corner, he spent his days furthering his education. His enemy was a cop, so the first thing he did when he got locked up was look for an inmate who was an ex-cop. Those were easy to find these days, because it was suddenly vogue for prosecutors to go after cops. He found three in the state pen who were willing to help him. One was doing time for payroll fraud to the tune of a quarter million, the second for involuntary manslaughter, and the third for rape. They were all too eager to teach him what he needed to know to defeat one of their own. Simon spat on the ground. While he needed them, he despised them. Not so much for being cops, but for being traitors. He would never betray one of his brothers no matter what happened, and cops were supposed to be brothers.

"Simon, the sun's going down behind us," David called over the walkie-talkie radio. "We've got the advantage back here now."

"Roger that," Simon said, tucking the radio in his belt. One of the cops he'd met in prison was a former SWAT member and he'd taught him the importance of communication. While his brothers had been busy running surveillance on the police department an hour ago, he had taken out the cell tower north of town. He then set up shop across the street and waited for the perfect time to launch an attack. When the door to the police department opened earlier, he opened fire and mowed down two people. They happened to be an old lady and the old man with one arm. While Simon didn't relish killing women—young or old—he would if he had to, and today he had to. That first assault kept Clint and his people busy long enough for David to take out the radio tower behind the police department and for Taylor to cut the phone lines to the building. Now, it was just a matter of time.

The tree Simon was hiding behind offered him a clear view of the sally port and he couldn't help but laugh to himself again. While he had kept the cops in the building occupied and off guard by delivering rapid fire from three different vantage points using three different weapons, Taylor and David had pushed an old pickup truck against the large garage door, blocking the vehicles inside. It was a brilliant idea. Other than two doors along the east side of the building and windows on the northern and western sides, the sally port was their only way out.

Simon pulled out his binoculars and scanned the openings at the front of the building. There were no cops in sight. Every now and then one would appear for a brief second and pop off a shot, but he hadn't been able to time them yet. He turned his attention to the block of explosives strapped to the rear tire of the old pickup truck near the fuel tank. One shot from his rifle would send the truck and that corner of the building up in flames. "This is your Alamo, Clint Wolf. This is where you're going to die."

After firing a few bullets into the front door window with the AR, Simon snatched up the AK and ducked as low as his large frame would allow. He then ran to the north, passing up the large cypress tree and stopping behind the old pickup truck across from the corner office. Trading the AK for his twelve-gauge, he squatted behind the front bumper and fired a round through the broken window to the corner office. It was hard to see inside because the lights were out and the curtains drawn, but, with luck, his bullet might find a human target.

He whisked back behind the truck and quickly moved to the front. He popped his head above the hood and snapped off another shot, this time aiming through the front door again. He dropped behind cover and paused before preparing for the move back to the cypress tree—waiting to see if there'd be return fire. He glanced up at the sky. The sun would be down soon and Clint and his officers would be able to escape under the cover of darkness. He couldn't let that happen. He finally had that murdering bastard where he wanted him, and he had to end it while he had the upper hand on the lawman.

Simon would never admit it out loud, but Clint Wolf scared him. While Thomas had been the youngest of his siblings, he was the toughest of the clan, and Clint had managed to beat him to death with his bare hands. Simon sighed and guilt flooded over him again, as it had many times over the past few years. When he'd looked into Clint's eyes right before killing his daughter, he had seen a look of cold determination that had given him pause. It should've served as a clue, but Simon was so filled with hatred and disdain for cops that he'd missed the warning signs. If only he'd left the little girl and woman alone, maybe Thomas would be alive today. He shrugged as he considered this. He'd killed women before and nothing bad had happened, so it couldn't have been that. Maybe killing the kid had brought a curse down on him and his brothers. It certainly haunted his dreams from time to time. While he didn't believe in God, he did believe in the devil, and his name was Clint Wolf.

Simon shook his head to clear it. He hadn't been around to avenge the killing of his father at the hand of a cop, but that was because he was too young to jump in a car and go find the bastard. He remembered Pops well. He would take the boys to the beach and buy them nice things. He never knew what Pops did for a living, but he knew he worked nights, and only a few each week. Pops would leave when the boys went to bed and he'd return sometime during the morning hours while they were still asleep. On one rainy night, Simon had awakened to his parents arguing in the kitchen. He'd slipped quietly down the stairs and peered through the spindles, watching as his mom stuck her index finger in his dad's wet face and told him she was tired of *this life*. Young Simon didn't understand what she meant, because Pops was always bringing home cash money—lots of it—and fancy things that he'd later trade for more money, and Mom liked money.

But then there was another night a few months later when everyone in the house was awakened by a loud banging noise downstairs. Before he and his brothers could wipe the sleep from their eyes, cops in black uniforms and masks flooded their bedroom pointing guns at them. All the boys were handcuffed and marched downstairs, where Pops and Mom were lying on their faces. It was the only time he'd seen Pops cry, and it wasn't until he looked up and saw his four boys handcuffed that he broke down.

Pops spent a couple of years in jail after that night. When he got out he promised Mom he'd clean up, but he was shot to death a week later in a midnight robbery. Simon wiped a tear that spilled from his eye and he gritted his teeth. He might not have avenged Pops, but he sure as hell was going to avenge his baby brother—and in a big way. The plan was to kill Clint Wolf and every officer in his department. Maybe even take out a few towns people while they were at it. The world had to know if you messed with a Parker there would be hell to pay. They were going to make history today and they were going to make Pops and Thomas proud.

Simon took a deep breath. He was about to step out from behind the pickup and make his way to the cypress tree when he heard an explosion of gunfire and a crashing sound from the area of the sally port.

CHAPTER 24

I caught my breath and whirled around, searching wildly for the source of the painful scream. I was relieved to see Susan and Amy in the doorway looking over their shoulders. They were okay, but someone was in distress and needed medical assistance right away.

I lurched out of Susan's office and followed her and Amy into the patrol section, where we found one of the deputies hollering in pain.

"Jesus!" he screamed, rocking back and forth on his side and clutching at his stomach with both hands. "I'm hit! I'm hit bad!"

His pistol had fallen from his grasp and blood oozed from a wound in his abdomen. It looked like he took a round to the torso when he'd popped up from behind the desk. I belly-crawled toward him and ripped my outer shirt off on my way to him. Balling it up, I pushed his hands out of the way and shoved my shirt against the bullet hole. I glanced at his nametag. Nate.

"Hang on, Nate," I said. "You'll be fine. Just breathe…that's right, in and out, come on, keep it up." I waved one of the other deputies over and pushed his hands onto my shirt. "Apply pressure."

When Nate's partner took over, I glanced around the room. Broken glass littered the floor and the back wall was so riddled with bullet holes it looked like a honeycomb.

"We need to get him to the hospital." Amy had joined us and was shaking her head. "He doesn't look good."

Even if we could get him through a back window without getting all of us shot, we still needed a vehicle to transport him to the hospital. I pointed toward the door to the processing room, which led to the sally port. "I'll get in my Tahoe and drive it out of there. I'll hit the horn to let y'all know when I'm ready to move and—"

"You'll never make it," Susan argued from where she knelt near the front door. "They'll light you up as soon as the garage door starts going up."

"Then I'll drive right through it," I said flatly. "I'll hit the horn when I'm ready. As soon as I do, direct every bit of firepower y'all have out the front windows to make them keep their heads down. If I see any of them out in the open when I hit daylight, I'm running them down. If not, I'll circle to the south and set up a position where we can triangulate our fire on their location." I pointed to the deputy who was holding pressure on the wounded deputy's gunshot. "While we keep them busy, you get Nate in one of the Chargers and head to the hospital."

Shifting from her knees to her heels, Susan said, "I'm coming with you."

"What if they've already moved positions?" Melvin asked.

I considered his point. They were only firing intermittently now and hadn't fired a shot in a couple of minutes, so they could be gearing up for another frontal attack or they could be circling around to the back. I cursed myself for not investing in security cameras to cover the outside of the building. I turned toward Susan's office. Seth was still in there, so I moved where I could see him. "Seth, do you have eyes on anyone?" I asked.

"If I did they'd be dead," he said. "They're moving like ghosts and using the shadows like a blanket. I haven't gotten a good look at a single one of them yet. They've had tactical training, that's for sure. They're displacing after each volley and changing their plane of attack constantly."

I pursed my lips. I needed to get south of them and light up their position to take away their advantage. "I'm going for the Tahoe." I looked at Susan. "Are you coming?"

She nodded and ducked as she passed by the window and followed me into the sally port. Once we were belted into our seats, I fired up the engine and backed up as far as I could in the sally port to give me some running room. When I was ready, I pressed the horn and smashed the accelerator. The tires screeched on the smooth concrete and our heads were pinned to the headrest as the Tahoe shot toward the garage door. At that same moment, the interior of the police department erupted in gunfire. I sucked in my breath and prepared for crunching metal and daylight as the Tahoe made contact with the garage—

The Tahoe lurched violently to a complete stop, throwing me forward. The seatbelt dug into my collarbone and chest, wrenching me to a halt. The airbag exploded in my face, filling the interior of the cab with gases and particles. I choked on the powder and tried to free myself from the seatbelt, wondering what the hell had just happened.

I could hear Susan coughing to my right and I reached out for her. My hand brushed against her shoulder and I could feel she was moving. She was cursing out loud and quite fluidly, so I figured she was okay. As soon as I got my seatbelt unfastened, I shrugged out of it and pulled the handle on my door. Nothing happened. Holding the handle, I slammed my shoulder against the door. It moved a little and then stopped. I twisted in my seat and pushed my foot against the door frame, straining to force it open. It opened partially, but not enough to squeeze through.

"Can you get out?" I asked Susan.

She coughed several times and then said she was busting out the window. I watched as she drew her pistol and, grabbing it by the barrel, slammed the butt against the glass. It broke easily and she used the metal frame of her pistol to rake the edges clean.

"Let's get out of here," she said when the window was free from shards of glass and safe to crawl through. Grabbing my AR-15, she slipped through the window and squatted low, peering through a break in the garage door.

"Do you see anything?" I pulled my shotgun from the floorboard where it had flown and leaned it against the broken window.

"No, it looks clear." Susan moved around to the back of the Tahoe and opened the rear gate. "Do you want to come through the back?"

I shook my head and crawled over the center console. Once I was in her seat, I leaned my shotgun on the ground and went through the window feet first. The gunfire from inside was starting to fizzle out. They must've shot themselves blank and were probably reloading. I pulled my T-shirt down and hiked up my gun belt, trying to figure out our next move.

The *splat* of a bullet hitting the back wall of the sally port caused me to duck involuntarily. Light appeared through a hole in the garage door where the bullet had just passed. It was about five feet off the ground—too low for comfort.

"Let's get out of here," Susan said. "The garage door can't stop those rounds."

We rushed toward the door to the processing center and had just cleared the opening when a loud explosion erupted behind us. The percussion took my breath away. Smoke and heat shot toward our backs and the entire room turned black.

CHAPTER 25

I bumped into Susan as I stumbled forward and we both fell to the ground. I choked as I crawled away from the explosion, covering my face with my T-shirt and feeling my way through the dark with my hands. Susan moved beside me and we pushed through to the patrol area together. Smoke had already enveloped that part of the building and we could hear everyone choking and gasping for air.

"What's happening?" Lindsey screamed from the back of the police department.

"Keep yelling, Lindsey," I called. "Everyone, move toward the sound of her voice!"

Lindsey continued screaming, but it didn't sound forced—the poor girl was terrified. I put my hand on Susan's back and pushed her forward. "Get to the back and keep it secure," I said through gasps. Keeping my burning eyes squeezed tight, I felt my way toward where I thought Nate to be. Within a few seconds I crawled upon him and started to shove him forward. I could hear others choking and scrambling around the room. They bumped into furniture and I heard the clanking of metal hitting the hard ground as someone dropped a firearm.

Nate's body gave way when I pushed him. I shook him, but there was no movement in response. Lungs burning and feeling like I could no longer hold my breath, I pushed my fingers toward his throat and quickly felt for a pulse. There was none. I crawled over him and stumbled forward on my hands and knees. I yelled out in pain when I slammed headfirst into what had to be Lindsey's desk. It wasn't where it was supposed to be, and it was only then that I remembered them flipping it over for cover. Making my way around it, I scrambled toward the hallway and was relieved to find the smoke lighter there. Someone bumped into me on the right and I heard a woman gasp. It was Amy.

We helped each other forward until we reached the door to the shower room. It was closed, but opened immediately and several pairs of hands grabbed at us and dragged us inside. I saw Melvin shut the door behind us and then sink to the ground against it, heaving as he tried to catch his breath.

"What the hell happened?" Seth asked. He was squatting in the corner wiping sweat from his face.

I quickly took a few breaths of my own and gathered my feet under me. Smoke was trickling through the crack under the door. I hurried and opened the faucets on the showers and sinks. "Let's get that crack closed up," I said.

As I told Seth about the explosion in the sally port, Susan helped me wet some towels and shove them at the base of the door to block the smoke. When we were done, I looked around the room. Lindsey and the two deputies were huddled next to each other beneath one of the windows. Susan stood on one side of me still holding my AR-15 and Amy leaned against the wall on my other side, holding her pistol in her hand. Melvin had moved over to sit on the floor next to the door. He looked tired. Seth had climbed up on the sink to the left side of the room and was peeking through the window there.

Several small explosions sounded from the front of the police department and it caught us off guard. Lindsey let out a scream with each explosion and the rest of us turned toward the door—guns at the ready—expecting someone to burst inside shooting. Realization struck me. "My bag of ammo was out there."

"We need to get out of here," Susan said. "This place is coming down in a hurry."

I knew she was right. There were three windows spread out across the back wall that faced the west. I frowned. If we tried to escape through one of them, we'd be like turtles on a log—just waiting to get shot. "Do you see anything?" I asked Seth.

He shook his head. "If they're out there, I can't see them because of the sun."

I suddenly remembered that the back side of the building formed an alcove—with the south side of the shower room making up one side—and there was a window in the toilet room on that side. I pushed through the sliding door to the toilet room and opened the window. Staying to one side, I peered out the opening and scanned the back of the building. Everything looked clear.

"I think we can make it out of here," I called over my shoulder. The alcove was cloaked in shadows, which would help to conceal our movement. The sun had all but disappeared over the horizon and that was to our advantage.

Melvin had joined me in the toilet room. He pointed toward Seth's truck that was parked behind the building next to his. "Seth has two SWAT radios from the sheriff's office on his front seat. If we can get to them, we can communicate with his office and we'll be back in business."

"They're the walkie-talkie type and they're good for sixteen miles." Seth had walked up behind Melvin. "I'll make a run for them. Y'all can cover me from the other windows."

"I'm going first." I stood on the toilet and slowly stuck my head out the window to get a better view of the back of the building. Other than the rustling of the tree branches in the back yard, nothing moved.

"Please be careful," Susan said.

Without responding, I quickly dove through the window. I landed on my hands and collapsed into a controlled roll, ending up on the balls of my feet. I scurried to a nearby tree and drew my pistol, scanning the area for the Parker brothers. Directly to my left, smoke billowed from the sally port and the smell of burnt material clung to the evening air. Other than that, nothing was out of place.

I heard Seth's gun belt scrape against the metal window frame as he squeezed through it. He appeared next to me within a few seconds. "I'm going for it," he said, fishing the keys from his pocket and pressing the *unlock* button on the keyless remote. With a nod, he bolted from the safety of the tree and sprinted across the open ground as fast as his legs could take him.

I kept my pistol at the ready. My mouth and eyes were wide open, listening and looking for anything that might represent danger. Seth was two steps from his truck and I started to relax. He was going to make it and we would be back in business.

The area to my distant right lit up in gunfire and bullets zipped toward Seth, riddling his body. I jerked in my skin as Seth's right leg went limp in mid-stride and folded right under him, dumping him headfirst into the side of his truck. His head slammed against the frame of the truck and bent at an odd angle. He fell hard and remained motionless. I immediately returned fire, aiming toward where I'd last seen the bright flashes. Melvin let out a rebel yell and jumped from the window calling out his friend's name.

"Stay inside, Melvin," I yelled. "It's too dangerous out here."

His boot snagged on the windowsill and he lost his balance, falling to the ground. Ignoring my warning, he gathered himself and ran toward Seth's lifeless body, shooting his shotgun from the hip as he advanced.

Having shot my pistol dry, I dropped the empty magazine and reloaded. I then chased after Melvin, yelling for Susan and Amy to cover us. I heard gunshots from the friendly part of the building and I holstered my pistol as Melvin and I reached Seth. After securing Seth's truck keys in my pocket, I grabbed his legs and Melvin grabbed his arms and we began dragging him to the alcove. Once there, I dropped to my knees and turned him onto his back. He'd been shot at least eight times—six times through the body, once through the neck, and another through the forehead. I frowned and looked up at Melvin, whose face was burning red in the dim light of the setting sun.

Through gritted teeth, he said, "I'm going to kill those bastards!"

"Calm down, Melvin," I cautioned. "We need to keep our wits about us."

He glanced around and then stared toward Seth's truck. "My shotgun...I left it behind!"

"Wait, we can get another one."

Melvin sprang to his feet and made a dash for the shotgun. I pushed off the ground and followed after him, drawing my pistol and screaming for more cover fire. I heard the familiar report of an AR-15 and the boom of a shotgun behind me and I knew Susan and the others had the shooter pinned down. I relaxed a bit. I was down to my last magazine and didn't want to waste precious rounds shooting at shadows, so I held my fire. Melvin reached his shotgun and snatched it from the ground. Before I could get to him, he charged the shooter's position to the right.

"Stop, Melvin!" I started to run after him, but, out of the corner of my eye, I caught flashes of gunfire from the left and bullets kicked up the mud at my feet. I bolted for Seth's truck and dropped behind the rear wheel well, trying to hide from the glow of the burning building behind me. I popped my head up and tried to see the shooter's position, but it was gray with dusk and his location was outside the glow of the fire.

I turned to look in Melvin's direction, but he had disappeared into the darkness and I couldn't see him any longer. He had fired a few rounds from his shotgun, but then everything had gone quiet on that end of the property. There had been no return fire or any other sounds from that direction.

I scanned the back of the police department—or what was left of it. Flames licked at the sky and I could feel intense heat emitting from the area of the sally port. Susan and the others had ceased firing from the back windows and I could see them at the window to the alcove. It looked like they were helping Lindsey out of the window. They were all coughing at this point and smoke was pouring from every window.

I hesitated, trying to figure out what to do next. Melvin could be in danger or he might even be down and in need of help, but the shooter to my left might be in position to start picking off Susan and the others as they crawled out of the window.

As though reading my thoughts, a shot sounded from my left and someone screamed in pain behind me.

CHAPTER 26

I slipped through the passenger's side of Seth's truck and cranked it up while lying across the seats. Working the accelerator with my left hand and steering with my right, I propelled the truck forward, turning it in the direction of the shooter. A few more shots were fired and a bullet smashed through the windshield, but then all went quiet. I pushed the brake pedal, hitting it a little too hard and sending my body rolling onto the floorboard.

I shoved the gear shift in *park* and scrambled out of the crack between the seat and the dash. I slid into the driver's seat just in time to see a large dark figure dart out of sight around the south side of the police department. I started to drive him down, but Susan yelled for me to wait, so I lurched to a stop. She jumped in through the passenger's door, shoving my shotgun upright in the crack between our seats and cradling the AR in her hands.

"Let's go!" She buzzed her window down and leaned out of it, ready to shoot anything that got in our way.

"Who got hit?" I asked, gunning the engine. The rear tires kicked up mud as they tried to gain traction.

"Lindsey took one to the shoulder, but it went clean through," Susan explained. "She'll be fine."

I could feel the heat from the fire as we rounded the corner of the building. I half expected bullets to pepper the windshield, but I saw Melvin running toward us instead. I brought the truck to a stop and lowered my window.

"They all piled into an old red pickup with a rusted out bed." Melvin was out of breath and pointing behind him. "Three of them. They're heading south on Main and they're heavily armed."

"Take one of Seth's radios," Susan said. She leaned across me and tossed a radio in Melvin's direction. He caught it with one hand and she pointed to the knob. "Turn it to channel six."

Melvin nodded and ran toward his truck. "I'm right behind y'all!"

I smashed the accelerator and raced out of the driveway and onto Main Street. Fire trucks were lined up along the highway and the local fire chief flagged me down. He was bunkered out and his eyes were wild. I recognized him from a fire scene we worked a year ago.

"Clint, we tried to put out the fire, but some man started shooting at us. We had no choice—we had to back out."

I nodded my understanding. "It's clear now, but be careful—there might still be some live ammo inside."

The fire chief began barking orders and firemen sprang into action. I drove around the trucks and sped south. Traffic was heavier than usual and I had to use my lights and siren to clear a path along the highway. We were two miles down the road when I saw a car in a ditch to the right. A lady in a dress was leaning against the back of the car rubbing her head. I slowed down and Susan leaned out her window.

"What happened, ma'am?" Susan asked.

"Some asshole in a red truck ran me off the road!" She pointed south. "He just kept going that way and didn't even stop to check on me. He probably doesn't have insurance."

I started to pull off, but the lady stopped me. "Do you think it has something to do with the fire at the police department? We heard there was an explosion. Do you think it was a terror attack?"

I waved her off and continued south. When the glow of the town was in my rearview mirror, I shut off my siren and strobe lights. The road was completely black, with no traffic in sight. My headlights seemed dim against the backdrop of utter darkness. An uneasy feeling started to form in my belly.

"What if they're waiting to ambush us?" Susan asked, apparently sensing the same thing I was feeling. "Right up the road is where they attacked Amy."

"Then they'll be easy to find." I gripped the steering wheel. "Keep your rifle ready."

We drove for about five minutes and were nearing the end of the highway when I saw headlights approaching. Susan pointed. "It's them!"

I jerked the steering wheel to the right and parked sideways in the roadway. The truck saw the maneuver and slowed to a stop a couple hundred yards away. Grabbing my shotgun from where Susan had secured it, I slipped out the driver's door and stood facing the truck. Susan jumped out of the truck and rested the AR-15 across the hood. "Get behind cover," she said.

The driver of the truck revved the engine several times. The headlights brightened each time the engine roared. I slowly pulled the shotgun to my shoulder and took aim at the driver's side of the windshield, my finger resting on the trigger. As I readied myself to kill the men responsible for murdering my family, I couldn't help but wonder what they had done with Chloe.

"Clint," Susan said, "please get behind the truck."

I focused like a laser on the front sight of my shotgun and ignored her plea. The engine revved again and tires screeched as the driver let off the brake and allowed his mechanical horses to run. Susan screamed one last time at me and then began firing into the oncoming vehicle. I stood like a statue and waited as the truck drew nearer and nearer. I was blinded by the headlights and couldn't see inside, but I knew where the driver's head was supposed to be.

When the truck was about fifty yards away, I pulled the trigger. The butt of the shotgun punched my shoulder as it bucked like a canon in my hands. Without thought, I pumped another round into the chamber and fired again, but the truck swerved violently to the left, taking the shoulder of the road. Loose rocks shot into the air and the wind from the near-miss brushed my hair back. I whirled around and leaned the shotgun against the bed of the truck to steady it. Taking careful aim at the back glass, I fired off a third round.

Brake lights lit up briefly, but the truck continued toward town.

"Let's go!" I called to Susan. "We need to catch them before they get out of town!"

As I whipped the truck around, Susan got on the radio and called for Melvin and asked for his location.

Amy came on the radio. "We're on Main Street, passing Mechant Groceries—heading your way."

I suddenly remembered driving into town from Tennessee and a thought occurred to me. "Tell them to get to the bridge and have the bridge tender raise the lift span."

Susan glanced sideways at me. "Why?"

"Because they'll have nowhere to go—they'll be cut off from the rest of the world." I pursed my lips and nodded. "They'll be stuck in town like mice in a trap."

Susan got on the radio and relayed my orders.

A second later Melvin's voice came through the speakers. "Chief, we don't have a bridge tender. Never have for as long as I've been here."

"Tell him one was working last night," I told Susan. "I know because he opened and closed the bridge for a boat."

Susan passed the information on to Melvin and the radio went silent for about three minutes. As we sped toward town, I wondered if they would get it up in time. If the Parker brothers made it past the bridge, we might never catch them.

When the radio scratched to life again, Amy came on to say there were no bridge tenders onboard. "It looks like someone kicked the door open at some point," Amy said, "but no one's here."

Susan keyed up the radio. "Just do whatever you have to do to get it open. Blow the damn thing up if you have to!"

We were a mile from town before we finally caught up to the red pickup truck. I had the needle on Seth's unit buried at 120 miles per hour. The trees on the shoulder of the road blurred by and the wind rocked the unit. Lights flashing and siren blaring, I crept up close to the bumper of the pickup, trying to see into the back windshield. There was a hole on the driver's side where my slug had passed through, but I couldn't see blood or flesh around the hole. I cursed silently to myself. The driver must've ducked down.

"You might want to ease up a bit," Susan warned as she clutched at the dashboard. "If they crash or stop suddenly, we'll go right up their asses."

I slowed a little and turned the bright lights on. "Can you see inside the cab?"

"No," Susan said. "Why? Do you not think it's them?"

"I want to see if they're all inside. If not, one of them might be holding Chloe somewhere else."

Susan was quiet as we took the first curve into town and raced toward the northern end. She finally put a hand on my arm. "I'm so sorry, Clint."

It was all she said and I knew she thought Chloe was dead. I gritted my teeth and thought about ramming their truck.

"Look!" Susan said, pointing about a mile ahead of the truck. "They got the bridge up!"

She was right. The lights on the side of the lift span burned bright in the sky and the gates were down. A dim glow burned from the windows of the bridge cabin. I smiled my approval. Melvin and Amy had figured out how to work the bridge. This was it—the Parker brothers were trapped! I eased off the accelerator in anticipation of them stopping.

"Are you loaded?" I asked Susan.

"I am, but I've only got half a mag left—sixteen at the most." Susan hoisted the rifle in her hands. "But that's plenty, right? There're only three of them."

I looked up at the bridge cabin. It was on the northern side of the bridge, but it wasn't too far. I'd seen Melvin shoot a rifle and I knew how good he was. He and Amy would have a decent vantage point from up there. I told Susan to radio them and tell them to prepare to pin down the Parker brothers if they got out shooting. Susan nodded and made the transmission.

I suddenly realized the truck was steadily pulling away from us. They weren't slowing down! It even seemed to pick up speed as it whisked by Cig's Gas Station and approached the ramp to the bridge.

"What in hell's name are they doing?" I asked, stealing a glance at Susan. She stared wide-eyed out the windshield and just shook her head.

I slowed our vehicle and waited for the splash of red taillights on the pickup. It had to come at any moment, because they were running out of roadway.

"Clint, I don't think they're…" Susan's voice trailed off as the truck crashed right through the safety gates, sending splintered wood and lights flying skyward. The brake lights never came on as the pickup raced forward and plunged over the edge, disappearing from our view.

CHAPTER 27

"Holy shit!" Melvin called over the radio. "Did y'all see that?"

I drove up the ramp, through the safety gate debris, and stopped a few feet from where we'd last seen the truck. Susan and I both jumped out and ran to the edge of the deck and peered over. Other than the lapping of waves against the bank and a gurgling sound from the throat of the bayou, everything was quiet.

I heard boot heels clanking against metal and looked across to see Melvin and Amy hurrying down the catwalk from the cabin, two beams of light bobbing up and down as they ran. When they hit the landing to the stairs, they sprinted to the edge of the opposite deck and aimed their lights into the water below.

"Do y'all see anything?" I hollered, straining to penetrate the darkness below.

After a brief moment, Melvin yelled back that he couldn't see anything. It was difficult to understand him because of the distance and him being out of breath.

"I can't believe they did that!" Amy called. She was in better shape than Melvin and wasn't as winded. She aimed her light at where we thought the truck would be, but Bayou Tail had swallowed it up.

Susan had retrieved a spotlight and she lit up the northern bank, but there was no sign of life. I couldn't see the southern bank because it was somewhere under us, so I asked Amy and Melvin if they could see anything. They couldn't.

"Susan, come with me." I turned and ran toward Seth's unit, calling over my shoulder, "Keep those lights on the water. If anything moves, shoot it!"

Susan and I backed off the bridge in the truck and proceeded to Grace Street. After driving a couple of blocks, we turned north on a cross street and then left on Bayou Tail Lane. I hugged the grassy shoulder, heading toward the underside of the bridge, and Susan used the spotlight to scan the banks of the bayou.

I stopped directly under the bridge and angled the truck so the headlights lit up the water. We jumped out and I drew my pistol as I rounded the front of the vehicle. Susan had the spotlight in one hand and she was cradling the AR-15 in the crook of her other arm.

We moved out of the glow from the headlights and scanned the surface of Bayou Tail.

"I don't see a thing," Susan whispered from beside me. "It's like nothing happened down here."

She was right. The water had grown still—deathly still. Had the Parker brothers perished in the crash? A sinking feeling fell over me. If they were gone, I might never find out what they did to Chloe. The bayou was at least two hundred feet wide and the water depth under the bridge was over twenty-five feet. That was far beyond most people's swimming capabilities—even if the water were clear. Here, the water was black and foreboding. Even if they did escape from the truck, they wouldn't know which way was up or down. We'd definitely need a boat and some experienced divers to search for their bodies.

I kicked at the ground. Before Chloe had disappeared, I'd prepared myself for a confrontation with the Parkers. I'd thought carefully about what I would do when I came face to face with them. Had planned what I would say. Those plans had changed when Chloe went missing. I needed them to tell me where she was and what had happened to her, which would require some smooth talking. But that was before they attacked my office.

Susan pulled out her phone and checked the time. "It's been about seven minutes since they disappeared," she said. "I think they're gone."

I sighed. "I'm afraid you're right."

"You sound disappointed."

"I needed them to tell me where to find Chloe."

"What if they had nothing to do with her disappearance?"

I asked what she meant.

"What if she simply left the area?"

"For what reason?"

"What if she needed a change of scenery? Or just made a run for it? Some girls get spooked when relationships get too serious."

"Our relationship wasn't too serious."

"Right, because moving in isn't a major commitment."

"It's not like we were talking marriage or anything."

Susan grunted and didn't say another word for a while, but her suggestion continued burning in my brain long after she'd spoken it. I found myself hoping she was right, but suspecting she wasn't. Stepping out on me was one thing—scaring her parents was something different.

Susan and I stood there silently looking out over the water. She stabbed the light at every little ripple of water, the faintest snap of a twig, or slightest rustle of grass, but there was no sign of the brothers. What if they'd escaped before we could get to the edge of the deck? I'd had survival training and time was of the essence if one wanted to escape a vehicle alive. If they'd had similar training, they would've been out of that truck in an instant and could've been heading downstream before we made it to the top of the bridge and out of the unit. I posed the question to Susan.

She mulled on it for a while and then said, "Anything's possible, Clint. Anything."

I started to walk west along the bank in case they had made it out and were headed in that direction, but I stopped when I heard sirens in the distance to the north. Melvin must've gotten word to the sheriff's office that we needed help.

The large pillars that held up the bridge began to vibrate slightly, followed shortly afterward by squealing pulleys and rattling chain. I looked up to see the lift span slowly coming down. The earth shook when it finally settled into place.

"Melvin's getting good at driving bridges," Susan said, but neither of us laughed.

CHAPTER 28

8:30 a.m., Friday, October 30
Mechant Loup Bridge

Sheriff Turner stood beside me under the Mechant Loup Bridge on the southern bank of Bayou Tail and we watched as his divers prepared to launch themselves off of Melvin's boat. They were closer to the northern bank and we used binoculars to watch their movements.

Although I tried not to show it, I was tired. My officers and I had spent a restless night along Bayou Tail Lane watching for any signs of the Parkers. Amy and Melvin had taken first watch while Susan and I returned to the scene of the shooting and helped Sheriff Turner's detectives sift through the rubble at the police department. At my request, the sheriff had agreed to have his detectives take lead on the investigation into the gun battle at my office.

Within minutes of speaking with Detectives Doug Cagle and Mallory Tuttle, it became painfully obvious that we didn't have a case against the Parker brothers, because not one of us could identify the men who attacked us. I had immediately named them as the shooters when first speaking with them, but when Mallory asked which Parker brother was at which firing position, I had to acknowledge I hadn't seen any of them. I didn't like it one bit, but that was the way it went.

After the fire department had put out the fire, Mallory and Doug had asked me to pinpoint the locations of each body to help with the identification process. Once we were done at the fire scene, Susan and I had returned to the crash site and watched the bayou for signs of life while Amy and Melvin napped in the back of his truck. We had switched places two hours later, and each pulled two shifts before Sheriff Turner's dive team had arrived at daybreak.

I was having a hard time keeping my eyes open, so the first thing I did was walk to Cig's for a cup of coffee. I hadn't gotten a wink of sleep, because each time I dozed off I kept seeing Abigail's face. Once, when I'd jerked awake, it caused Susan—who was snoozing at the far end of the truck bed—to stir from her sleep, and she'd asked if everything was okay. Not wanting to interrupt her any more, I focused on remaining awake.

Standing there with the sheriff, I'd just taken my last sip of coffee and wanted another one. There had been no signs of life on the water or either bank during the night, so we all knew it was a recovery mission. Whoever was down there was already dead and there was nothing anyone could do for them. I, on the other hand, was alive and in dire need of coffee, so I was going get another—

"Do you think those bastards are still down there?" Sheriff Turner's voice startled me.

"I…I don't know, Sheriff. I really don't know."

"Mallory tells me you think they're the same pieces of shit who murdered your family."

I wanted to say I did, but ever since Mallory pressed me on what I'd seen, I'd begun to question my theory. After all, the district attorney's office in the city had dropped the charges against them due to lack of evidence, and who was I to argue with them? I had to admit to myself it *was* possible someone else was responsible for the attack on our office, and the murder of the bar tender, and Chloe's disappearance.

"Damn it!" I shook my head to clear it. This all *had* to be the work of the Parker brothers. I couldn't think of anyone else who had the motive or the stones to take on an entire police department. "It has to be them, Sheriff."

I found myself starting to hope their bodies were down there. It would be all the proof we needed that they attacked us, and it would bring closure to the investigation. If they weren't down there, they might just get away with murder again—and I couldn't let that happen.

Either way, I still didn't know what had happened to Chloe, and it made me sick to my stomach. *Here's hoping Susan was right,* I thought, *and Chloe had made a run for it.*

Within minutes, one of the divers dropped into the bayou and floated beside the boat, waiting for his partner to join him. When they were both in the water, they gave a nod and slowly disappeared into the blackness below. Melvin and a water patrol deputy named Sean manned the ropes attached to each of the divers and stood hunched over, feeding just enough slack for their descent.

Melvin's face was taut and his eyes narrow. I'd never seen him so serious. I wondered if he was thinking of his wife and toddler back home. After living through a night like last night, it could cause any officer to reevaluate his priorities and to question his reason for doing this job.

Things were a bit too quiet, so I thanked Sheriff Turner again for his assistance and apologized for the loss of his deputies. "They risked their lives to save ours," I said. "They fought to the very end. I'm proud to say I knew them."

"Seth was one of my best deputies." Turner's tone was somber. "Nate was new, but he had a ton of potential. Making the notification to their families was the hardest thing I've ever had to do." He removed his cowboy hat and rubbed beads of sweat from his forehead. "They sure don't warn you about that kind of thing in sheriff school."

I nodded my agreement. It was one of the worst parts of the job and something I'd never grow accustomed to.

"I have to get back to the office," Turner said after a few minutes. "If you don't mind, I'll take Seth's personal belongings from his truck and then leave it with you. You can use it as long as you want. Let me know if there's anything else my department can do for you …anything at all."

I thanked him and turned as Susan walked over from where she'd been talking on her cell phone. Phone crews had worked late into the morning repairing the cell tower north of town and they'd gotten things running in quick order—much quicker than after a hurricane, where they'd have to contend with high winds and widespread damage.

"Lindsey's fine," she said. "They patched her up and sent her home."

"Think she'll ever come back to work?" I asked. "She seemed pretty freaked out in there."

Susan frowned. "Is there anything to come back to? Our office is completely destroyed."

I just shrugged. She had been there when I'd run into one of Mechant Loup's councilmen at the fire scene earlier in the morning. When I'd asked about using some offices in the new town hall building, he said he would have to run it by the other members. He was concerned that our presence there would put the entire council and their employees in danger. "If you find the Parker clan at the bottom of Bayou Tail, we'll move y'all in today," he had said. "If not…I just don't know."

I couldn't say I blamed him. It seemed everyone who stood next to me was in danger. I didn't like being the cause of so much pain and misery. First, it was my family. Now, it was everyone else in my life. Why couldn't the Parker brothers have kept things between them and me? By going after Amy, Chloe, Dexter, and everyone else, they'd done nothing more than reinforce my desire to see them dead. They'd started a war…a war I planned on winning.

"Let's have a seat over here," Susan said, nudging my arm and waving me toward a shady spot under the bridge where large rocks cropped up out of the bank. I sat next to her and watched as she took stock of her ammunition. Soot was smudged on her forehead, and her uniform shirt was ripped in a couple of places. There was blood on the outside of her left hand and I wasn't sure if it had spilled from her own body or someone else's. After she'd finished counting rounds, she leaned the AR against one of the nearby rocks and folded her arms across her chest. "You think they'll find anything?"

I followed her gaze. Melvin was still watching the water intently. A large wrecker had arrived and parked on the opposite side of the bayou.

"At this point, I sure hope they do. I'm ready for this to be over. Enough people have died over those assholes." My thoughts returned to Chloe and I asked Susan if I could borrow her phone. I hadn't seen mine since we'd crashed my Tahoe in the sally port. She handed it to me and I found myself just staring at it.

"What's wrong?"

"I don't even know my own girlfriend's phone number." Although I'd recently been given her dad's number, I couldn't remember his either, so I handed the phone back to Susan.

It was cool under the bridge and would've been pleasant under different circumstances. The gentle breeze caressed my face. I wanted to lie down on the ground and fall asleep, but I knew I couldn't. I was about to get up and walk to Cig's for more coffee when Susan spoke.

"So, I've been thinking," she began slowly, and then stopped.

When she didn't continue, I asked, "About?"

"I know I told you I didn't want to know if my dad had done something terrible. I wanted to remember him like I knew him."

I nodded.

"Well, I believe I want to know what you found out. I don't think I can live in peace knowing Bill Hedd knows something about my dad that I don't know."

"It's your choice, Sue. I'll do whatever you want me to do...whatever makes you comfortable."

She took a deep breath and blew it out forcefully. "Okay, tell me—and tell me fast, like ripping off a bandage."

I didn't hesitate. I told her everything Conner had told me and explained what happened with Bill and her attorney. "He didn't want the world knowing his wife was a liar and a cheat, so he decided to drop the false charges against you."

Before she had time to process what I'd told her, Melvin hollered from the boat. "We've got movement! They're coming up!"

CHAPTER 29

Susan and I jumped to our feet and moved to the water's edge, watching through binoculars with bated breath. White bubbles rose slowly to the surface and increased in volume and intensity. Before long, the divers broke the surface of the water. Melvin and Sean helped them onto the deck of the boat, where they removed their breathing apparatuses. One of the divers shook his head and said something to Melvin, who immediately pulled out the radio loaner from the sheriff. The radio on my belt scratched to life.

"The truck's down there, but they think it's empty," Melvin reported.

My heart sank. "Do they think the Parkers got away?"

"They're not sure at the moment," he called back. "They're going back down to attach a cable to the truck. As soon as the wrecker pulls the truck from the water, they'll go back down and search the bottom for bodies."

Susan and I exchanged looks and I asked her what she thought.

"Let's wait and see what they find on the bottom. I'm hoping the truck landed on top of them."

While the divers went back under to attach a cable to the truck, Susan and I decided to walk to Cig's for more coffee.

We were about fifty yards from the store when I smelled food cooking. I shielded my eyes from the sun and saw a large tent in the parking lot. A dozen people were bustling about under the tent and several others were bent over massive metal pots that sat on top of large burners. When we got closer, I saw shrimp jambalaya in one pot and chicken and sausage gumbo in another. My stomach growled.

"What's all this about?" Susan asked.

I didn't know, so I nodded to a man wearing a dirty apron and asked what was going on.

"We heard what happened, so we figured y'all could use some food—and some backup." He shot a thumb over his shoulder and I looked where he pointed. There were at least ten men huddled near a van and they all carried long guns and had pistols strapped to their belts. By their clothes and choice of weapons—long-barrel shotguns and hunting rifles—I'd guess they were trappers or alligator hunters, and they looked ready for battle.

Susan and I sauntered over to where they stood and I introduced us. After shaking hands all around, one of the men spoke up. "I'm Brennan Boudreaux—Dexter's brother," he said. "And these are my friends. We figured you could use more fire power, considering what all happened yesterday. And if you're hunting the men that killed Dexter, I want to be a part of that posse."

I immediately saw the resemblance. Although a bit younger, the man could've passed for Dexter's twin.

One of Brennan's friends spat a stream of tobacco juice to the pavement. "I only wish we'd been around when the shit went down." His eyes turned to slits. "Things would've turned out different, that's for sure."

I wasn't ashamed to say I would've welcomed their help, and I did exactly that. "We could've used y'all."

There was a round of somber nods that was interrupted when an elderly woman walked up carrying two plastic bowls of jambalaya. She handed one to Susan and one to me. "Y'all must be starving."

We thanked her and I asked if there was more for Melvin and the divers. The woman laughed. "When we cook around here, there's enough to feed everyone…everywhere in the world."

Brennan and two of the other men offered to help us carry the food, and we waited while the woman made extra bowls. With drinks and food in hand, we made our way back to Seth's truck and drove across the bridge to the northern bank with the food. A couple of news vans were parked on the shoulder of the highway and crews were unloading their equipment. I frowned as I thought of Chloe. I fought the urge to panic. *Where the hell are you?*

The wrecker was just pulling the old red pickup from the depths of Bayou Tail when we drove down the embankment and parked. Mud and water gushed off the metal as the winch lifted it onto the shore and dragged it toward the wrecker. The operator stopped the truck near the wrecker and made preparations to drag it onto the flatbed. I stepped forward and looked through the open driver's door, hoping to see a body smashed up under the dash. It was empty. I scanned the back seat, but it was also empty. Even the weapons were gone—and that wasn't a good sign.

After the truck was secured on the flatbed and the divers had stripped out of their gear, Susan and I disseminated the food and we all huddled under the bridge—out of sight of the reporters—to eat.

As he munched on a bite of jambalaya, one of the divers mentioned finding the driver's door open when he approached the truck underwater. "I went to pull on the handle, but it was already open. Not by much, mind you, but it *was* open. I think they made it out the truck." He paused to take another bite of his food. "And if they did, they could've survived."

"We never took our eyes off the water," I said. "Wouldn't we have seen them come up?"

The diver shrugged. "Not always. We had a suspect crash his car in the bayou about a year ago in broad daylight. Patrol was right behind him and saw his car hit the water. He never surfaced, so they called me to recover his body, but I couldn't find him. He showed up at his grandma's house later that night."

"So," I said slowly, "are you saying we could've missed them?"

"It's quite possible."

Putting my empty bowl aside, I stood to my feet and looked toward the west, where Bayou Tail eventually spilled into Lake Berg. Could they have made it that far? I then scanned the southern bank of the bayou. We had been there all night and would've heard something if they had crawled their way out of the bayou. I turned my attention to the northern bank, looking first to my left and then to my right. The underbrush was thicker on this side of the bayou. What if they were hiding out in the bushes at that very moment, just waiting to attack us?

"They could be long gone," Melvin said. "Or they could be watching us right now."

I saw Susan's hand inch toward the AR-15. "I think we need to get a helicopter and a K-9 officer out here to start working the banks—just in case we missed something."

"That's not a bad idea." I turned to Melvin. "I'm open to suggestions."

He frowned and lowered his head. He was thoughtful for a while. Finally, he looked up. "Gretchen Verdin was Seth's sergeant and she's part Chitimacha Indian. She can track a roach across the surface of the water without her dog. Together, they're dangerous."

"Can you get her here?"

Sean stood and started toward his patrol car that was parked nearby. "I'll get her on the radio. I think she's working days, so she should be out and about by now."

One of the divers stood and tossed his garbage in a plastic bag we'd tied to the tailgate of Melvin's truck. "We'll get back in and search the bottom just in case they drowned."

Melvin nodded and made his way to where his boat was tied to a tree. As he and the divers boarded the vessel and cruised toward the middle of the bayou, Susan and I stood on the bank and watched.

Susan pointed across the bayou in the direction of Cig's. "Your house is a mile away. You don't think they know that, do you?"

I scrunched my face. "Who?"

"The Parker brothers." She searched my eyes. "If they survived the crash, they might be heading that way to ambush you."

"That would make my day." I turned away and started walking toward Seth's truck, calling over my shoulder, "I'll be back."

"Where're you going?"

"Visit with Chloe's parents."

CHAPTER 30

Mrs. Rushing burst through the front door of her house before I had a chance to get out of the truck. "Did you find her?" she asked, her face red and streaked with tears. "Is she okay?"

I frowned and simply shook my head. Chloe's dad walked outside and shoved his hands deep in his pockets. "Clint, what's happened to our baby girl?"

"I don't know." I crossed my arms and studied both of them. They were in genuine pain, so they obviously knew nothing. I tried to be objective. "Has Chloe ever done anything like this before?"

"What do you mean?" Mrs. Rushing asked.

"Has she ever taken off without telling anyone anything?"

"You mean run away?" Mr. Rushing asked. He looked at his wife and then stared down at the ground. When he didn't say anything, I prompted him for more.

"What is it?" I asked. "What aren't you telling me?"

Mrs. Rushing stood there wringing her hands as she explained how Chloe had run away when she was in high school. "It was all over a stupid fight. She wanted to go to a concert with some friends, but we told her she couldn't go. She became really angry and—"

"It was in the city," Mr. Rushing interjected. "Her friend had just gotten her license and we didn't trust her driving, so we told her she couldn't go. If was for her own safety."

"Did she go anyway?" I asked.

Mr. Rushing shook his head. "She went into her room and slammed the door. An hour later we called her in for supper and she didn't answer. When we checked her room we found her window unlocked. The screen was on the ground outside the window and she was gone."

"We called everyone she knew," Mrs. Rushing said, "but no one had seen her or heard from her. Andy drove to the city and tried to get into the concert hall to search for her, but they wouldn't let him in without a ticket."

Mr. Rushing nodded. "I found a payphone and got in touch with her friends' parents. Two of the dads met me out there and we found the car in the parking lot and waited. When the concert was over the girls came out to the car, but Chloe wasn't with them."

They explained how they had contacted the sheriff's office and made a report. "The detective on the case got her friends to talk and they finally told him where she was hiding." Mr. Rushing shook his head.

I raised an eyebrow. "Where was she?"

Mrs. Rushing lowered her head. "She was with some older boy she'd met at the mall. His parents didn't even know she was there."

"Yeah, he snuck her in through his bedroom window." Mr. Rushing took a deep breath and exhaled. "To say I was pissed is putting it mildly. When I questioned her, she said she wanted to get us back for not letting her go to the concert—she wanted to hurt us like we had hurt her."

I pulled at my dirty T-shirt and pondered everything I'd just learned. I'd done stupid things in my youth, as had everyone, but what if Chloe still had that wild streak in her? What if she was mad at me for going to Tennessee and wanted to make me feel what she felt? She did sound upset over the phone when I first told her I was making the trip. "If she were to do that sort of thing again," I began, "where might she run off to?"

The Rushings traded looks and then shook their heads in unison. "I have no idea," Mrs. Rushing admitted. "Ever since she moved out we've pretty much stayed out of her business."

I began searching the recesses of my brain, trying to remember if she had ever mentioned a name of a friend, but couldn't think of any. She had only talked about her work companions. Thinking they might know more about Chloe, I checked on Achilles and then hurried to the truck to go interview her work associates. I heard my name over the sheriff's radio when I got inside. It was Susan and she seemed impatient.

"Go ahead," I responded.

"They found another vehicle in the bayou," she said. "You need to get here quick!"

CHAPTER 31

I raced down Bayou Tail Lane and jumped from the truck in time to watch the wrecker driver work the levers on the winch. As the cable wound around the spool, it made an occasional popping sound and jerked into place, spraying water along its length.

Brennan Boudreaux and some of his friends were standing on the street. Brennan nodded in my direction. "Anything you need, Chief."

I nodded my thanks and hurried to where Susan and Melvin stood near the wrecker. "What's going on?"

Susan shot a thumb toward the divers, who were stripping their gear off in the shade under the bridge. "They said they were searching the bottom for bodies and came upon another car, but they think this one was heading south when it went into the water."

I glanced across the bayou. A team of reporters were crowding along the northern bank, their cameras aimed in our direction. A dark feeling suddenly fell over me. "Oh, shit! Do you think we caused this accident when we opened the bridge? The lights on the northern gates are burnt."

"No way!" Melvin shook his head from side to side. "Amy and I were up there and could see for miles. The only car that went off the bridge was the truck."

I relaxed a little, but suddenly remembered driving home Wednesday night and what Amy had said over the radio yesterday. "Melvin, did y'all really find the door to the bridge cabin kicked open?"

Melvin nodded. There was a blank look on his face. "We haven't had a bridge tender in years. It was probably some kids being stupid, or some teenagers finding a place to hook up."

"The bridge was up Wednesday night when I came home from Tennessee," I explained. "Someone dumped this vehicle over the edge."

"How do you know that?" Melvin wanted to know.

"The gates on the north side aren't broken," I explained. "That means someone drove up to the edge of the deck first, raised the lift span—which lowers the gates—and then pushed the vehicle over the edge." I pursed my lips and shook my head, remembering the ripples in the water that night. "And I showed up right after they did it."

"But why would someone push a car over the edge?" Susan asked. "What would be the point of that?"

I sighed. I had no idea why, but I couldn't think of another logical reason for a car to be at the bottom of Bayou Tail—and especially in that area. The only way to get a car down there would be by going over one of the decks.

One of the divers walked up to where we stood. His wet suit sloshed as he walked. "I felt around on the inside, but I didn't feel any bodies," he said.

"We'll know soon enough." I pointed to the edge of the bank, where the water was bubbling up and the front bumper of a red car emerged from the disturbed water. My knees suddenly went weak and I stumbled forward.

"Clint, what are you doing?" Susan asked, grabbing my shoulder.

"That's Chloe's car!" I brushed her off and rushed down the grassy embankment and into the bayou. Water immediately saturated my shoes, but I didn't care. The wrecker operator hollered a warning, but I continued onward, grabbing onto the side of the muddy car to steady myself. My heart raced in my chest and a fog of confusion filled my brain. How could this be? She couldn't be inside the car— I'd received text messages from her after Wednesday night. And who had been in the bridge cabin? Could she have done this? Was she trying to disappear?

My foot slipped on a slimy rock and I fell backward, splashing into the bayou. Dirty water shot up my nose and into my mouth. I twisted around and scrambled to my feet, choking on the muddy soup. I plunged forward, sinking to my chest as I reached for the open window frame. I pulled myself partially through the opening and stared wildly about, searching every inch of the car with my eyes. I relaxed and backed out of the window when I realized it was empty.

Susan appeared beside me and put an arm around my back. "Come on, Clint, we have to back away so the operator can get her car out of the bayou."

I nodded and allowed her to lead me back to the bank, where I plopped to a seated position in the wet mud. "It's empty," I said.

"She's not inside."

"That's a relief." Susan sat beside me and pushed her wet hair back. "If she's not inside, where is she?"

I stood and extended my hand. Susan took it and I braced myself as she pulled herself to her feet. While the wrecker finished pulling Chloe's car from the bayou, I turned to the divers. "Are y'all sure no one's down there?"

They shook their heads in unison, and one said, "There's no way we can be sure. We combed the bottom as best we could and didn't find anything, but there's a possibility the current could've moved the bodies downstream."

Melvin walked to Chloe's car and opened the driver's door. He knelt beside it for a moment and then hollered for me to walk over. Susan and I hurried to the car and I looked where he pointed. The driver's seat had been pushed completely forward and the car jack was propped between the seat and the accelerator. It had been fully extended and was lodged firmly in place, pinning the accelerator to the floor.

I rubbed my chin. "So, she wasn't inside when the car went off the bridge."

A puzzled expression fell over Susan's face. "Do you think Chloe dumped her own car in the bayou?"

That thought was already haunting me. What if she did do this? If so, she had stood in the bridge cabin watching me that night. I shivered, more from the thought than the cool breeze blowing over my wet body. After what her parents told me, I had to wonder if I really knew her at all. Sure, we hadn't told each other everything about ourselves, but that type of behavior seemed a bit extreme for a teenager.

Melvin removed the keys from the ignition. "I'll check if the jack is from her car," he said, making his way to the trunk.

I nodded idly and watched as he slipped the key into the hole. I was still trying to figure out why Chloe would've done this when the trunk lid swung up. I frowned when I saw Melvin's mouth drop open and his eyes grow instantly wide. He lurched backward and screamed, "Holy shit!"

I rushed toward the trunk, but he waved his arms and screamed for me to stay back. I ignored him, continuing forward. When he stepped into my path, I shoved him aside and craned my head to see what all the fuss was about. When my eyes came to rest on what he had seen, I jerked my head away and fell to my knees. Bile rose to my throat and I vomited on the ground.

CHAPTER 32

Susan rushed past me and stopped dead in her tracks, staring in disbelief. "Dear God," she said in a strained voice. "What in the hell's going on?"

My head swam. I felt weak. I thought I was going to pass out, but I somehow managed to hold myself together until the moment passed. As I slowly processed what I'd seen, anger began to grow in the pit of my stomach. After a dozen uncertain seconds, I stood on wobbly legs and approached the trunk.

"Jesus, Clint, just stay back," Susan pleaded.

I shook my head and reached for the trunk lid, steadying myself. I forced my eyes back to Chloe's lifeless face and bit down hard, trying to keep what was left of my lunch in my stomach. I felt numb. The woman I'd come to know was lying in a heap in the trunk of her own car—and it might very well be my fault.

Chloe's face was ashen and her eyes were wide open, as though she'd fought death to the very end, trying not to let the light fade to darkness. I reached out to touch her and jerked my hand back when I felt her cold skin. It was not how I remembered her. Her body had always been so warm and inviting.

"Chief, I'm so sorry," Melvin said. He put an arm around my right shoulder and Susan put an arm around my left one, and we all stared in silence.

After what seemed like forever, I allowed my eyes to take in the rest of her body, searching for clues as to why she was there. She was wearing a green sun dress and matching sandals. There were three dark stains on the front of her dress, and I winced when I realized it was blood from gunshot wounds. I moved closer on unsteady legs and tilted her head to the side. In her left ear there was a snowflake earring I'd bought her for Christmas, but the right one was missing. Her fingernails were intact and clean, and her knuckles didn't appear bruised. I lifted one arm and then the other, but none contained any defensive wounds.

"It's like she didn't know what hit her," I mumbled. "Like she didn't see it coming."

"Chief, didn't you say someone opened the bridge Wednesday night?" Melvin asked.

Not taking my eyes off of Chloe's body, I nodded.

"It must've been the killer," he said, "because someone broke into the bridge cabin, and it looked fresh. I'm going process the cabin. I'll search for prints, DNA, shoe patterns—anything I can find."

I nodded again, but I already knew what he'd find. The Parker brothers were responsible for this. They'd attacked Amy at the bridge and they dumped Chloe and her vehicle into the bayou.

When Melvin had driven away, I shook my head to clear it. I needed to tell Chloe's parents and then I needed to hunt down the Parker brothers and take them in. I was hoping they resisted arrest, because I wanted them dead. But I couldn't start tromping around in the swamps until that tracker from the sheriff's office arrived at the scene. If I messed up any potential scents, we'd never find them.

"Where's Gretchen Verdin?" I asked to no one in particular. "We need to start tracking these bastards right away!"

"She's on her way," Sean called out. "She should be here in fifteen minutes."

Susan moved in front of me and put her hands on my face. Looking me right in the eyes, she said, "You need time to grieve and you need some rest. We can take care of tracking the Parker brothers. I'll see to it personally."

I grunted and shook my head. "No way are you taking this from me, Susan. The Parkers are my problem and I'm going to deal with them."

Susan chewed on her lower lip for a moment. Finally, the hard lines on her face relaxed. "Okay, but I'm going with you."

"That's fine." I reached up and pulled the trunk shut. "I don't want people gawking at her like this."

"I understand," Susan said. "I'll get Mallory and Doug down here to process the car. It's best if they handle the investigation."

"They can handle the case, but I'm making the notification." We made our way back to the bank of the bayou and I pointed to where my AR-15 was leaning against one of the pillars under the bridge. "Do you need more ammo for that?"

She nodded.

"After we notify Chloe's parents, we'll drive to my house and load up on ammo. I want to make damn sure we have enough firepower to put an end to this shit."

We were about to leave when I heard the roar of an engine approaching at a high rate of speed. I turned to see Reginald's large F-250 skidding onto the shoulder. He jumped out and approached Susan and me at a brisk walk.

"Isabel said Chloe Rushing was found dead," he said. "Is it true?"

I nodded. "She was murdered."

"Damn." Reginald shook his head and frowned. "I'm sorry, Clint, and so is Isabel. She told me to let you know we're here if you need anything. She wanted to come here herself, but she's stuck in court."

I thanked him and told him we had to go. "We'll be back in a few," I explained. "Melvin can update you on what's been going on here."

CHAPTER 33

8:45 p.m.
Clint Wolf's House

Ringleader scanned the restaurant. His front tooth on the left side was missing and he pushed the tip of his tongue through the gap, then scowled. "When I give an order, I expect it to be followed. When it's not, there are consequences!"

"Sir, you're right. I disobeyed your order—"

"I know I'm right!" Ringleader jerked Abigail around in front of him as he stepped forward. She screeched in terror, tears pouring down her pale face.

"Abbie, it's okay," I said calmly. "Just look at Daddy. I promise you, everything's going to be—"

"Shut the hell up!" Ringleader pointed the pistol at me. "Are you a pig? You're acting like a pig right now." He sniffed the air. "You smell like a damn pig!"

There was too much distance between us for me to disarm him. I shifted my eyes from him to the other three men. I could see Paunchy dragging himself to his feet in my peripheral vision. The pistol was on the floor in front of him, but was too far from me.

Ringleader shoved the pistol roughly into the side of Abigail's temple, making her cry even louder. He glared at me. "Are you a pig?"

"No, I'm not a cop. I'm just a guy who took his wife and daughter out to dinner. Please, I'm begging you not to hurt her."

"Begging, eh? Get on your knees and beg me like you mean it."

I dropped to my knees, folded my hands in front of my face. "Please, sir, I beg you not to hurt Abigail. She's six years old. She just recently graduated from kindergarten and—"

"Cops," one of the other robbers called. "The cops are coming!"

"You should've stayed in your seat." Ringleader smiled and pulled the trigger.

———

I jerked awake and stared wildly about, not knowing where I was or what was happening.

"Are you okay?" It was Susan's voice and she was in the driver's seat of Seth's truck. There were worry lines on her face. "You must've fallen asleep. You were mumbling and grunting."

I took a deep breath and settled down, remembering. After notifying Chloe's parents about her murder, Susan and I had served as Gretchen's cover team as she worked her K-9 up and down the northern banks of Bayou Tail searching for a scent, but they'd found none. The sun had finally gone down on us and we were forced to abandon the search until morning.

I straightened and gathered up my shotgun and bag of ammunition. "Pick me up in the morning?"

Susan nodded. After a moment, she said, "I'm so sorry about Chloe. You've suffered so much in your life already and to have this happen to you…"

"Thanks." I fidgeted in my seat. "Do you know when they're doing her autopsy?"

"Mallory said they're shooting for tomorrow afternoon, but it depends on how long it takes to do the others." She sighed. "This has been the second worst day of my life, Clint."

I nodded my agreement. I knew what her worst day had been and she knew mine. We both sat in silence, each understanding the other. I finally opened my door and slid out. I paused to look at her before shutting the door. Her eyes were moist.

"Do you need anything from me?" she asked. "Anything at all?"

"Just get some rest. Tomorrow's going to be a long day."

When she was gone, I trudged inside and tossed my shotgun on my bed. After stripping off my gun belt, I hung it on the bedpost and walked into the bathroom. I didn't recognize myself in the mirror. I smelled like marsh mud and stale sweat, and looked even worse. I didn't feel like taking a shower, but I needed one, so I labored through it.

Smelling like soap and feeling a little better physically, I pulled on some shorts and a T-shirt and walked into the kitchen to look for a bottle of vodka. I squatted in front of the sink and smiled when I jerked open the cabinet doors. There were two bottles—one full and the other half empty. I reached for the full one and had just wrapped my fingers around it when a familiar voice from the living room startled me.

"Pig, are you ready to go to hell and meet your—"

Without hesitation, I whirled around and threw the bottle in the direction of Simon's voice as I lunged toward my bedroom door. I heard glass break, and Simon roared in pain.

As I bolted into my room, gunfire exploded from the living room and bullets riddled the kitchen cabinets behind me. I snatched the shotgun from my bed and dove into the closet, huddling behind my gun safe. Simon was belting out orders and I could hear at least one other voice as they directed their gunfire toward my bedroom. Light was still shining from the bathroom and it lit up my room enough for me to see the curtains jerking from bullet strikes. Holes appeared in the wall paneling of my room and stuffing from my mattress floated into the air. The barrage was relentless and I knew better than to step away from the cover of my metal safe. I patiently gripped my shotgun, waiting for the right moment.

Almost as suddenly as it began, the shooting finally stopped. A shell casing tinkered across the wooden floor and came to rest somewhere in the living room. After that sound, everything grew deathly quiet. I took slow, quiet breaths, holding my mouth open to try and hear over the ringing in my ears.

Having played enough hide-and-seek as a kid, I knew the seeker was always at a disadvantage, so I stayed put. If the Parker brothers wanted me bad enough, all I had to do was sit there and wait. Sooner or later, they'd come seeking.

Seconds ticked by and turned into minutes. After about fifteen minutes, I heard a coarse whisper, but couldn't make out what was said. The floor creaked in the living room and I knew someone was on the move. The sound grew steadily closer until it reached my bedroom door and stopped.

I stood and waited beside my safe.

"Can you see anything?" Although he was whispering, I recognized Simon's voice.

"I can't see behind the bed," someone said from the doorway. I didn't recognize the voice, but knew it had to be one of Simon's brothers. A beam of light shined from the doorway and stabbed at the dark corners of the room.

"Go check it out," Simon said, sounding impatient. His voice was closer to the door. "I'll cover you."

A boot scuffed against the floor just inside my bedroom, and I moved my finger to the trigger of the shotgun. The beam of light wobbled as the man took another step into the room. I took a deep breath and held it, waiting for the next step, which would put him right outside the closet.

The beam of light turned in my direction and I leaned deeper into the shadows of the closet, trying to hide from the probing light.

"Hey," the man called, "I think something moved in the closet!"

CHAPTER 34

I exhaled my lungful of air and stepped out of the closet. In one quick motion, I brought the shotgun to my shoulder and pulled the trigger. The blast was deafening. The flashlight fell from the man's grasp and he collapsed in a lifeless heap. In the dim glow from the bathroom light, I saw a gaping red hole in his throat. If my memory was right, the man was Thomas Parker. I gritted my teeth. One down, two to go.

"You *bastard!*" Simon screamed. "I'm going to kill you, pig!"

I quickly faded back into the closet as gunfire again erupted from the living room. Bullets ripped through the walls around me, but I stayed behind the fireproof gun safe. After a few long seconds, there was a brief lull in the action and I heard a magazine hit the floor. I quickly stepped out and fired another shot in the direction of the door. In that brief moment, I realized no one was there. I thought about running to the opposite side of the room, but there was no cover, so I dipped back into the closet.

"Taylor, get some gasoline," Simon yelled. "We'll burn him out!"

My heartbeat quickened. If they set fire to my house, I was toast. Unless…

As gunshots continued to rain in from the doorway, I reached around the safe and punched in the code on the electronic lock. When the door popped loose, I shoved it open. I then began grabbing boxes of ammunition and pulling them off the shelves. I tossed them to the floor beside me, trying to make a space large enough for me to fit inside. When I'd stripped everything from the safe, I grabbed the shelf and tried to pull it free. It didn't move. *Shit!* There was no way I was fitting inside the safe with the shelf still in place.

There was a brief lull in the gunshots being fired into my closet wall and my bedroom, and I heard the screen door slam at the back of my house. Taylor was heading for the shed to look for gas! That left Simon all alone in my house. I stood ready, trying to time the rhythm of his shots. I was about to step out and engage Simon when a voice called from the back yard.

"Taylor Parker, drop the gun—*now!*" It was Susan!

"Do it or you're dead!" Melvin hollered.

Simon stopped shooting in my direction and I knew he heard the voices, too. I peeked out of the closet and saw him in the doorway to my bedroom, looking toward the back of the house.

"Taylor, don't—" Susan's voice was cut off by a three-round burst of semi-automatic gunfire and a *boom* from a shotgun. Simon screamed Taylor's name and jumped to his feet, starting for the back door. He was raising an AK-47 semi-automatic rifle to his shoulder, but I had sprung from the closet and was on him before he took two steps.

With a grunt, I struck Simon in the back of the head with the butt of my shotgun. His knees buckled and he fell on his face, the floor shaking under his weight. I glanced out the door and saw Taylor lying on his back on my porch, his torso riddled with bullets. I kicked the door shut and pushed the table in front of it.

"Clint, are you okay?" Susan hollered from outside. "What's going on in there?"

I didn't answer. Instead, I leaned my shotgun against the kitchen counter and bent over to grab Simon by the back of his leather vest. He was heavy—probably just south of two-eighty—and I had to strain to get him to his knees. He was groggy and rubbing his head, but he seemed to know where he was. He sat on his heels and stared up at me, hate in his eyes. "I'm going to kill you, pig!"

I jerked my pistol from its holster and pushed it against his forehead. My hand shook as I applied pressure to the trigger. "Simon Parker, I'm going to—"

"Going to *what*, pig? Murder me in cold blood?" Simon grinned and shoved his tongue through the gap where his two front teeth used to be. "You don't have the balls!"

I cocked my head sideways and frowned. "I thought you had one missing tooth."

Simon spat on the floor at my feet. "That blonde bitch of a pig you got working for you knocked the other one out." His scowl turned to a smile and he licked his lips. "But I'll be seeing her real soon."

I tapped his forehead with the muzzle of my pistol. It was my turn to smile. "I don't think you appreciate the gravity of the situation you're in."

Simon shrugged. "So I'm going to prison again. Big deal. I've been to prison a bunch of times, but I always get out. And when I do, I'm coming—"

In one deft motion, Simon knocked my pistol away from his forehead with his left hand and wrapped his right arm around the back of my legs. He threw his shoulder into my knees and knocked me onto my back. I was caught off guard and my pistol went off when I crashed into the floor, but the bullet impacted the ceiling harmlessly.

Simon reared up and brought his right fist crashing down onto my face, splitting my brow open. Blood gushed down my face. I tried to blink it away, but there was too much of it. Through a blur, I saw him raise his fist into the air again. I quickly reached up with my left hand and shoved my thumb as far into his left eye socket as I could. Grunting like an animal, I tried to push his eyeball out the back of his head.

Simon squealed in pain and clutched at my hand with both of his. I hooked my left leg around his right leg and kneed him in the ribs with my right leg. At the same time, and using his right eye socket as a handle, I pulled his head toward the left while smashing my pistol into his temple, sweeping him off of me. Now on top of him, I slowly returned the muzzle of my pistol to his forehead.

Susan and Melvin continued calling from outside, demanding to know what was going on. I knew it was only a matter of time before they kicked the door down and came in to arrest Simon.

"Simon Parker, you murdered my wife and my little girl," I said slowly. Although I was the one speaking, it sounded like someone else's voice.

Simon's hand was covering his right eye, but his left eye grew wide and he lay still. I thought I detected a shiver in his bottom lip.

"You also killed my girlfriend, the mayor and his wife, Seth, and Nate." I gritted my teeth and nodded. "For all of that, you have to pay with your life."

"What in hell's name are you talking about? You can't kill me." Simon's voice was trembling. "You're a cop, for Christ's sake! That would be murder."

"You broke into my house to kill me, Simon," I said coldly. "I can do whatever the hell I want with you. I own your ass."

Simon stammered, desperately searching for words to get him out of his predicament. Finally, he resorted to begging. "Please, officer...I beg you. I'm sorry for what I did. I didn't know what I was doing at the time. I swear it! I'll even plead guilty if you take me in—to all of it. I don't want to die. I want to live. My dad was killed by a cop and it ruined our lives. I don't want to be like my father. I want to be different—"

I shoved the muzzle of my pistol deep into his mouth to shut him up. The blood rushed to my head as I remembered the desperation I'd felt that evening three years ago as I begged for Abigail's life. Now here he was begging for his own life. He had shown no mercy to my innocent baby girl, and now he expected me to show him mercy. Gritting my teeth, I shoved the muzzle deeper into his throat, wanting to push it through to his brain stem.

Simon let go of his right eye and clutched at my hand, trying to push my pistol out of his mouth. I knocked his hand away and shoved it even deeper. His left eye was wide and bulging and tears flowed down his face. He was gagging and mumbling something I couldn't understand. My trigger finger was tense, my hand shook. I'd wanted him dead since the day he murdered Abigail and Michele. I had prayed for the chance to do it myself and that chance had arrived, but I suddenly found myself conflicted. I was always prepared to take a life in defense of myself or of someone else, and I had hoped to be involved in a gun battle with Simon and his brothers, but I'd never considered murdering any of them in cold blood.

I heard pounding on my back door and it interrupted my thoughts. After more pounding, the door burst open and the table slid across the kitchen. I didn't look up, but I could see Susan and Melvin standing there in my peripheral vision. A moment later there was a crash behind me and footsteps approached, but stopped abruptly.

"Holy shit," Amy said from behind me. "Clint, hold up...don't do what you're about to do."

"Chief, put the gun down," Melvin pleaded. "It's over. We've got them. We won."

"Listen to them," Susan said in a soft voice. "Put down the gun so we can bring him in. It's over. He's going to prison and he'll face the death penalty for sure. His life is already over, so don't throw everything away for him."

Simon nodded his head up and down, begging with his good eye. I eased up on my pistol. This bastard wasn't worth my freedom. Susan was right...he was finally going to pay for what he did. He'd just confessed to all of the murders and he would be locked up in a hellhole until the day the state executed him. He'd have to live with the loss of his brothers like I'd had to live with the loss of my wife and daughter. That, I realized, would hurt more than the split second of pain he would feel if I shot him. Death would be the easy way out for this monster.

Susan took a step closer to us. "Come on, Clint. You're better than him. Stop and think about what you're doing. Please, think it through."

"You're right." I sighed and removed my pistol from Simon's mouth.

Simon's face relaxed and he licked his dry lips. "I knew you didn't have the balls to do it, you little prick." He smiled wide and pushed his tongue through the gap where his front teeth used to be— just as he'd done right before he shot Abigail.

My vision blurred and my head swam as an overwhelming sense of rage engulfed my every fiber. Abigail's innocent face came back to me and I could hear the fear in her voice as she begged me to help her. I relived the very moment her soul left her body—could see her expression go immediately blank when Simon's bullet sucked the life right out of her.

Letting out an animalistic growl that sounded like it came from somewhere above me, I shoved my pistol back into Simon's throat and screamed down at him, "You murdering piece of shit! You killed my baby girl!"

I could feel Susan grabbing at my shoulder...could hear Melvin and Amy screaming at me to put the gun down...could smell the fear emitting from Simon's body, but my senses were dull to all of it, as though it was all a dream. The one thing that felt real was the gun in my hand. Knowing what I had to do, I stared unblinking into Simon's eyes—not wanting to miss a thing—and pulled the trigger.

CHAPTER 35

4:37 a.m., Saturday, October 31
Chateau Parish Sheriff's Office

Reginald Hoffman walked into the interview room to join Detectives Mallory Tuttle and Doug Cagle, who had finished interviewing me an hour earlier. Doug's sleeves were rolled up and it looked like he wanted to beat a confession out of me. He'd eyed me with contempt during my entire statement, often referring to Simon as the *victim*.

My left brow was starting to sting from the stitches I'd received. Doug had handcuffed me in my kitchen, read my rights, and then reluctantly transported me to the hospital before bringing me to the sheriff's office. My head ached. I glanced up at Reginald when he walked in and nodded. His dark hair was usually slicked back with some kind of gel, but tonight it was thick and bushy, making him look every bit of his forty-seven years.

"I just got off the phone with Isabel," he said, speaking to Mallory and Doug. "And she says our office won't be pursuing charges against Chief Wolf."

"What?" Doug's mouth fell open. "He murdered a man in cold blood—and he confessed to it!"

Reginald shook his head. "It was a justifiable homicide. Simon Parker broke into his home to kill him, which makes him fair game in the eyes of the law."

"But he wasn't in fear for his life," Doug argued. "Simon was unarmed and helpless."

Mallory slid a criminal code book toward her partner and said, "Like I already told you, he doesn't have to be in fear for his life to use deadly force in his own home. The only requirement is that he felt deadly force was necessary to compel the intruder to leave."

"But the *intruder* was lying on his back with a gun in his mouth, so how in the hell was he supposed to leave?" Doug threw the criminal code book across the room. "That's a loophole and you know it!"

Mallory shrugged. "Then have the law changed."

"Oh, you can bet your ass I will!" Doug folded his arms across his chest and fixed me with a cold stare. "You swore an oath to uphold the laws of this state and you violated that oath. You're no different than the murderer you killed and you're certainly not fit to be a chief of police."

"Doug, you're right, I did swear an oath to uphold the laws of the great State of Louisiana, and I do feel like I've failed my profession and my department." I stared down at the floor and frowned. "Three years ago I remained true to that oath, and my wife and baby girl were killed because of it. Last night I remained true to the memory of Michele and Abigail." I looked back up at him. "It was selfish of me. If the state would've decided I'd committed a crime and they wanted to charge me, I'd have taken my medicine like a man. If some higher power decides I've committed some sort of moral sin...well, I've retroactively paid a heavy price for that, haven't I?"

"But you didn't have to kill him! You could've taken him in and he would've been tried and convicted for murdering your family, Chloe, Mr. Dexter, Seth and—"

"He doesn't need a lecture, Doug," Mallory interjected. "The DA's office gets the final call and they've made their decision. You don't have to like it, but you damn sure will abide by it."

Doug stood and stormed out of the interview room, slamming the door behind him. When he was gone, Mallory apologized for him. "He doesn't have kids, so he doesn't get it."

I waved it off. "I understand where he's coming from and he's right—I'm no longer fit to be chief of police. Once this investigation is concluded and things are back to normal in Mechant Loup, I'm going to resign."

"That won't be necessary." Reginald leaned back in his chair and kicked his feet up on the desk. "Isabel and some of our brightest assistants have been researching this for hours, and they all agree the law can't touch you. You were lawfully inside your home, he made an unlawful and forcible entry into your home, and you knew he made that unlawful and forcible entry. That there, my friend, is presumptive evidence that the deadly force was necessary to compel the intruder to leave. You're free and clear."

"The thing is," I began in a quiet voice. "I didn't care about the law—I was going to kill him wherever I found him. The fact that he was in my house was just dumb luck. I had murder in my heart and that disqualifies me from serving as chief of police."

Mallory and Reginald sat in silence for a few moments. When Mallory spoke, her voice was firm. "I would've done the same thing had that bastard killed my daughter."

Reginald nodded in agreement. "And the fact remains he broke into your house, where it was legal to take him out. Since you didn't find him anywhere else, what you *would* have done is not relevant and no one will ever know—or care—what you were thinking."

"Well, I know, and I won't lie to myself or the people I serve."

Reginald dropped his feet to the ground and stood. "Well, suit yourself, but you're a free man. If I have my way, you'll get an award for killing the piece of shit who murdered Seth. He was my friend."

Mallory stood with Reginald and opened the door. "Susan's waiting for you in the lobby."

I followed them down the long hallway and into the lobby, where Susan was pacing the floor. She spun around when we opened the door and rushed toward me, throwing her arms around me and squeezing. Her mouth was pushed up against my neck and it muffled her voice, but I understood perfectly when she told me how relieved she was to see me. After thanking Reginald and Mallory, we walked out into the cool night air and she announced I was staying at her place.

"Your house is shot to shit," she said. "So, you can stay with me until everything is back in order."

I didn't argue. As she drove, I told her my plans to resign and my reasons for doing so. She didn't say a word until we were in her driveway and she had shut off the engine. She twisted in her seat to face me. "You know how we all tried to talk you out of shooting Simon?"

I nodded.

"We didn't do it to stop you from killing him." She paused and shook her head for emphasis. "No, the reason we tried to talk you out of killing him was because we didn't want you going to prison. We didn't want you throwing your life away for that piece of shit."

"Cops can't go around doing things like that, so I have to resign."

"But Reggie said it was justifiable homicide—you did nothing wrong."

"The fact that the statute is ambiguous doesn't give me the right to exploit a loophole." I smiled to reassure her. "Please understand that, as a father and a husband, I'm proud of what I did and I'll sleep good knowing I removed that evil bastard from this earth. I just can't be a cop anymore."

Susan sat there shaking her head. "What am I supposed to do with you gone?"

"You'll be the next chief of police," I said. "And you'll make a damn good one."

She grunted and led me into her house. I'd been there before, so I knew the lay of the place. "You can have my bedroom," she said. "I'll crash on the couch."

"No indeed!" I insisted on taking the couch and we argued about it for a minute. She finally relented and disappeared in her room to retrieve a pillow and some blankets. When she reappeared, she also had a clean shirt and some shorts. "These are too big for me," she explained. "And don't worry—they're unisex fighting gear."

I thanked her and walked toward the bathroom. I stopped in the doorway and looked back to where she stood in the kitchen. "How'd you know to come to my place earlier?" I asked. "I didn't even hear them break into my house, so how'd you know to go there?"

"One of your neighbors tried calling our office to report hearing gunfire in the neighborhood. The line was dead, so she called the sheriff's office and asked if they knew how to get in touch with you. Mallory heard it over the radio and called me immediately."

"How many times have you saved my ass now?" I asked.

"I'm not counting, and neither should you." She frowned and the dimple over her lip deepened. "It's what we do for each other, and I'm hoping we get to keep doing it for many years to come."

CHAPTER 36

"Look at me, Daddy!"

I smiled as Abigail skipped across the rich meadow in her white dress, stopping often to pick up flowers and tuck them into a basket that hung from the crook of her elbow. "Mommy will love these flowers!"

I turned to my left and saw Michele standing under a bright light. Her smile was as beautiful as I remembered. "Look at her, Clint. Look at our beautiful daughter."

"Michele, it's you," I said softly.

"Of course it is. Who else would it be?"

I hesitated, not knowing what to say next. I finally managed to ask if she was happy.

Her smile was all the confirmation I needed, but she said, "As happy as I've ever been."

Abigail was running back toward me. I squatted to take her in my arms, but she stopped just out of reach and turned her back toward me. "Do you like my wings, Daddy? I'm an angel now! Want to see me fly?"

———

I heard the sizzling of bacon before I smelled it. Disoriented, I slowly opened my eyes and sat up. My vision was blurry at first, but Susan's figure slowly came into view. She was bustling about the kitchen wearing nothing but a long shirt. The muscles in her tanned legs rippled, but her feet barely made a sound as she padded back and forth from the counter to the stove.

I rubbed my messy hair and wondered how long I'd slept. The last thing I remembered doing was lying wide-eyed in the dark, staring blindly at the ceiling. My last thought was whether or not Susan had a bottle of vodka stashed somewhere in her cabinets. I must've fallen asleep immediately thereafter, because here I was, awake and not knowing what the hell happened.

"What time is it?" I asked, suddenly realizing I hadn't had a nightmare.

"Good, you're up." Susan turned from the stove, holding a spatula in one hand and tongs in the other. "I could use some help before I burn my house down."

I hurried to the kitchen and took the tongs from her, taking care of the bacon while she dealt with the grits and eggs. She indicated with her head toward the microwave clock. "It's a little past noon."

"Wow," I said, grinning large.

Susan stopped what she was doing to study my face. "I…I don't think I've ever seen you this happy. What's going on?"

"I slept for like six hours."

"Congratulations. You're an average American. But I still don't get why you're so giddy."

"I just feel different." I lowered the fire on the bacon and explained how I couldn't remember the last time I'd slept without having a drink—or a nightmare. "And I had this weird dream that I saw Michele and Abigail, and they were happy. Abigail even showed me her back. She had the most beautiful wings attached to it. She said she was an angel."

I looked from the bacon to Susan. Her eyes were misty and she was smiling. "I'm not religious, or anything," she began. "But I think that's their way of telling you it's okay now—that you did the right thing last night. You brought closure to their case and enabled them to move on in the afterlife."

I nodded my head, not knowing if she was right or not, but feeling better than I had in years. If she was right and the dream *was* a sign, what was I supposed to do next? *Where does my life go from here?*

Without saying more about it, Susan and I finished cooking brunch and sat at the table to eat. I didn't know if her cooking was that good or if I was that hungry, but it was the best eggs, bacon, and grits I'd ever eaten. We were almost done eating when Susan's phone rang. She answered with a smile, but her smile slowly faded as she listened.

"Okay, we'll be right there." She disconnected the call and placed her phone down on the table. "We have to go to the sheriff's office right away."

"Is there a problem?"

I already knew the answer, because her brown eyes looked

troubled and she was chewing on her lower lip. She nodded slowly. "It seems the Parker brothers didn't kill Chloe."

I dropped my fork. "What? Are they sure?"

"Mallory was pretty positive. She said she's got something she wants you to hear."

I sat there stunned. "If Simon and his brothers didn't kill Chloe, who was it?"

Susan shook her head. "She didn't say. She just wants us to get there as fast as we can."

CHAPTER 37

Chateau Parish Sheriff's Office

Mallory met Susan and me in the lobby at the sheriff's department and ushered us into an office at the end of a long hallway. Her name and rank were displayed in gold letters above the doorframe. Once we were inside, she sat at the desk and fired up her computer.

"What's going on?" I asked. "Why'd you say the Parker brothers didn't kill Chloe? What proof do you have?"

Mallory reached into a leather bag and pulled out an evidence envelope. After donning a pair of latex gloves, she removed a small black device from inside and placed it on the desk in front of her. "Do you know what this is?"

I nodded. "It's an undercover recording device."

"It's the same kind we use in some of our undercover sting operations." She reached back into the leather bag and pulled out a wire. She connected the wire to the device and then plugged it into one of the USB ports on her computer. "We found this bug in Chloe's bra."

"In her bra?" I asked. "I've never seen her with that thing before. What was it doing in her bra?"

"She was recording a conversation between herself and Megyn Sanders," Mallory explained.

"Megyn Sanders…wait a minute!" I was thoughtful. "Why would Chloe be talking to the manager from the Bayou View Pub?"

Susan shrugged and glanced at Mallory. "Do you think it has something to do with Megyn's murder?"

"I didn't listen to all of it," Mallory acknowledged. "When I realized what it was and that it might relate in some way to your case, I figured y'all needed to hear it." She frowned and stared into my eyes. "And I felt you should hear it first, since she was your girlfriend. In fact, if you want, we can step out and let you listen to it alone."

"That's not necessary." I said it like I was sure, but my heart started to pound in my chest as I realized I might be hearing the very last recording of Chloe's voice.

Mallory turned toward the computer and began working the mouse. "Now, I did hear enough to know they were talking about the Lance Duggart case."

Susan began chewing on her lower lip. "Isn't he the guy who killed Bill Hedd's wife?"

"Yep," Mallory said.

My mind began to race. Chloe's intern had been going through old newspaper film from twenty years ago to see if she could dig up some dirt on Bill that might explain his animosity toward Susan's dad. Last I heard, the intern hadn't found anything significant, but what if she'd stumbled upon something?

I voiced my concern and asked Mallory how she knew the recording pertained to that case.

"One of her first questions had to do with Lance Duggart." Mallory clicked the mouse and leaned back in her chair. "Here it is…"

I crossed my arms as the recording began to play. I heard a door slam and shoes echo against a wooden floor. Finally, Chloe's voice came through the speakers.

———

Chloe: Mrs. Sanders? Mrs. Megyn Sanders?

Megyn: Yeah, that's me.

Chloe: Hi, I'm with the paper. [Pause] *It's pretty quiet in here today.* [Pause] *So, I wanted to ask some questions about your former boss, Lance Duggart.*

Megyn: Lance? What for? He's been in prison for about twenty years. I haven't seen him since he got arrested and I don't visit him in prison.

Chloe: I wanted to ask you about the day he got arrested. [Paper rustling] *I've obtained a copy of this police report from back then. You're listed as a witness in the murder case. Do you remember giving a statement?*

Megyn: Some detective came talk to me. Yeah, I remember that.

Chloe: The evidence custodian couldn't find the cassette tape containing your statement. [Paper rustling] *I also obtained this witness list from the trial, but your name isn't on it. Were you called to testify at the trial?*

Megyn: The detective had come by the bar a few weeks before the trial and asked if I'd been subpoenaed by the defense, but I told him no. He said I didn't have to talk to them if they came around. He told me they had all the evidence they needed and Lance had confessed after they matched his DNA to the lady, so I wasn't needed in trial. To be honest, I was relieved, because I was scared to death about going to court. The detective said I helped him break the case, because I confirmed the connection between Lance and the lady. I felt bad about that, you know? Lance was my boss and my friend. I mean, I was honest with the detective, but I certainly didn't want to testify in court. I didn't want to help them send him to prison.

Chloe: Do you remember what you told the detective?

Megyn: I remember it like it was yesterday. You don't forget things like that, you know what I mean?

Chloe: Absolutely. So, what'd you tell him?

Megyn: Well, first he came in with a picture of the lady who had gotten raped and murdered. Asked me if I ever saw her in the bar before.

Chloe: Did you?

Megyn: A few times. She'd come in and go to the corner of the bar—right over there—and wait. When Lance would finish doing whatever he was doing at the time, he'd go talk to her and then the lady would leave. It never failed, Lance would come over to me and make up some excuse about why he had to leave, and then he would disappear for an hour, or so. In fact, I even saw her on the night she was murdered.

Chloe: She came here the night she died?

Megyn: Oh, yeah, I told that to the detective. He got real interested when I told him about their relationship. I didn't know why, but then I saw on the news that she was the district attorney's wife. I swear, I had no clue she was married. If I would've known, I would've told Lance to stay away from her.

Chloe: Wait a minute...are you saying Lance was having an affair with the DA's wife?

Megyn: Oh, yeah, they were carrying on like high school kids sneaking around on the parents.

Chloe: And you told this to the detective?

Megyn: Yes, ma'am.

[Long pause]

Chloe: Did you tell the detective anything else?

156 | BJ Bourg

Megyn: Well, I did tell him Lance came back to the bar that night after meeting the woman. He asked a bunch of questions about how he looked, what he was wearing, and stuff like that.

Chloe: What did you say to that?

Megyn: Lance looked normal. He was clean, you know? No blood or anything. The detective said he probably cleaned up and changed his clothes. I told him I didn't think Lance was capable of murder or rape. I told him they must have had volunteer sex and there was an accident or something, but he laughed at me. Can you believe that? He just stood there laughing at me.

Chloe: [Short pause] *Did Lance say anything to you when he came back to the bar that night?*

Megyn: [Short pause] *He mentioned something about being tired. When I asked him what he meant, he said he was tired of being used. That's it—that's all he said.*

Chloe: What time did you say Lance got back from seeing his girlfriend that night?

Megyn: I didn't say, but it was a quarter after ten.

[Paper rustling]

Chloe: How sure are you?

Megyn: I'm positive. I looked at the clock when he came in. It was actually ten-fourteen, to be exact. I remember it, because I told it to the detective and he told me I had to be wrong. We went back and forth about it and I told him I was positive, but he insisted it couldn't be possible.

Chloe: Did Lance leave again that night?

Megyn: Yeah, he left when we closed up at two.

Chloe: He was arrested about a week after the crime, right?

Megyn: Something like that.

Chloe: Did he act any different during that week?

Megyn: Oh, yeah. He wasn't himself. He would come in late and leave early—on the days he actually showed up. I think he missed three days during that week, which is unusual for him.

Chloe: What if I told you the woman was alive at eleven o'clock that night, which means there's no way Lance killed that woman?

[Long pause]

Megyn: I...I mean, how could you know that? I read that they had his DNA and they found the knife at his house.

Chloe: According to the police report, a burglar alarm went off at her house exactly seven minutes after eleven. If you're positive he was here at ten-fourteen and he stayed here until two, then there's no way he committed the crime.

[Long pause]

Chloe: It's okay, don't cry. Look, you told me on the phone that Jolene once mentioned to Lance that her husband was having an affair. When I confronted Mr. Hedd about that he got really angry, so I think there's some truth to it. I need a name.

[Door slams]

Chloe: Hey, what are you doing here? Wait—what's going on? What are you doing? No!!!

———

I jerked in my skin as gunfire and screams blasted through the speakers.

CHAPTER 38

I leaned forward and dropped my head to my hands, listening to Chloe and Megyn scream for their lives as gunshot after gunshot was fired—at least five of them. There was a crashing sound and, due to the muffled amplification, I knew the device had recorded Chloe hitting the floor. I squeezed my eyes shut and fought back the tears as I listened to Chloe gasping for air in a struggle for her life.

Susan leapt from her seat and shut off the recording. "Jesus Christ, Mallory! Couldn't you have vetted this recording before playing it for him?"

I heard Mallory stammering for words and felt Susan's hand on my shoulder, but it all seemed like a dream. After a long moment, I lifted my head and tried to collect my thoughts.

"Do you need a minute?" Susan asked.

I thought about walking out, but I knew the best thing for me to do was get busy on the case. As long as I was being productive and working toward finding her killer, I knew I'd be okay. "No, there's too much work to be done."

"I'm so sorry, Clint," Mallory said. "I just thought you should be the first to hear it. I had no idea—"

"It's okay. We need to hear it—all of it." I nodded. "You can put it back on."

Frowning, Mallory clicked the *play* button and we all sat there listening as Chloe put up a gallant fight for her life. It was difficult to listen to, but I needed to know every detail of what happened to her. I had failed to be there to save her, so the least I could do was bring her killer to justice.

Just as Chloe took her last breath, footsteps pounded the floor and faded away from the recording device. I heard a woman's voice pleading with someone to help her, and then I jumped again as another gunshot sounded.

Footsteps moved toward Chloe and then faded away again, seemingly moving in a different direction. A door slammed shut and everything grew quiet. We all looked at each other. "Is that it?" I asked.

Mallory shrugged and pointed at the time indicator. "There's still ninety minutes on the recording."

We continued listening and finally heard the door slam again. The footsteps echoed across the wooden floor and grew loud as they walked past Chloe's body. The killer walked around for a while, but we weren't sure what he was doing. We heard a *dinging* sound at one point and I knew he was removing the money from the register. A few minutes later it sounded like he grabbed Chloe and began dragging her across the floor. Her body plopped to the wooden floor and we heard the door slam again. A car started somewhere in the distance and then drove nearer. It stopped and a car door slammed. The sounds we heard next indicated he had dragged Chloe across the porch and hoisted her body into the trunk of her car. The trunk then slammed shut and the only other sound we heard was rumbling from a short car ride. After the engine was killed and the door slammed shut, there was no other sound for about thirty minutes.

Finally, someone entered the car again and cranked the engine, taking Chloe's body for a ride. Somewhere along the way, the memory card on the recording device filled up and the audio file shut off.

Things were starting to come together inside my head, and I didn't like the picture that was forming. "I received a text message from Chloe Wednesday evening at about six o'clock saying she was in an interview. It had to be the interview with Megyn, but Megyn had been dead between eight and twelve hours when we found her, and that old man we talked to Thursday said the bar was closed at five."

"What are you getting at?" Susan asked.

"The killer must've had Chloe's cell phone and was using it to keep me at bay." I turned to Mallory. "Do we know what time she made the recording?"

"The date and time stamp showed Wednesday at quarter to five in the evening."

Every text message I'd received after that point was from the killer. I grew nauseous at the thought of communicating with the person who murdered Chloe. But who could it be? And why were both women killed?

I rubbed my chin. "The killer took Chloe's body away from the bar and cleaned up the scene."

Susan nodded her agreement. "Those two bullet holes in the wall weren't misses at all—those were the two bullet holes that went right through Chloe's body."

"The coroner recovered one bullet from Chloe," Mallory said. "If you give me the bullets y'all cut from the wall and the ones y'all recovered from Megyn's body, I'll have the lab compare them to the bullet from Chloe. If they match, we can prove they were killed by the same person."

"That won't happen," I said. "The evidence from Megyn's murder was secured in our evidence lockers at the police department."

"And it all went up in flames!" Mallory cursed. "Did y'all recover any other evidence from the scene?"

"We got some fingerprints—most of which were smudges—and we swabbed for DNA," Susan said. "But everything's gone."

"Any spent shell casings?"

"Nope—the killer picked them up."

"Megyn was shot three times," I said. "Twice from some distance and once point-blank in the head. Chloe was shot three times and from some distance. Six shots total from at least three different shooting positions, but not a single shell casing was recovered." I shook my head. "I understand why the killer would take the shell casings, but why move Chloe's body from the scene and clean up the blood? That doesn't make sense."

"Maybe Chloe is like one of those shell casings," Susan offered. "Her body might offer a clue as to who the killer is."

"Or," Mallory said softly, "they didn't want you finding Chloe because then you wouldn't be on a case—you'd be on a mission."

I considered both of their points. "This new revelation could be a coincidence, and the Parker brothers could still be responsible for her death."

"Think about it, Clint," Susan said. "Right before the shooting started, Chloe said, *what are you doing here?* That means she *knew* her killer."

My mind began to race. If she knew her killer, that might mean I knew her killer. "We need to run a search warrant on her phone," I said. "We need to trace her steps in the hours leading up to the shooting—find out who she spoke to and where she went."

"Already done," Mallory said. "Follow me."

CHAPTER 39

Mallory led us to a large conference room in the detective bureau and slammed the door shut. She ran her fingers through her long brown hair and pointed to a large map on the wall. "The red push-pins represent pings from Chloe's phone on Wednesday," she explained. "The time she was at each location is written on the little pink tabs."

I studied the map and recognized most of the locations, but not all of them. When I asked about them, Mallory handed me a document she had prepared. "This details the times and corresponding locations for you," she explained. "As you know, we can't pinpoint her exact location from the phone records, but we're pretty sure we'll be able to verify all of it when we start doing interviews. We know she did stop at the sheriff's office that morning, so that location has already been verified."

"She stopped here?" I read through the list, running my finger across each time and location:

7:30 a.m. – The Rushing residence
7:45 a.m. – At news station
8:13 a.m. – Still at news station
9:46 a.m. – Sheriff's Office
10:31 a.m. – Between Sheriff's Office and news station
10:40 a.m. – At news station
4:37 p.m. – Bayou View Pub
6:00 p.m. – At news station
10:26 p.m. – At news station

"Why'd she stop here?" I asked.

"She stopped in our records division to pick up a copy of the

Lance Duggart investigative report and then she stopped in CID to speak with Doug."

"Why Doug?" I asked.

Mallory shrugged. "I guess she saw that he was the lead detective on the case initially."

"Did he speak with her?" I wanted to know.

"He did. He said she asked about some missing witness—we now know it was Megyn Sanders—but he had no clue what she was talking about." Mallory looked over her shoulder to make sure the door was still closed. "I wasn't here back then, but they say there was some bad blood between Reginald and Doug over the case. Doug wasn't making enough headway, so the sheriff brought Reginald in to take over."

"Apparently a good move," Susan said, "because Reginald solved it."

The stitches above my left eye were starting to itch, so I rubbed the cut as I thought things over. I needed to know everything I could about the case. If I could find out what Chloe found out, maybe that would point me in the right direction. I finally asked Mallory if I could see the file. With a nod of her head, she disappeared out the door and returned about ten minutes later with a large binder that was labeled, *Jolene Hedd Murder Book*.

I pushed the binder aside and continued running down the list of times. I stopped when I reached the six o'clock hour and stabbed the paper with my finger. "Chloe texted me at six to say she was in an interview."

"That's impossible," Mallory said. "She was already dead."

"Precisely." I pointed to the location on the document. "Someone from the news station used her phone to text me."

Susan sucked in her breath. "You're right. And they were still using it at ten twenty-six that night."

"That was a text from her phone to tell me she had just arrived at her dad's house and she would call me in the morning." I turned to the binder. "There's something in here that made someone at the news station want to kill her, and I need to find out what that reason could be."

"Find the motive, find the killer," Susan said, echoing my words from long ago.

"While you get acquainted with the murder file," Mallory offered, "Susan and I can head out to interview Chloe's intern. We need to verify the times on the phone records and find out if she had any appointments scheduled—either on this case or on something else." She handed me a list of telephone numbers. "These are the numbers that communicated with Chloe on that day. We haven't identified any of them yet—other than yours—but we'll get on it right away. Do you recognize any of them?"

"Once I put a number in my phone, I never look at it again." I frowned. "I don't even know Chloe's number. I just press her name every time I want to call or text her."

Before they walked out, Susan handed me her phone in case something came up. She told me to call Mallory's phone if I needed her. She grinned. "It's under her name, so you won't have to remember the number."

I nodded and dropped to the chair in front of the murder book. When I was alone in the room, I ran my hands across the top of the binder, aware that Chloe had touched this same object just three days earlier. I closed my eyes and tried to imagine her sitting there…tried to imagine what would be going through her head. When nothing came to me, I sighed and opened the binder.

I turned to the photographs first and found a picture of Jolene Hedd's lifeless body. She was lying on her back on the floor in the master bedroom of her house. Her clothes had been ripped from her body and she was completely nude, except for the straps of her black bra clinging to her shoulders. She had been stabbed in the neck and there was blood on her body and on the blue carpet around her. It was a horrific scene.

I flipped though the report, searching for information on Lance Duggart. Why had this successful bar owner killed the woman with whom he'd been having an affair? And why rape her if he was having consensual sex with her on a regular basis?

Susan's phone began ringing and I glanced at the number. I didn't recognize it, but I answered it anyway. It was Reginald.

"Clint, I've been calling your phone all morning."

"Oh, yeah, it got lost in the fire at the police department. What's up?"

"I need to talk to you right away," he said. "We were all thinking Simon Parker and his brothers murdered Chloe, but the audio recording Mallory recovered changes everything. I strongly suspect her murder is linked to the Lance Duggart case."

I remembered hearing that Reginald had solved the case when no one else could, and realized he probably knew more about it than anyone else. I told him I was at the sheriff's office and he said he'd be right over.

CHAPTER 40

Susan sat at the small kitchen table holding Ali Bridges' hand. Ali was crying hysterically and shaking uncontrollably. Mallory walked over with a tissue and sat on the other side of her. After she'd calmed down a little, Ali took the tissue and wiped her face. She finally nodded. "I'm...I can talk a little. It's just so...so hard, you know? Chloe wasn't just my boss, she was my friend. She was such a nice person."

Susan frowned. "I know this is hard. I'm sorry we had to bother you with this, but it's important we know everything Chloe did on Wednesday."

Ali took a deep breath and exhaled. Her brown eyes were bloodshot and her long hair was tucked into a rough bun. "Okay, I'm ready."

"What time did she get to work Wednesday?" Susan asked.

"I'm not sure. I got there at eight and she was already there."

Susan jotted down the information. "What time did she leave and where did she go?"

Ali was thoughtful. "She left not long after I got there. Maybe nine o'clock? Earlier in the week she had asked me to look up old articles involving the district attorney and a man named Isaiah Wilson. I found a bunch of articles about the DA, but only one about that man."

Susan caught her breath at the mention of her father. Mallory glanced at her, but Susan nodded to let her know she was okay to continue questioning Ali.

"Did you find any connections?" Susan asked.

"No, not really. The article about the man named Isaiah was just mentioning how he had died during a boxing match." Ali dabbed at her eyes with the tissue. "It was a good write-up. It talked about all the things he had done as a boxer. Now, Chloe was real interested in the picture from his funeral, because she said one of the ladies in the picture was the DA's wife."

Susan pursed her lips. She knew the article well—a copy of it was folded neatly in a box of keepsakes back home—but she hadn't realized Jolene Hedd was in the picture. "Did you know why Chloe thought to look into this Lance Duggart case? What did that have to do with Isaiah Wilson?"

"Well, Chloe thought it odd that the district attorney's wife was pictured at Isaiah Wilson's funeral and then six months later she was raped and killed."

"Did she think there was a connection?"

Ali shrugged. "I don't really know, but she did ask me to call the sheriff's office to see if they had a report on the case. It took a while and they transferred me a half dozen times before I finally spoke with a lady who was able to help me." Ali explained to Susan that the clerk had to dig around for a while, but she finally found the box containing the case file. "She called me first thing Wednesday morning and told me she would make a copy for Chloe, but it would cost fifteen cents per page. Chloe didn't care about the cost—she just wanted to get her hands on that file."

"Is that where she went when she left the office Wednesday morning?" Susan asked.

"Yes, ma'am."

When Susan asked what time Chloe returned to work, Ali tucked a lock of hair behind her ear and said, "It was sometime in the afternoon. Two o'clock maybe?"

Susan glanced at the timeline Mallory had created. "Are you sure about that? Her phone records show she was at the news station at ten-forty."

Ali nodded. "I'm positive. She called me about ten-thirty to tell me she had left the sheriff's office and was heading to the district attorney's office to speak with Bill Hedd. Afterward, she was planning to have lunch with her boyfriend—"

"Wait, what?" Susan asked, looking from Mallory to Ali. "Clint was in Tennessee."

"No, not Clint," Ali said. "It was some new guy. Chloe said she broke up with Clint."

Susan sank into the chair. "Are you sure?"

Ali nodded and continued. "I don't know what time she got to the DA's office or left, but she came into the station around two o'clock. I'm not sure what time she met her boyfriend for lunch, but they probably ate somewhere in town. That's what they usually do."

"What was this boyfriend's name?" Susan asked.

Ali shrugged. "I don't remember her ever saying his name and I've never seen him."

Fighting to stay focused, Susan glanced at her notes and then back up at Ali. "Is it possible Chloe came back to the news station earlier than two o'clock and you didn't see her?"

Ali nodded. "She usually leaves her car parked here when she goes to court or the district attorney's office, because it's only a block down the street. Besides, there's never any place to park over there, so she probably just parked here and walked over."

"What time did she leave the office again?" Susan asked.

Ali was thoughtful. "I believe it was three-thirty, four o'clock."

"Did she say where she was going or if she was meeting anyone?"

"No, ma'am. If she's working a story, she doesn't really talk about it until it hits the paper." Ali started crying again. "I wish she would've said something to me, because I might've been able to do something to help find her before it was too late."

"Don't even think about blaming yourself." Susan put her arm around Ali's shoulders. "There's nothing anyone could've done to save her."

When she was sure Ali was calm enough to be alone, Susan led Mallory outside. The fall air was cool on her face. It was normally her favorite time of the year, but her heart was heavy and filled with emotions she didn't understand. When Clint had murdered Simon Parker in cold blood she had panicked. She was certain he would end up in prison for the rest of his life and it killed her inside. When Mallory and Doug tried to question her about what happened, she did something she'd never done before—she refused to cooperate with an investigation. She later spoke with Melvin and Amy, and they said the same thing.

"I told Doug and Mallory to kiss my ass," Melvin had declared defiantly when they were alone on the street outside of the sheriff's department. "That piece of shit Simon deserved to die and I'm glad Clint had the stones to kill him."

"I told them I wasn't saying a word either," Amy said. "Doug tried to play me like a fool, telling me I could be indicted if I stood idly by and watched Clint murder Simon. I told him to go to hell and charge me if he wanted to, but I wasn't saying a damn thing."

"I'm just glad they decided not to charge Clint," Susan remembered telling them. "Because I know he went in and told them exactly what he did."

Susan shivered, trying to shake the foreboding cloud that still hung over her. All of the hurt and desperation she had felt when Clint was shot a year ago came flooding back last night. Although going to prison was better than dying and she would've still been able to visit him on a regular basis, she wanted him in her daily life—*needed* him in her life. Just the thought of wanting him and needing him caused a wave of guilt to wash over her. She had no right to have those feelings, much less allow herself to verbalize them internally. Clint was Chloe's boyfriend and, even though Chloe was gone, it would be improper for her to make a move at this point, or any point, really. He was her boss, which meant they could never be an item. Period.

As Susan reached Mallory's unmarked cruiser, she remembered Clint's words from the night before, *"Cops can't go around doing things like that, so I have to resign."* A new wave of panic came over her as she wondered what that meant. Where would he go? What would he do? Would he move back to the city? What if he—

"Where the hell are you, girl?"

Susan jerked her head around and saw Mallory standing with her hands on her hips, staring with her head cocked to the side.

"What? Did you say something?"

Mallory frowned. "Your body's here, but your mind is a million miles away. It's him, isn't it?"

Susan felt her face catch fire. "What are you talking about?"

"Don't play dumb with me," Mallory said. "I've seen the way you look at him, and I've seen the way he looks at you. There's a connection."

Susan turned her head, embarrassed. "He's got a girlfriend."

"Not anymore," Mallory said softly, taking her place in the driver's seat. "You heard Ali—they broke up before she was murdered. He's available."

"Jesus, Mallory! He hasn't even had a chance to bury Chloe yet. Give it a rest." Susan slipped into the passenger's seat shaking her head.

"All I'm saying," Mallory explained, "is that he's available now and so are you—and you're what he needs right now."

"What are you talking about?" Susan felt guilty for even entertaining Mallory's idea, but she was curious.

"He needs a strong woman who can take care of herself when

he's not around," she said, cranking the engine and pulling out of the apartment parking lot.

"Now you've lost me."

"Think about it—his wife and daughter were killed right in front of him and there was nothing he could do to save them. That kind of thing can bring a strong man to his knees." Mallory nodded her head for emphasis. "I promise you he'll never have kids again. I wouldn't be surprised if he's already gotten a vasectomy."

"You're talking crazy," Susan said.

"Hear me out. As for the women in his life, he's tired of falling in love just to have his heart ripped out every time they die on him." Mallory stopped at a red light and turned to face Susan. "He already knows you can take care of yourself, so he knows his heart will be safe with you."

"If what Ali said is true, he lost Chloe before she was murdered."

"Either way, he's coming for you. It might not be today, or next week, or next month, but he's coming. I saw it in the way he looks at you."

Susan's eyes misted over and she turned her head so Mallory wouldn't notice. She was sorry Chloe was dead, but angry at her for two-timing Clint. Her hands began to shake and her heart raced as she wondered what to do about this revelation. Clint hadn't shown any signs of having problems at home, and he spoke of Chloe as though they were still together. Should she tell Clint, or leave it alone?

CHAPTER 41

Chateau Parish Sheriff's Office

It was almost four o'clock when Reginald walked into the conference room. I stood and shook his hand, then pointed to the open murder book on the table. "I bet this brings back some bad memories."

He nodded, taking a seat across from me. "This was a terrible case, that's for sure. At the time, I didn't know Bill personally, but I knew of him, as did all the cops who worked it. We figured if it could happen to him, it could happen to any of us. It made us all feel vulnerable."

"You mentioned you think this case has something to do with Chloe's murder," I said, getting right to it. "What makes you think so?"

"Chloe came to the district attorney's office on the day she was murdered."

"That's not uncommon. She was always at the DA's office or the courthouse. It was part of her job."

"But this time was different."

My brows furrowed and I studied his face. "How so?"

"She walked in asking to speak with Bill. She told the receptionist she wanted to do a feature piece on him. She made it sound like she wanted to highlight his accomplishments since taking office. I mean, what politician doesn't want a little positive press every time they can get it?" Reginald pointed to the file in front of us. "But that was a lie...she really wanted to ask questions about his wife's murder."

"Did he meet with her?"

"Of course, he did. My buddy, Danny, who's one of our new

prosecutors—I played ball with him in high school—was in the meeting with them, and he said it went from cordial to contentious in seconds." Reginald took a deep breath and exhaled, explaining how Chloe had barely sat down when she began questioning Bill about one of the witnesses in his wife's murder case. "Chloe told Bill she'd obtained a copy of the investigative report and saw that Megyn Sanders was a witness, but her name hadn't appeared in the transcript from Duggart's trial. When Bill acknowledged knowing about Megyn, Chloe wanted to know why she hadn't been called."

"What did Bill tell her?" I asked.

"He told her the truth—that Megyn was a friend to Duggart and the prosecution figured she would try to say something that would jeopardize the case against Duggart, so they didn't call her."

"Isn't she the one who broke the case?" I asked.

"She did, but the prosecutor from Magnolia Parish was calling all the shots." Reginald lifted a finger, shaking his head. "I take that back. Although Bill recused himself, I think he was calling the shots from behind the scenes. After all, he's good friends with the district attorney in Magnolia."

"You said it got contentious...what happened?"

"She straight up accused Bill of killing his wife."

My mouth dropped open. "She did *what*?"

Reginald nodded and said Chloe had accused Bill of murdering his wife so he could be with his lover, and she accused him of using his position as DA to pin the murder on Duggart, whom he knew was sleeping with Jolene.

"Bill had a lover on the side?"

Reginald shook his head. "Not that I know about, but Danny said Chloe claimed to have a witness who was going to name his lover and it would break the case wide open."

"How'd he react to that?" I asked.

"Danny thought he was going to hit her—he was that mad." Reginald frowned. "He kicked her out of the office and told her she was never allowed back in the building."

I sat quiet for a while, processing this new information. I needed to know what she knew. She went to Bayou View Pub sometime after confronting Bill, so Megyn must've been the witness she was talking about. If Megyn did know something that would implicate Bill in the murder of his wife, and she was willing to give that information to Chloe, it would be motive enough for Bill to want both of them dead.

I asked Reginald if Chloe ever tried to interview him about the case, but he said she hadn't. I told him what I knew about her conversation with Doug and asked why he thought she would speak to him about the case. "You wrote the primary report, so I would've guessed she'd have spoken with you."

"Doug handled the initial investigation," Reginald explained. "I was brought onboard when the case started growing stale. I don't know if you know it, but there was some bad blood between us during the investigation. He was mad that the sheriff gave me the lead role over him."

I pointed to the investigative report, which I'd read from cover to cover, and asked what had led him to Megyn Sanders. "Lance Duggart wasn't on anyone's radar until you met with Megyn, but there's no mention of how you got to her."

"I was actually looking for Duggart when I stumbled upon Megyn."

"Duggart?" I rubbed my chin. "I thought you got his name from Megyn. That's what the report says, anyway."

"Bill's the one who turned me on to Duggart—handed him to me on a silver platter, come to think of it." He ran his hand through his slicked-back hair and shook his head. "Looking back now, it does seem a little convenient."

He went on to explain how he had marched into the district attorney's office and demanded to know where he was when his wife was murdered. Bill claimed he was at a conference two hours away, and when Reginald asked who could verify that fact, he grew belligerent and said there were four hundred lawyers and judges who would back him up.

"But when I told him I'd spoken to every one of those judges and lawyers," Reginald said, beaming, "and not one of them remembered seeing him between the hours of nine o'clock at night and one in the morning, he lost his shit."

"That was pretty slick," I said, knowing he hadn't spoken to any of them. "I'm surprised he bought it."

"I was, too, but after his wife died, he'd spent the week in a drunken fog, so he had no idea what we'd done—or hadn't done—on the case. I used it to my advantage and it paid off." Reginald shrugged. "That's where Doug went wrong. He treated Bill like a district attorney instead of like a regular husband who might have killed his wife."

"But how'd that lead to Duggart?"

"My ploy scared Bill into coming clean about his wife's affair. He realized he'd have to cough up something or risk being a suspect in his wife's murder, and—true or not—those kinds of suspicions could wreck a campaign."

"I didn't read anything in the report about an affair. Are you talking about her affair with Isaiah Wilson?"

"I had no clue about Isaiah until Susan's lawyer came by the office Thursday." Reginald shook his head and recalled how Bill had found a receipt in his wife's purse for a hotel room in the city. "That prompted him to follow Jolene one day and he saw her meet up with this guy in a black pickup truck. He copied the license plate number and had one of his investigators run it. It came back to Lance Duggart." Reginald explained how Bill had confronted Jolene and threatened to divorce her, but she begged him not to leave her and promised to break it off with Duggart.

"But why isn't any of that in the report?"

"Professional courtesy." Reginald shrugged. "Bill had been through enough, so I didn't see any reason to cause him further embarrassment by speculating about his wife's infidelity."

"It's not speculation—Bill told you about it. And wouldn't that tidbit of information be huge during the trial?"

"The information I had from Bill was pure hearsay and Duggart never admitted to the affair. In fact, he flat denied it." Reginald grunted. "It wasn't until we got the results back on the semen found inside Jolene that he wanted to talk."

I went back to the picture of Jolene's nude body, processing what I'd just heard. "So, do you think Jolene was trying to break it off with Duggart and he got angry and attacked her?"

"That's basically what he told me when he confessed."

I flipped through the report, locating a synopsis of Duggart's statement to Reginald. "I read that, but I couldn't find a transcript or an evidence form for a recorded confession. Everyone was using cassettes back then and I'm guessing y'all were, too, right?"

"Yeah, but he refused to give a recorded statement," Reginald said. "I told him it would protect him by keeping us from putting words in his mouth, but he told me to go screw myself."

I asked Reginald if Bill's revelation was what led him to the Bayou View Pub, and he said it was. He said Duggart wasn't there, but Megyn was and she was willing to tell him everything he needed to know. "She confirmed the affair and even said Duggart told her he was tired of being used by Jolene," Reginald said. "I immediately went out to his house to question him. He gave us consent to search his house and we tore it apart, but didn't find anything."

"I saw that in the report. It looked like y'all found the bloody knife outside…in the garage, right?"

"Yeah, Doug went rummaging through the garage and found it hidden in a rusty toolbox. It made him feel better about losing the case to me." Reginald smiled, thinking back. When he continued, he said Duggart went crazy when they showed him the knife and he accused them of planting it.

I'd read the crime lab report and saw that the blood on the knife came back to Jolene. I mentioned it to Reginald and he nodded.

"I arrested Duggart as soon as the preliminaries came back on the blood. Once he was in custody, I asked for consent to swab his cheeks for a DNA sample, but he refused." Reginald chuckled. "I got a search warrant and we tied him to a table and swabbed his cheeks anyway. Considering how hard he fought, I wasn't surprised when the lab matched his DNA to the sperm recovered from Jolene's dead body. Needless to say, the jury deliberated for less than an hour when they heard that key piece of evidence."

I stared down at the file. What was I missing? Chloe had hit on something—and that something had gotten her killed. But what was it? Could the name of Bill's lover be the key to everything? Or was it simply the time issue?

"Reginald, did you listen to the recording Chloe captured right before she died?"

"No, I haven't had the chance yet."

I explained how the evidence custodian couldn't find Megyn's recorded statement, and asked if Megyn told him what time Duggart returned to the bar that night.

"Damn, that was twenty years ago, Clint." Reginald stared at the ceiling and squinted. After a moment he said, "I think she gave an exact time, like eleven-thirteen, or something. When I asked how she could give an exact time, she pointed to some clock in the bar and said she looked at it when he got there." Reginald smirked. "When I compared the time on the clock to my watch, it was off by an hour and eleven minutes."

"Did Megyn or Lance ever mention Bill having a girlfriend?"

Reginald shook his head. "If he was having an affair, we would've known about it."

I leaned back in my chair and shook my head. "What was Chloe after, Reggie? What did she find that we're missing?"

Reginald scowled and leaned over, staring down at the ground. "I don't even want to consider what she might've found," he said softly.

"Why's that?"

"For most, their first instincts aren't always right, but for me, they are." When he looked up his eyes seemed drawn. "My first instincts were that Bill Hedd killed his wife, but I let him talk me out of it."

"What are you saying?" I asked, my blood slowly turning to ice. "Do you think Chloe found evidence that implicated Bill in the murder of his wife and he killed Chloe to keep her quiet?"

Reginald stood and paced back and forth, shaking his head. "I can't even go there in my head. I've known Bill for too long. He's a bit bullheaded and brash, but he's honest. I don't think he's capable of that sort of thing. Hell, he hired me as his top investigator because I had the stones to stand up to him. He admired that and respected me for it."

"Then what is it, Reggie?"

He stopped pacing and pursed his lips. "Considering how mad Danny said he got at Chloe, I just don't know anymore."

I suddenly remembered the text I'd received from Chloe's phone while it was pinging in the area of the news station. "Does Bill have any friends or allies at the news station?"

"Bill's got friends everywhere. Why?"

I explained what we learned about her phone being used in the area of the news station after her death, and he dropped to a chair, mulling it over. After sitting there for a while, his mouth dropped open. "Shit, Clint, our office is a block away from the news station!"

"And?" As soon as I said it, my own mouth dropped open. "If Bill was using her phone it would've pinged in that same area!"

Reginald stood and nodded. "The text messages weren't coming from the news station…they were coming from the district attorney's office!"

CHAPTER 42

Susan had seemed especially quiet on the drive back to Mechant Loup. Other than laying out the timeline they received from Chloe's intern, she didn't say much. I told her everything I remembered about the file and shared Reginald's suspicions, but she didn't have much to say in return. She had received a call from Amy earlier saying the interim mayor wanted to meet with all of us at the town hall when we were finished our duties, so we headed that way.

"Did Amy say who the council picked as the interim mayor?" I asked when we arrived in the parking lot and stepped out of the truck.

Susan shook her head. "She didn't even know. One of the council members saw her in the lobby at the town hall and asked her to get the word out to all of us."

I nodded my understanding and we marched up the large concrete steps, pushing our way through the double glass doors just as Melvin and Amy strode from the section of the building that had been loaned to us. They both stopped and stared at me, a strange look on their faces.

I approached them and nodded. "Is everything okay?"

Melvin walked up and wrapped me in a bear hug. "I was so scared you'd go to jail last night, Chief," he said, his voice trembling. "We need you here. We can't do this without you."

I slapped his back a couple of times. "I'm still here, Melvin."

When he let go, Amy gave me a light fist-bump with her injured hand. "I just started working for you," she said. "They can't take you away just yet."

We all laughed and walked down the hall together, heading for what used to be Dexter Boudreaux's office.

"Any idea who it is?" Melvin asked.

"Not a clue," I said, reaching for the knob. When I turned it and opened the door, I nearly choked on my tongue.

Pauline Cain was sitting behind the desk. She quickly stood to her feet and took a deep breath. "Why, hello, Chief. It looks like we'll be seeing a lot more of each other."

"Mrs. Cain...what the hell?" I couldn't believe what I was seeing.

"The council approached me and asked if I'd serve as the interim mayor until a special election could be organized." She straightened the front of her suit jacket and nodded. "I agreed to do it and, if this job suits me, I might officially run for the office."

I smiled. "Wow, that's great. I'm proud to serve under you."

Susan, Melvin, and Amy echoed a chorus of agreements. When they were done, Pauline said she would allow me to run the police department as I saw fit, the same as Dexter. She then grabbed a box from her desk and tossed it toward me. I caught it in the air and glanced at it.

"It's your new phone," she explained. "I understand you lost your old one in the fire, and I need to be able to keep in touch with you. It's the same as your old number."

I thanked her and took it out of the box, grumbling silently over the thought of reentering contact information for everyone I knew.

"Now, I have to get to work planning some funerals," Pauline said. "We have to honor those who have fallen in the last few days. Afterward, I'll be meeting with the council about rebuilding the police department. Until then, please make yourselves at home here. Our house is your house."

We thanked her and talked briefly before walking out into the cool night air. Amy had been out on the streets all day, so she bid us goodnight and headed home.

"I'm on nights, Chief," Melvin said. "Anything you need, just holler."

"Susan and I will be out of town again tomorrow," I said. Susan's brow furrowed and I explained. "We're going to prison—I want to pay Lance Duggart a visit, see for myself what he has to say."

"Good idea," Susan said.

"I'll be here to help Amy if she needs anything," Melvin said. "I don't sleep during the day anyway, with my wife and baby home."

He started to walk away, but I stopped him. "Hey, did you recover any evidence from the bridge cabin?"

"Oh yeah, I recovered a dozen shoe prints, but that's about it." He frowned. "I think the killer wore gloves, because I didn't find any fingerprints except my own."

"Where're the shoe prints?"

"I turned them over to Mallory and she entered them into their evidence."

I thanked him and got into the truck with Susan. She hesitated before cranking the engine.

"What is it?" I asked.

"Are you coming back to my place?"

I stammered, finally muttered, "I mean, is it okay? I haven't had a chance to fix up my place yet. I can pay you rent, if you like."

"No, it's great," Susan said quickly. "You can stay as long as you like—or until I run out of food—and I'd never accept a penny from you, so don't even mention that again."

I thanked her and suddenly slapped my forehead, remembering Achilles. "Shit! Achilles is still at Chloe's dad's house. He must think I abandoned him."

"My back yard is fenced and my house is dog-proof," Susan offered. "We can pick him up now and bring him with us. I'd love to have him around."

"That'd be nice…thanks."

When she still didn't start the truck, I turned to her and demanded she tell me what was on her mind.

She lowered her eyes and spoke so softly I could barely hear her. "Chloe's intern mentioned that you and Chloe had broken up, and I wanted you to know how sorry I am for you."

I furrowed my brows. "We didn't break up."

Susan looked me right in the eyes. "I was afraid you didn't know."

"Didn't know what?"

"Ali said Chloe called her and said she was having lunch with her boyfriend. When I told her you were in Tennessee, she said Chloe had broken up with you and she was seeing some new guy."

I laughed off Susan's comment. "No, Chloe and I were still very much together, and she didn't have some new boyfriend. Ali must've misheard her. Hell, between her job and hanging with me, Chloe didn't have time for anything else."

Susan forced a smile. "You're probably right."

I studied her face as she fired up the engine and drove out of the parking lot. She was visibly troubled, and that worried me. I'd never suspected Chloe of being unfaithful, but now a sliver of doubt was starting to wedge its way into my mind.

CHAPTER 43

7:15 a.m., Sunday, November 1
Susan Wilson's House – Mechant Loup, Louisiana

The sun was shining through the curtains in Susan's living room when I awakened. I heard snoring from the corner and wondered if that was what had stirred me from my sleep. I sat up and glanced in the direction of the noise. Achilles was fast asleep, snoring like a human. He had gone crazy with delight when we picked him up, nearly knocking me off my feet. While he had run around the yard showing off, Susan and I had sat on the porch with Chloe's parents, answering every question they had. They had scheduled her funeral for Monday morning and asked that I serve as a pallbearer. I'd agreed and Susan and I had left shortly afterward. We'd made a brief stop at my house to gather more of my clothes and some toys for Achilles, and then headed for her place.

I stretched and reached for the arm of the sofa, where I'd thrown my T-shirt last night. As I was pulling it on, I caught movement from the kitchen and looked up to see Susan leaning against the wall, watching me. She wore a long orange cotton shirt that made her tanned figure seem even darker, and she was sipping from a cup of coffee. Her face turned red and she quickly looked away. "Sorry," she said. "I was trying not to wake you."

"You didn't." I pointed to Achilles. "That air horn of a nose woke me up."

I joined her in the kitchen and poured a cup of coffee for myself. Achilles' ears had perked up and he watched me walk by, but then went back to chasing lady dogs in his sleep.

Susan dropped to a chair at the table, crossing her legs as she sat. "I've got muffins in the oven."

"You'd better stop doing that," I said. "You're going to spoil me."

Susan ignored the comment, instead asking how I slept.

"Like the dead."

In a quiet voice, she asked if I'd had any nightmares.

I smiled. "I haven't had one since I killed Simon and had that dream about Abigail being an angel."

That seemed to please her and her eyes glistened. "I'm really happy for you."

We didn't talk much during breakfast, each lost in our own thoughts. I didn't know what she was thinking, but I was mulling over what she'd said about Chloe having a new boyfriend. While I was fairly certain Ali had misunderstood what Chloe told her, that sliver of doubt was growing inside my mind—especially when I remembered what her parents had told me about her runaway—and I was starting to question every incident where she'd come home late or missed one of my calls. I wasn't prepared to accept it yet, but if she did have a new boyfriend, I needed to know his name and where he was when Chloe got murdered. But how was I supposed to find out now that Chloe was dead?

After Susan and I ate, we took turns showering and dressing for work. I was just snapping my gun belt in place in front of the bathroom mirror when a strange ring sounded from the living room. I looked toward Susan's bedroom, where I could see her putting the finishing touch on her braided hair.

"What's that noise?" I asked.

"It must be your new phone," she called. "I've never heard that sound before."

I hurried into the living room and dug through my bag, finally locating my phone. It was Mayor Cain.

"I hope I didn't wake you, but I wanted you to know I pulled some strings with Rupe's Dealership—I'm good friends with Julie Rupe, as you know—and had them deliver your new police package Tahoe this morning. They didn't have time to put the stickers on, but it's here whenever you're ready to pick it up."

After thanking her, Susan and I headed for the town hall. Melvin was in the office reserved for us and he tossed me a set of keys when I walked in. "This is from the mayor. She said it's for the black Tahoe in the parking lot."

Lindsey was sitting at a desk in the corner of the large room, a portable radio in front of her and a bandage across her exposed shoulder.

180 | BJ Bourg

I smiled when I saw her. "I'm glad you came back to work. How's your shoulder?"

"It's hurts a little, but I'll be fine. To be honest, I didn't think I'd be back," she admitted. "I've never been that scared in my whole life."

"None of us have," Amy said. Her wrist was still bandaged, but she was in good spirits. "You took your gunshot like a real hero."

Lindsey's face beamed and she turned toward the radio log, making a note of some traffic that had come across the waves.

Susan pulled me aside. "Why don't you go to the prison and interview Duggart alone?" she said. "I'll stay here and give Amy a hand."

I agreed it would be better to have Susan there, given Amy's injury, and I followed Melvin outside. I asked about his wife and daughter before climbing into my new Tahoe, and he said they were fine.

"Claire wants me to hang up my badge," he said slowly. "She doesn't want to be a widow at such an early age."

I couldn't say that I blamed her, but it was a personal decision and I didn't want to influence him either way, so I just waved and headed for my new Tahoe. The state prison was two hours away and I wanted to be back before sundown.

CHAPTER 44

10:45 a.m.
LA State Prison – Chetimaches, Louisiana

Sitting in the small interview room in full police uniform, I felt naked without my gun belt. The prison smelled of rotten feet and disinfectant—an unsettling combination. The building was ancient and dank, like an old dungeon, and I was sure if the walls could talk they would tell tales of unspeakable horror—both in history and in the not so distant past. When all of the world's evils come together in one place, demons are sure to come out and play.

I had to wait ten minutes before the steel lock on the large metal door shifted and the door opened, squeaking as it did. Two prison guards stepped through the door, escorting a man in tan coveralls. He was cuffed and shackled and had to shuffle to keep from falling. He moved like a well-trained dog, with the guards only needing to point their commands rather than speak. He'd been here a long time, and that was plain to see.

Duggart eyed me with suspicion as he took the seat across from me. His eyes were gray and cold, filled with hate. What hair he had left was styled into a flattop and matched the color of his eyes. The lines in his face were deep and angry and he didn't flinch when the guards slammed the door shut behind him, leaving us alone.

The chains on his wrists rattled as he lifted his pale arms and dropped them onto the steel table. "What the hell do you want, law man?" His voice was raspy and hard.

I placed my own arms on the table and leaned closer. "I want to talk to you about your reason for being here."

"Unless you're here to get me out, I got nothing to say to you."

I pointed to a tattoo on his arm. It was shaped like a kick pedal for a bass drum. "You play?"

He smirked. "Stop trying to play cop with me. I know the routine. You pretend to find some common ground and we talk about it. You get me saying *yes* to a lot of things and then you try to trick me into saying *yes* to committing a crime. I'm not stupid, copper."

It was my turn to smirk. "You seem a bit paranoid for acting so sure of yourself. When I ask if you play the drums, it's because I'm curious to know if you play the drums...nothing more, nothing less."

Duggart squinted, but didn't say anything.

"I'll dispense with the pleasantries and get right down to it, then," I said. "Did you rape and murder Jolene Hedd?"

He leaned forward and said, "No!"

I grabbed my accordion file folder from the floor and placed it on the table. After removing the synopsis of his statement, I turned it so he could see. "Then why'd you confess to it?"

"That statement is bullshit! I didn't confess to nothing."

"So, you didn't say you killed her because she tried to break up with you?"

"Hell, no!"

"Then why don't you tell me what really happened?"

Duggart grunted. "Why? So you can twist my words like that other cop did? No thank you."

"Trust me, we want the same thing."

"The last time I trusted a cop I got life in prison without parole." Duggart stood to his feet and turned toward the door. "This visit is over."

"Bill Hedd might be responsible for killing my girlfriend," I said. "I'd love nothing more than to have him trade places with you."

Duggart froze in place. "Is this some kind of trick?"

"I wouldn't joke about my girlfriend being murdered."

Duggart grunted and returned to his chair. "How'd it happen?"

I explained how Chloe had been murdered while interviewing Megyn in the bar. "I think she was trying to find evidence to help you," I said, "and that got her killed."

"Wait, what about Megyn?"

"She was gunned down, too."

I thought I saw his eyes water up. He hung his head and was silent for a moment. "Megyn blamed herself for my arrest." He sighed. "It actually was her fault, but I can't say I blame her. She only told the truth and that cop twisted everything she said."

"What do you mean?"

"She's the one who told the detective about me and Jolene. They would've never known I was sleeping with Jolene had she kept her mouth shut."

"That's not entirely true," I explained. "Bill found a receipt for a hotel room in the city, so he followed Jolene one night and saw her meet up with you. He got the license plate number off of your black truck and had one of his investigators run it. That's how he knew who you were. When he was pressed on his whereabouts for the night of the murder, he gave up your information and that's what led the detective to the bar."

Duggart was thoughtful. "So, Bill followed us that night?"

"What night?"

"The night Jolene was murdered."

"No, it would've been a different night. He confronted her after her rendezvous with you and she promised to break up with you."

"The detective tried saying the same thing. He wanted me to confess to killing her because I was angry about her breaking up with me." He shook his head. "She never tried to break it off with me. I didn't even know Bill caught us. In fact, I never took her to the city, so I don't know what receipt you're talking about."

I squinted. "What do you mean?"

"I mean I never took her to the city. That receipt had to be for someone else."

I hadn't considered that angle. "So, you think she was seeing someone else? A second person?"

Duggart shrugged. "It's not impossible. I mean, she was screwing around on her husband with me, so what would keep her from screwing around on me with someone else? Women like that, they've got no loyalties."

I folded my arms across my chest and leaned back in my chair. Jolene had been sleeping with Isaiah Wilson, but he died in January—six months before she was murdered. At the time of her murder, she was having an affair with Lance Duggart, but Duggart never took her to the city, so that means she was sleeping with someone else. Did Duggart really kill her? Or was it Bill? Or this mystery man?

I rested my elbows on the table and studied Duggart closely. "If you didn't rape Jolene, how'd your DNA get inside of her?"

"Because I slept with her that night."

"The night of the murder?"

"Yeah." Duggart frowned. "It was our last night together. We met in the cane fields like we always did and had sex in the back of her Escalade. I can describe every inch of her SUV for you, if you like, and I can take you to the exact spot we'd meet."

"The second part might be hard," I said. "A lot has changed in the twenty years since you've been locked up."

He described the road they'd meet on and the route they'd take to get back home. While some of what he said sounded familiar, it was obvious some of his landmarks were no longer there. I shuddered at the thought of him being innocent. That would be unspeakable. How do you get twenty years of your life back? I turned to the file folder and dug out the investigative report. "What time did you meet Jolene that night?"

"Roughly ten o'clock. She said she had to hurry home in case Bill called. He was at a conference or something." Duggart frowned, staring at the concrete ceiling. "I still remember what she looked like, standing in the headlights of her car, completely naked with her arms in the air. She was so beautiful. Bill didn't deserve her. To him, she was just a trophy to show off, like a deer mounted on the wall. I saw through her beauty to the woman on the inside. I don't know what she saw in me, but I know she always told me I made her feel free."

Duggart paused for at least a minute, appearing to be lost in the moment from twenty years ago. I brought him back to the present with a wave of my hand and a question. "You were saying she was standing naked in front of the headlights..."

"Yeah, she was. I tackled her to the ground—easy like, you know?—and we rolled around for a while. Afterward, I talked to her about our future, and what her intentions were. I didn't like going home to an empty house while she was going home to her husband."

"Did that make you angry?" I asked.

"Well, it upset me, but not enough to murder her, if that's what you're getting at. I loved her and would never hurt her." Duggart's shoulders slumped. "Bill didn't love her, so I'd say he was quite capable of killing her. In fact, I always suspected he had come home early from the conference that night and attacked her when she got back from seeing me."

"Did you tell the detective your suspicions?"

"Not exactly, but I did tell him he should probably investigate the husband, because they were the ones who usually murdered their wives."

"Did you and Jolene fight that night?"

"Look, I've never touched her! I already told you, I'd never hurt her."

"No." I lifted a hand. "I meant argued. Did y'all argue that night?"

"I mean, a little. I accused her of having a number two on the side."

"You accused her of cheating on you with someone other than her husband?"

Duggart nodded.

"Why would you accuse her of that?"

"She always had to hurry off, even when Bill was out of town, so I got suspicious." Duggart sighed. "But then she told me she loved me, so I figured I was just being paranoid and dropped the issue. She promised to see me the next day and then we left our spot. I followed her to the Central Chateau Bridge, like I always did, and flashed my lights at her when I turned off to head home. It was our goodbye sign—I'd flash my lights and she'd tap her brakes."

"Lance, I have to ask you this," I said slowly. "If you didn't kill Jolene Hedd, why'd they find a knife in your garage with her blood on it?"

The veins in Duggart's temples protruded. "Someone planted it there, that's how! I'd never seen that knife in my life."

I pulled out the photograph of the knife in his toolbox and slid it across the table. "So, you're saying someone planted this knife in your toolbox?"

Duggart nodded. "That's exactly what happened. Look at that toolbox—I hadn't touched it in years."

"Who would've done that?"

"You're the detective, you figure it out."

"You're stuck in prison for the rest of your life, and you've had twenty years to think about it." I tapped the picture with my index finger. "So, you tell me who you think planted this knife."

"I don't know, copper, but my best guess would be Bill Hedd. The only thing I know for sure is I didn't kill Jolene."

I wanted to believe him, but I wasn't sure. I asked him where he went when he left Jolene, and he said he went straight to the bar. He talked to Megyn for a while and then went home. When he heard about the murder on the news the next morning, he freaked out and laid low.

"They were talking rape and murder and saying the person could get the death penalty," he said. "That scared the shit out of me. I knew my DNA would be all over her and I figured it was a matter of time before they'd come calling."

"Why didn't you come forward and tell them what you knew?" I asked. "That's what an innocent person would do."

"Well, most innocent people aren't screwing the district

attorney's wife," he countered. "Jolene told me how vindictive he was, so I knew better than to cross him."

I stared down at my notepad, assessing the information I'd gathered. In a nutshell, a convicted rapist and murderer was professing his innocence and claiming to have been framed...not an original assertion. I knew if I polled every inmate in that prison, the vast majority of them would also claim to be innocent of the crime that landed them there. I looked up at Duggart. "Can you give me something that'll help prove you didn't do this?" I asked. "Anything at all?"

"Like what?"

"I don't know...maybe another alibi witness? Did anyone other than Megyn see you that night?"

Duggart shook his head.

I was thoughtful. "My girlfriend—Chloe Rushing was her name—seemed to think Megyn had some information that would implicate Bill in the murder of his wife. Any idea what Megyn might've known?"

"Whatever Megyn knew, she would've heard from me, and I didn't have any proof that Bill killed Jolene."

"Chloe seemed to think Bill had a lover on the side." I lifted my hands. "Do you know anything about that?"

Lance explained how Jolene had always suspected Bill of messing around when he'd go out of town, but she never had any proof. "To be honest," he said, "I thought she was using me just to get back at him."

"Is that why you killed her?"

Duggart's eyes turned to slits and he rose slowly to his feet. "You were bullshitting me about your girlfriend being murdered, weren't you? This was all a trick to try and get me to confess! Who sent you? Was it that bastard, Hedd?"

I stood and met his hard stare with one of my own. "If you did rape and kill Jolene Hedd, I hope you get raped on a regular basis here and then die a slow and horrible death. But if you didn't commit this crime, then I hope to God I can find the evidence to clear you, because no innocent person should ever have to spend a single day in jail for something he didn't do."

Lance sighed and sank back to his chair. "I am innocent, but no one wants to listen to me. My own lawyers tried to convince me to take a plea because they thought I did it. How can you defend somebody if you think he's guilty? My goose was cooked before that trial even started."

"Let's get back to the girlfriend bit." I flipped through my notes and found where I'd detailed Chloe's conversation with Megyn. "It seems Megyn said that Jolene told you her husband was having an affair, and Chloe seemed to think Megyn knew the name of his girlfriend." I looked up at Lance. "She must've gotten that name from you, right?"

"Yeah, but I don't remember." He rubbed his head with his chained hands. "That was twenty years ago. I can't even remember what day it is today, much less some name from that long ago."

"Damn it, Lance! Give it some thought, man." I slammed my palm on the desk and stood up. "You're going to spend the rest of your life in here if you don't start remembering something. Give me a name. A first name…last name…nickname…anything."

Lance threw his head back and faced the ceiling. He began mumbling to himself with his eyes closed. He remained like that for so long I thought he had fallen into a trance and was speaking in tongues. After some time, his eyes flew open and he jumped to his feet. "I've got it!"

Excitement coursed through me. "What is it?"

"I remember his girlfriend's last name—it was Ridley."

My shoulders drooped. The name meant nothing to me. "What about a first name?"

"A first name?" Lance scoffed. "You're lucky I came up with anything."

"Come on, can you remember anything at all about the first name?"

"Just that it was different. It wasn't a common name like Jennifer or Mary or something like that."

CHAPTER 45

1:00 p.m., Monday, November 2
Chateau Parish Church of Christ

Susan and I stood amongst several hundred other law enforcement officers as the mournful bagpipes paid tribute to Seth and Nate. Their families were standing at the front of the church, all of them crying. Susan grabbed my hand and squeezed. I squeezed back.

We'd attended Chloe's funeral at nine in the morning. Mr. Rushing had asked me to say a few words and, despite my uncertain and bitter feelings, I said some nice things and then sat quiet through the rest of the ceremony. After Chloe had been laid to rest, Susan and I drove straight to the service for Dexter and his wife. The small cemetery in town was overcrowded with people from far and wide. Dexter was well known as an alligator trapper and was a favorite among the tour guides in the area. I recognized a lot of the townspeople, but there were many strangers from out of town who had made the long drive to pay their respects. Dexter was the kind of man you could meet once and remember for the rest of your life.

As people took turns talking about what a great person he was, I had thought back to the first day I met him and frowned. I'd always thought my inexperience on the water was what had contributed to him losing his arm to Godzator, but he had selflessly gone out of his way to make me feel better about it. During the service, I'd glanced out over the swamp behind the cemetery and wondered if the monster was still out there somewhere waiting for me.

After Dexter and his wife had been buried, Susan and I labored through a miserable lunch and then drove to the service for Seth and Nate. When we arrived at the Church of Christ, we had to park several blocks away. I'd never seen so many law enforcement officers in one place, nor had I ever seen so many different police uniforms. Marked patrol cars had come from as far west as Utah, as far east as New Jersey, and as far north as Michigan. But the number of officers was dwarfed by the number of civilians who had come from all across the country to pay their respects and show their support.

Although I'd spent most of the night and day wondering about Chloe cheating on me, right at that moment, with the bagpipes playing and muffled sobs chorusing throughout the cathedral, my mind was on one thing—the tremendous hole that would forever be in the hearts of all those who loved Seth and Nate. There was nothing quite as final as death, and those poor people were about to find it out the hard way. The children would soon realize their fathers would never be attending their baseball games or dance recitals or birthday parties again. The wives would soon realize their husbands would never kiss them or hold them or comfort them again. The mothers and fathers would soon realize their sons would never come over for Christmas or stop by after work or give them any more grandchildren. I knew the pain they felt and it broke my heart for all of them.

As for Chloe, if she *had* cheated on me, it would sting a bit, but my heart would immediately go to work purging any feelings I felt for her. It was a defense mechanism I'd acquired as a teenager and it had served me well over the years of my youth. I glanced around and shook my head. Perspective was everything, and the betrayal I might feel would be nothing compared to the loss these poor families felt for their deceased loved ones. Now, if Chloe hadn't betrayed me, I would certainly feel guilty for second-guessing her, but I'd at least be able to mourn her passing without a cloud of doubt hanging over my head.

After the bagpipes had stopped playing and everyone was seated, the sheriff and different members of each family walked to the stage and honored the heroes with beautiful words of love and sorrow. There wasn't a dry eye in the house and every individual in the place remained focused until the very last speaker. The pastor closed the ceremony with a prayer and then everyone broke rank and started making their way to the doors for the funeral procession.

My phone vibrated in my pocket and I glanced at the screen as I waited for our row to start moving. It was a text message from Mallory. She'd called earlier in the day to say she and Doug were heading out to Bayou View Pub to spray the place with luminol. Her message said she was able to confirm that Chloe was killed inside Bayou View Pub. The spot in front of the two bullet holes in the wall lit up like a Christmas tree. They had cut out sections of the floor and found dried blood in some of the cracks, and she was certain it would come back to Chloe.

I shoved my phone back in my pocket and looked wistfully toward the nearest exit. Now that we knew for sure where Chloe had been killed, I needed to question Bill about his whereabouts on Wednesday.

I leaned over and whispered the news into Susan's ear. She nodded and we slowly made our way toward the end of the pew with the rest of the officers in our row. Just as we reached the crowded aisle, I felt a hand pulling on my wrist from behind. I turned and saw Isabel squeezing toward me from between two officers. Reginald was right behind her and they were trying to stand their ground and not get sucked up with the crowd stampeding toward the exits.

"Where are you parked?" Isabel asked, raising her voice to be heard over the buzzing crowd. "The sheriff wants you in the procession that's heading to the cemetery."

I tried to explain where we were, but she waved me off. "Forget your car—y'all are getting in with us."

I didn't even try to object. Seth and Nate had died fighting for us and I wanted to be front and center paying tribute to them. I looked toward Susan, but didn't have to say a word. She had heard Isabel and was already leading the way toward the side door.

Once we were outside, Isabel pointed toward the road, where dozens of cop cars were lined up behind the two hearses. Reginald's F-250 was about four cars behind the second hearse. "We're already in line," she said.

Susan and I followed them across the grassy front yard and climbed into the back of the truck while they climbed into the front seat. We all made small talk as we sat in the truck and waited, and the conversation eventually turned toward the investigation into Chloe's murder.

"I wanted to ask you about the case at Chloe's funeral," Reginald said, "but I didn't think it was appropriate. Anything new? Any developments?"

I told him about the text message I'd received from Mallory and he nodded. "I think it's time to have a conversation with Bill."

Isabel groaned. "God, this is getting bad. My stomach's been in knots for days."

"I went into work last night," Reginald said, "and searched every inch of his office for that phone."

Isabel shook her head. "I already told you he wouldn't keep it in his office. If he's got it, it's in his car."

Sirens started wailing and six officers on motorcycle patrol pulled out onto the road and started leading the procession toward the funeral home. Reginald took his place in line and we settled in for the long, slow ride to the cemetery.

My uniform pants were grabbing, so I shifted in my seat and adjusted them, wondering why I made myself and my officers wear the polyester pants. I was the chief, after all, and could change the uniforms to whatever I liked. As I moved my feet to a more comfortable position in the spacious back seat, my eyes caught a glint of shine from the floor. I leaned over to see what had made the sparkle and saw a tiny object just under the driver's seat.

"What is it?" Susan asked.

I shrugged and lifted the object from the floor. My mouth dropped open and the blood in my veins turned to ice as I brought the object close enough to my eyes to identify it. My stomach ached and I felt sick. I scanned the back seat in disbelief, searching the floor first, and then the seat, and then the ceiling. My heart nearly stopped beating in my chest when I saw a bare footprint in dust on the ceiling. It suddenly all made sense to me.

Susan noticed something was wrong. She leaned close to me and whispered, "What's up?"

Not taking my eyes off the bare footprint on the ceiling, I handed her the tiny object. I heard her gasp when she saw Chloe's missing snowflake earring clutched between my fingers.

CHAPTER 46

I finally tore my eyes from Chloe's bare footprint on the ceiling and stared out at the trees whisking by on the shoulder of the road. I didn't want to jump to conclusions, but it was difficult not to see the writing on this wall. Chloe had met her new boyfriend on Wednesday for more than just lunch, and her new boyfriend was Reginald Hoffman. I cursed myself for not reading Reginald better. His shock and concern when we recovered Chloe's body, his appearance at Chloe's funeral, his interest in the case...all of it should've set off warning bells. The only reason he was so concerned was because he cared about her—the same as I did.

Susan grabbed my hand and squeezed. I turned to face her and she mouthed the words, "Are you okay?"

Squinting in anger, I nodded and tucked the earring in my shirt pocket. I didn't say another word on the drive to the cemetery. When we stepped out of the truck, I made my way to the burial plots and stood beside Susan. As the master of ceremonies belted out commands to the seven officers on the honor guard, I stood with fists clenched and jaw set, wanting nothing more than to confront Reginald. I had the good sense to wait until after the ceremony, but it took everything in me to hold myself back.

As the seven officers fired the three-volley salute, I stood motionless, unmoved and feeling numb. My fears had been realized—Chloe was a cheater and I'd been played as a fool. More than hurt, I felt anger at myself for having been such an idiot. How could I have been so blind and trusting?

I was finally able to block out my thoughts and focus on the end of the service. When it was over, I stood in line to walk by the family and bid them well. Reginald was about ten people ahead of me and I kept my eyes on him. When we were done, I turned to Susan. "Call

Melvin to come pick us up. I'll be right back."

"Where are you going?"

"Have a word with Reginald."

She took a deep breath and exhaled, but didn't say a word as she fished her phone from her pocket.

Reginald was laughing with a couple of other officers when I walked up and grabbed his arm roughly. "We need to talk."

There was a look of confusion on his face as he followed me down a long corridor of tombstones. I didn't bother saying a word in explanation, preferring to let him wonder. Deep down, he probably already knew what was up. Our shoes clanked against the concrete sidewalk and I didn't stop until I'd gone about fifty yards and we were well out of earshot of the crowd.

I rounded a corner and stopped between two large gray tombs, turning to face him.

"What's going on?" he asked.

"How was your lunch date with Chloe Wednesday?"

I saw the color drain from his face. He stammered for a second, but quickly regained his composure. He took a deep breath and exhaled slowly. "So, you knew about us."

I nodded. "You're the worst kind of scum—a cop who'll sleep with another cop's wife or girlfriend. It's a good thing you left the sheriff's office and went to work at the DA's office, because you'll never have another partner."

The color had returned to Reginald's face and he suddenly seemed defiant. "Well then, if you knew about us, I have one question for you." He took a step closer to me and I saw his hand inch toward the pistol at his side. I relaxed the muscles in my right arm, ready to go for my own gun. I studied his eyes, waiting for the slightest twitch.

"Go ahead, ask your question," I said calmly.

"Did you murder Chloe and shove her in the trunk of her car because you were mad at her for cheating on you?"

"If you were my friend, you'd know three things about me...I don't believe in violence against women, I don't compete for women, and I don't fight over women."

The lines in Reginald's face slowly began to disappear as he began to relax. He sighed. "Then what do we do from here?"

"We find her killer and bring him to justice."

Reginald frowned. "I'm really sorry, Clint. I didn't mean for this to happen. She started coming around during the grand jury hearings and she interviewed me a few times over lunch. We got to talking and found out we had a lot in common, you know? One thing led to another and we ended up—"

"Save it," I said sternly. "I don't care how it started and I don't want to hear how you cheated on your wife with Chloe."

"I didn't cheat on my wife with Chloe. My wife left me over two weeks ago."

"Well, I'm glad to hear it," I said. "Maybe she can find someone who's more honorable and trustworthy than your sorry ass."

"Don't act all high and mighty with me." Reginald sneered. "We all know how Susan was caught bringing cake to your house on your birthday."

"What's that got to do with anything?"

"Chloe knew y'all were having an affair, so she decided to give you some of your own medicine."

I felt my face grow hard as I took a step closer to Reginald. "I'm not a cheating piece of shit like you," I said. "I'm loyal and faithful to the woman in my life—a concept that's foreign to you. If Chloe didn't realize that, she didn't deserve me."

He gulped audibly and his face turned pale. I realized he probably thought I was going to hit him, so I stepped back.

"Look, I'm sorry for spreading that rumor," he said. "I was just repeating what Chloe told me. I was certainly wrong for being involved with her when I knew y'all were dating. You can call me whatever you want and you'll be right...I won't even try to argue. I just hope we can put our differences aside and work together to find the person who killed her." Reginald hung his head and I thought I saw tears dripping to the ground. "I know it's not what you want to hear, but I did love her and I want to find who killed her so I can put that bastard in the ground."

After a long moment of staring him down, I sighed. "I told you the latest on my end, what've you found out on yours?"

"Nothing, really." He squeezed his eyes with his hands and looked away for a moment. When he turned back to face me, his eyes were red and his chin was trembling. He busied himself pulling his cell phone from a leather pouch attached to his belt. After messing with the phone for a minute, he turned it so I could see the screen. He'd received a text message from someone named *True Love* at six o'clock on Wednesday evening stating she was in an interview and was working late. *True Love* sent another message at ten twenty-six to say she'd made it to her dad's house.

"Am I correct in assuming you saved Chloe's contact information under *True Love*?"

Reginald's face flushed a little, and he nodded.

"Jesus, Reggie...are you in grade school?" I stifled a chuckle and studied the messages. "So, the killer texted you from Chloe's phone at the same time he texted me." I rubbed my chin. "Everyone knew Chloe and I were together, but who knew about you and her?"

Reginald's eyes grew wide. "Shit, that's a great point. The only person who knew I was seeing her was Bill. A couple of the prosecutors and one or two of the secretaries suspected something was going on, but Bill knew for sure."

"How do you know he knew about it?"

"After Chloe had come in there accusing him of killing his wife, he pulled me aside and told me I needed to keep a tighter leash on my bitch of a girlfriend."

I clenched my fists. "He called her a bitch?"

Reggie nodded.

"What did you tell him?"

"What do you mean?"

"What did you say in response to his comment?"

"Nothing, really. I mean, what was I supposed to say?"

"Twenty years ago you had the courage to accuse him of killing his wife, but now you keep your mouth shut when he calls your girlfriend a bitch?" I shook my head. "What kind of man have you become?"

"I'm two years away from retirement and smart enough to pick my battles carefully."

I was bored with the conversation and needed to start figuring out my next move, so I turned and started walking toward where Isabel and Susan were waiting for us. Reginald put away his phone and strode along beside me.

"I need to talk to Bill," I said.

"Good luck with that."

"I need you to get me in to see him."

Reginald shook his head. "He has to think I'm on his side, or he won't let me close to him. That phone is our only real evidence against him, and I'll never find it if he fires me."

I knew he was right, so I didn't argue.

"What's up?" Isabel asked when we reached them. She looked inquisitively from Reginald to me and back to Reginald. "Y'all look pretty intense."

"Can you get me in to see Bill?" I asked. "I have some questions for him."

Isabel pushed a lock of blonde hair behind her ear and cocked her head to the side. "About?"

"Chloe's murder."

"Do y'all really think he did it?"

Reginald nodded and told her about the text messages we'd both received from Chloe's phone while it was pinging in the area of the district attorney's office.

Isabel's brow furrowed and she opened her mouth to speak, but then clamped it shut.

"Can you get me in?" I asked.

Still distracted, Isabel said, "Um…he has coffee every morning at this little café two blocks from the office. There's a big sign out front that reads, *Fresh Beignets Daily*—can't miss it."

"What time should I be there?"

"He arrives at seven sharp every morning. There's a little private room in the back where he sits and reads the newspaper." Isabel turned away from me and shoved a finger in Reginald's direction. "And why was Chloe texting you again?"

"I'll let you two catch up," I said before he could answer. I waved for Susan to follow me and we walked to the front of the church to wait for Melvin.

CHAPTER 47

5:00 a.m., Tuesday, November 3
Susan Wilson's House – Mechant Loup, Louisiana

I reached blindly for the phone and slid my thumb across the screen to turn off the alarm. As quietly as I could, I rushed through my morning routine, trying not to disturb Susan. I had let Achilles out and fed him and was just pouring a cup of coffee when she stumbled out of the bedroom rubbing her eyes. "That time already?" she asked. "It felt like I just went to sleep."

I nodded and handed her the cup, grabbing another for myself. "I want to get to the café early so I don't miss Bill."

She nodded and dropped to a chair. After placing her cup on the table, she reached behind her head and pulled her hair to her right side, covering up that shoulder and leaving the left side of her neck and collarbone area exposed. She took a slow sip of her coffee and asked if I wanted her to tag along. "After all," she said. "You'll be interviewing a potential murder suspect and could use the backup."

I tore my eyes away from her smooth skin and concentrated on the smoke rising from my cup. "That might not be such a good idea, considering how he feels about you."

"I can wait in the Tahoe," she suggested. "At least I'll be close by in case something happens."

I nodded my agreement and decided to take Achilles into the back yard while she got dressed. As soon as I opened the back door, he bolted outside and went straight for a squeaky chicken toy Susan had bought him. Once he snatched it up, he ran in circles with what looked like a giant grin on his face. Each time his front paws hit the ground, the chicken would squeak and he would try to run even faster. He passed close to me on one of his circles, so I lunged for the chicken and got a hand on it, knocking it from his mouth. After an intense scramble, with both of us fighting for the toy, I managed to get it away from him and held it high into the air. Without warning, he leapt effortlessly into the air and clamped his jaws shut around the chicken, jerking it from my grasp.

I laughed and watched as he shot across the yard like a bullet, determined to keep the toy away from me. Just then, my phone rang and I pushed it idly to my ear.

"Is this Chief Clint Wolf of the Mechant Loup Police Department?"

The voice sounded official. "This is Clint."

The man identified himself as the assistant warden for the Louisiana State Penitentiary in Chetimaches. "An inmate named Lance Duggart requested to speak with you, but I wanted to verify you all had official business before allowing him to speak with you. According to Inmate Duggart, he was assisting you with a homicide investigation."

Immediately alert, I verified Duggart was working with me, and a few seconds later he came onto the phone.

"Chief, I've been thinking about it all night and I think I remember the name of the woman who was sleeping with Bill Hedd."

"Shoot," I said, grabbing a pen and a small notebook from my pocket. Holding the phone against my ear with my shoulder, I wrote down the name he mentioned. It sounded familiar to me, but I couldn't be sure I'd heard it before. "Is that a nickname?"

"I'm not sure," Duggart said. "I just remember her saying she thought he was sleeping with some girl named Izzy Ridley. She only mentioned it one time and didn't say more than that, so it's really all I know. To be honest, I didn't care what her husband was doing—I just cared about her."

I thanked him and hung up. Once Susan was ready to go, I rubbed Achilles' head and let him back into the house. Susan and I then jumped in my Tahoe and headed north while I told her about my conversation with Duggart.

"Izzy Ridley..." Susan scrunched her face and whipped out her phone. "The name doesn't sound familiar. I'll have Lindsey run it."

Within minutes, we were crossing the Mechant Loup Bridge and leaving the town behind us. I frowned as I glanced in my rearview mirror. If only I had thought to go up into the bridge cabin Wednesday night I would've caught the murderer and put an end to all of this. *Or you would've gotten yourself killed*, I thought. The murderer would've had the drop on me for sure, so there's no telling how that would've ended.

After talking with Lindsey and waiting for her to run a name inquiry, Susan hung up her phone and turned to me. "You're not going to believe this shit! Izzy is a nickname and Ridley is a maiden name."

When she didn't say anything more, I asked, "Are you going to tell me or do I have to beg?"

"I...I don't know if I believe it." She stared down at her notes and shook her head. When she finally told me the name, I shook my own head.

"That can't be right," I said. "There's no way."

"Lance must be shooting you a line of shit."

We rode in silence, each of us in disbelief. If Izzy was who we thought she was, things were about to get real ugly.

After I'd driven for about fifteen minutes, Susan turned to me. "I just want you to know I'm sorry for what you've gone through."

I cocked my head sideways. "What're you talking about?"

"I've been cheated on before," she said softly, "and it sucks."

"Don't apologize for something she did." I shook my head, not really knowing how to express my feelings—and not really knowing how I felt. "I don't even know what I was thinking getting involved with Chloe. On one hand, it felt good to have someone show interest in me and to have someone to hang out with, but on the other hand, I was often overcome with guilt. If you're feeling guilty about being in a relationship, something's wrong."

"Did you feel guilty because you felt like you were cheating on Michele?"

I was thoughtful, and then nodded.

"Clint, you have to know it's okay to move on with your life. Michele would've wanted you to."

"The thing is...I never asked her for permission to move on. I know it sounds crazy and I know she can't hear me or anything, but I think I should've at least asked her what she thought or let her know that I planned to move on before actually doing it."

"How do you mean?"

"I think I should've visited her grave and talked to her about my plans. Should've given her a chance to show me a sign or something—to let me know it was okay to move on." I stole a glance at Susan. "Does that sound crazy?"

"No, it actually sounds very romantic."

"Nice try, but I know there's nothing romantic about me...and

I'm okay with that. I'm a man who understands his weaknesses."

"Oh, shut up." Susan laughed and playfully punched my arm. "You don't fool me, Clint Wolf. I know there's some sweetness under that tough exterior."

I grunted and kept driving. When I pulled into town I found a parking spot along the street in front of the café. "Call my phone," I said. "I'll leave the line open so you can hear what's going on."

Susan nodded and made the call. I answered and slipped my phone back into my uniform shirt pocket. After giving her a nod, I stepped out into the cool morning air and strode toward the front door. "Here goes nothing, Sue."

CHAPTER 48

The café was darker than I expected, so I stood to the side of the doorway to let me eyes adjust to the dimness. Both walls of the building were lined with round metal tables and chairs, leaving a narrow aisle down the middle. A sign to the right side of the room boasted hot beignets daily and listed a lunch special containing crawfish etouffee, popcorn shrimp, salad, and desert. The hostess walked up wearing a white button-down shirt and black pants. She greeted me with a smile and asked if I'd be dining alone.

"Actually, I'm supposed to meet the district attorney here," I lied, pointing to my badge. "I'm the chief of police over in Mechant Loup and we need to meet about a case. He's expecting me."

She smiled and led the way down the narrow aisle until we reached the back of the café. She then stood aside and pointed toward a dark hallway. "It's the first door on the right. Can I bring you something to drink?"

"I'll have a cup of coffee." I strode down the hallway and glanced through the doorway before entering. It was a small private room with a large window overlooking a giant pond. An egret was swooping in for a landing at the far end of the pond and an alligator was sunbathing on the near bank.

Bill was seated at the only table in the room and his back was to me. I took a deep breath and approached the table. He looked up when I stopped beside him, and immediately lurched back in his chair and gasped, the newspaper slipping from his fingers. "What in hell's name are you doing here?"

I lifted my hands in a surrender position. "I'm just here to talk about a personal matter, and I was hoping you could help me."

Eyeing me suspiciously, he regained his composure, gathered up the newspaper, and folded it neatly. Seemingly back in charge, he placed it aside and waved toward one of the chairs. "Please, sit."

I took a seat—leaving my right leg angled away from the table so I would have easy access to my pistol—and thanked him.

Bill glanced at his watch. "What is it that you need to discuss? I have to be getting back to the office."

"I don't know if you're aware of this, but my girlfriend, Chloe, was murdered the other day."

His face was thick and blank beneath his Elvis Presley hairstyle. "I was sorry to hear about it. No one should have to endure that pain."

"And I'm sorry you had to also endure that same pain."

He only nodded and stared at me, waiting for me to get to my reason for being there. I knew better than to be confrontational, because that would get me nowhere. I had to make him feel like I needed his help.

"I understand Chloe went into your office sometime on Wednesday," I said. "I was hoping you might tell me what she was after. It might help me retrace her steps and hopefully lead to the killer."

"I thought that Simon Parker fellow murdered her and then you justifiably killed him in your home. At least, that's what the sheriff's office reports indicated, and it was the basis of my decision to not bring charges against you." Bill leaned back and folded his arms across his belly. "Was that a mistake on my part?"

I didn't need anyone to point out the idle threat, but I didn't take the bait. "You see, sir, it turns out Simon Parker didn't kill Chloe." I told him about the hidden recorder and how it was connected to Megyn's murder. "It seems Chloe was looking into your wife's murder when she was killed herself."

Bill waved his hand dismissively. "That case has been closed for twenty years. Lance Duggart killed my wife and he's spending the rest of his life in prison where he belongs."

"Would it surprise you to know that Lance Duggart was having an affair with your wife?"

The veins in his temple began to throb and I knew he was getting angry. "My wife was not having an affair with that creep! That bastard broke into my house, raped my wife, and then brutally murdered her."

I looked toward the door and leaned close, lowering my voice. "I'm sorry, but I don't want anyone to hear any of this. After all, it's no one's business."

He looked over his shoulder, suddenly remembering that we were sitting in a public café. Lowering his own voice, he said, "Jolene never met Duggart. Even if she had, she wouldn't have had an affair with that piece of shit."

"So, the relationship with Isaiah Wilson was her only indiscretion?" I thought Bill was going to reach across the table and punch me in the face, but he managed to hold it together.

"That animal stalked and raped my wife!" He glanced over his shoulder and then turned his red eyes back to me. "He's lucky he died in the ring, because he would've died in jail otherwise."

Ignoring his last comment, I pulled a folder from where it had been tucked in the back of my beltline and placed it on the table. I opened it and removed the sheriff's office report from twenty years earlier. "I understand the murder weapon containing your wife's blood was found in Duggart's garage and his DNA was linked to her rape."

Bill nodded again, but his face was still red with anger.

"If Duggart wasn't having an affair with your wife at that time, then who was?"

"Son, if you think I'm going to sit here and let you disparage my wife, you've got another thing coming!"

I leaned back and raised my hands. "I'm sorry, but that's not my intention. I'm just trying to solve a murder—nothing more, nothing less. I want to keep your wife completely out of it, but I need to know what Chloe was after, because it might lead me to her killer."

"Are you saying you think Chloe's murder was connected in some way to my wife's murder?"

"Absolutely." I told Bill about the conversation I'd had with Duggart, but I left out the part about his mistress. I wanted to save that for later.

"The man's a rapist and a murderer, so you can take everything he said and wipe your ass with it." Bill's face twisted into a sneer. "If I had my way, he would've gotten the death penalty and he wouldn't be around for you to interview anymore."

"During the course of this investigation," I began, trying to keep Reginald out of it, "I've obtained information about a receipt you found in your wife's possession before she was killed."

"Receipt? What receipt?"

"Oh, I think you know the one—it was a receipt from a hotel room in the city for a trip you knew nothing about."

Bill's eyes narrowed. "Who told you that?"

"Who told me is not as important as who she was seeing," I explained. "It seems Duggart never took her to the city, so she had to be seeing someone else." I paused and let him process that information before continuing. "Or, maybe the receipt wasn't for your wife after all. Maybe it was your receipt."

"Son, you've got some wild theories. If you don't watch it, you might find yourself in some real trouble. After all, you just murdered a man in cold blood, so I would tread very softly if I were you."

"Except you're not me and I'm not you. Now, are you going to tell me who you were screwing, or am I going to have to guess?"

"I don't like your tone of voice." Bill pushed his empty coffee cup and plate of half-eaten beignets to the side and rose to his feet. "I hereby put you on notice that I will be launching a grand jury investigation into your actions with regard to the shooting death of Simon Parker. Now, you try to have yourself a good day."

"What do you think Isabel's husband will do when he finds out you were sleeping with his wife?"

"You ought to be ashamed of yourself!" Bill's face turned to crimson. "After all she's done for you, you're going to sit here and slander her good name? Is this how you're going to thank her for fighting for you and that Wilson girl? Do you realize I almost fired her for standing up to me on your behalf? *Do you?*"

While a strong feeling of guilt cut me to the core, I couldn't let him know it. I stood and faced him with a confidence I didn't feel. "Are you going to make me tell Isabel's husband, or will you face this head-on like a man and leave her out of it?" Bill didn't say a word, but he also didn't walk away, so I figured I had him contemplating his options. "When Jolene cheated on you with Isaiah, it nearly killed you. I know you loved her and I know she hurt you, but you gave her a second chance. And what did she do? She squandered it. You knew she was sleeping with Duggart and you confronted her about it. She promised to break it off, but she didn't, so you ran into Isabel's arms." I paused and nodded for emphasis. "You thought if only you could get revenge on Jolene it would help to even the score—perhaps make the pain go away—but it didn't."

"You don't have a clue what you're talking about." Bill's eyes were bulging and I knew he was on the verge of exploding.

"Then deny coming home early from the conference to find the house empty. Deny waiting in the shadows for her to return from her rendezvous so you could attack her. Deny ripping her clothes off to make it look like a rape, knowing her boyfriend's DNA would be all over her. Deny planting the knife in—"

"You go to hell, Clint Wolf!" Bill spun on his heel and stormed out of the private room, nearly ripping the door from its hinges as he did so.

I stood staring after him and slowly pulled out my phone. "Did you get all of that?"

"Yeah," Susan said. "It was pretty intense, but he didn't confess to anything."

"I know." I sighed. "We need concrete evidence before we can go after him, but how are we supposed to get that?"

"Let's lean on Isabel and see what she has to say. She might even be in on it."

"Damn, Sue, she's been good to us—she really has."

Susan agreed with me and I walked outside to find her standing on the sidewalk near my Tahoe. We both put our phones down when we met up and I frowned. "Is there a way we can get to Bill without involving Isabel?"

"A wise man once told me if you find the motive, you find the killer." Susan shook her head. "If Isabel's the motive, there's no way we can keep her out of it."

CHAPTER 49

After grabbing a bite for breakfast, Susan and I drove to the sheriff's office and met with Mallory.

"Do y'all think Isabel's involved?" Mallory asked after we told her everything we knew to that point.

Susan and I traded looks and I shook my head. "She doesn't strike me as the type to go killing off her competition."

"What if Jolene was threatening to tell Isabel's husband?" Susan suggested. "That would be reason enough to kill her."

"But why kill Chloe?" I asked.

"Chloe was about to expose her relationship with Bill, which could blow the Duggart case wide open." Susan reached back to fix her ponytail. She had elected not to braid her hair into cornrows that morning, because we had been in a hurry to leave. After she was satisfied with her hair, she pointed to the case file on Mallory's desk. "She's got motive, so we need to figure out if she had opportunity."

"Opportunity to murder is one thing, but if someone other than Duggart killed Jolene, they'd need to possess the knowledge that Duggart was having an affair with Jolene *and* they'd need the opportunity to hide the murder weapon in his garage." I folded my arms across my chest. "Bill fits two out of those three elements. We just need to figure out if he had the opportunity to hide the murder weapon."

"Not so fast," Susan said. "If Jolene told Duggart who Bill was sleeping with, doesn't it make sense that Bill would tell Isabel who Jolene was sleeping with?"

Susan had taken a seat on a leather sofa in Mallory's office and I dropped beside her, my mind turning over every piece of information I'd learned about the case. We all sat in silence for a few minutes until it finally dawned on me. "The knife—we start with the knife that killed Jolene." I jumped to my feet. "Where's Doug?"

"He's been reassigned to patrol," Mallory explained. "He got drunk one night after you shot Simon and started running his mouth in a bar, telling everyone in the place that they could commit cold-blooded murder if they wanted, just as long as they dragged the victim in their house first."

I scowled. "Well, one of us needs to talk to him about that knife, and it probably shouldn't be me."

Susan and Mallory nodded their agreement.

"What are we trying to find out?" Susan asked.

"We need to know what made him look in the garage." I rubbed my chin, remembering what I'd read in the file and the pictures I'd seen. "He found that knife in such an obscure place. It was either dumb luck, good detective work, or he knew it was there."

Susan's head snapped around. "Do you think Doug's involved in this? That he planted the knife or—"

"Oh, shit!" Mallory leaned back in her chair. "Why didn't I think of that? Bill Hedd is Doug's uncle. He and Doug's mom are siblings."

I snapped my fingers, remembering how Reginald said Doug wouldn't even consider Bill as a suspect because he was the DA. What if the real reason was that Bill was his uncle? "Get his ass in here and interrogate the shit out of him!"

"What're you going to do?" Susan asked.

"I'm going to have a long conversation with Isabel."

Susan pulled me aside before I left. "Look, if we clear her of any involvement in the murders, let's try to minimize the damage to her personal life."

I nodded my agreement. "She's been a strong advocate for us and I'd hate to cause her any undue hardship."

"Right, but don't let your guard down, either," Susan warned. "She seems all nice and innocent, but she might be a cold-blooded killer on the inside."

I smiled to let her know not to worry and left the building. I headed north again to the district attorney's office, enjoying the sunshine on my face and the wind blowing my hair through the open window as I drove. My mind wandered to Michele as I traveled the lonely highway. *How I wish you and Abigail would still be around to see days like today.*

CHAPTER 50

An hour later…

Susan sat beside Mallory and they both stared at Doug, who slouched in the chair across from them in the interview room. He looked different in a uniform, and Susan noted how the buttons on the polyester shirt strained to hold the flaps together. It must've been a while since he'd worn it and he hadn't had the chance to upgrade to a larger size.

"Why am I here?" Doug sneered at Mallory. "What's the matter? You didn't screw me over enough by having me kicked out of the bureau? What are you trying to do now—get me fired?"

Susan put a hand on Mallory's arm before she could reply. "Doug, would you prefer to speak with me alone?"

Doug's face softened a little. "I mean, I'm not sure what this is about, but I don't trust her anymore."

Susan turned to Mallory, who nodded and left the room.

When they were alone, Susan opened the folder containing her copy of the Duggart file. She removed the initial investigative report and slid it across the table. "Do you recognize this report?"

Doug studied it and nodded absently as he skimmed the pages. "Yeah, this was a long time ago, when I first made detective."

"As I understand it, there was some bad blood between you and Reginald Hoffman over this case."

"Reggie was a know-it-all. He kept telling me I was going soft on Bill because he was the district attorney. He told me I needed to treat him like any other husband of a murdered wife." Doug leaned back and grunted. "Dumb bastard 'bout shit his pants when he realized he'd wrongfully accused the district attorney of murdering the wife he loved."

"Did Reginald think your relationship with Bill was clouding your judgment?"

"It didn't cloud my judgment. When I interviewed Bill, I treated him like any other suspect—I approached him with respect and pretended to believe he was just a poor grieving husband. I certainly didn't want to scare him into asking for a lawyer or shutting down." He shook his head. "Being nice to a murder suspect doesn't mean your judgment is clouded—it means you're a smart interviewer."

Susan nodded and asked again about Reginald's perception of Doug's relationship with Bill.

"He didn't know Bill was my uncle. Hell, no one did until that chief investigator job came open. I applied for it, but Bill did some research and found out he couldn't hire me because of nepotism rules." Doug sneered. "Reginald really thinks he got the job because of his great detective work, but he didn't even solve the Duggart case—I did—and the only reason Bill hired him was because he couldn't hire me."

Susan could hear the resentment in Doug's voice—could almost feel it leaking from his pores. She removed a supplemental report Doug had generated toward the end of the Duggart investigation. "What about this report?"

"Yeah, this was the supplement I wrote when we executed the search warrant on Duggart's house."

"So, you're the one who found the murder weapon and that knife is what sealed Lance Duggart's fate, right?"

Doug nodded.

Susan removed a picture of an open toolbox from the file. The rusty box had seen better days. The tools inside were covered in a rusty film and there were cobwebs in the corners. It looked as though the tools hadn't been used in ages. Resting atop all the tools was a new knife covered in dried blood. After studying the picture, she slid it to Doug. "Is this what it looked like when you found it?"

Doug glanced at the picture and immediately nodded.

Susan pointed to the cluttered garbage around the toolbox. "How was it that you were able to find the box under all of that clutter? I mean, what made you think to look under that junk?"

Doug shifted in his seat. It was a slight shift, but Susan caught it.

"Well, you know how it is," he said, buying time. "When you execute a search warrant, you make it a point to touch everything in the place to be searched. That's what I did—I didn't leave a stone unturned or a pile of garbage untouched."

Susan removed another picture from the file. This one depicted an overall view of the garage. "Is this what the garage looked like when y'all left?"

Doug nodded. "That's how it looked when we pulled out."

She pointed to several piles of undisturbed garbage scattered around the garage. "If what you're saying is true, why didn't you rummage through all of these piles? It appears to me you went straight to that pile and then stopped—as though you knew exactly where the murder weapon would be."

Doug fidgeted in his seat again, hesitating for a brief second before answering the question. "Look, when you find what you're looking for, you stop searching, you know? The murder weapon happened to be in the first pile I searched." He shrugged. "After finding it, there was no need to rummage through the other piles of garbage. After all, I could tell no one had been through there in a while."

"Earlier, you said it's your practice to touch everything in a place to be searched, did you not?"

Doug was squirming now. "Look, Susan, you know how it is. Sure, you usually touch everything during a search, but if you find what you're looking for, why go through the trouble? We knew the murder weapon was a knife. Once I found it, we were done. I mean, none of the other detectives went through the garage either, so I don't know why you're giving me shit over it."

Susan decided to change her angle of attack. "Why were you mad that Clint didn't go to jail for killing Simon Parker?"

"Are you kidding me right now?" Doug threw his hands up. "Clint murdered that man! He put a gun in the man's mouth while he was lying helpless on the ground and shot a hole through the back of his head. He should be in jail, not running around wearing a badge."

"Clint killed a murdering piece of shit who was—and would've continued to be—a menace to the public at large. He risked his freedom to save God knows how many future victims."

"A murderer is a murderer, and he's no different than Simon Parker." He pounded his chest and then waved his arm around. "We don't get to play judge, jury, and executioner out here. We're the law, not vigilantes. I believe in the system and I swore an oath—"

"Shut your self-righteous mouth." Susan propped her elbows on the table and stared coldly into Doug's eyes. "Do you read the Bible?"

"What's that got to do with anything?"

"Ever read the passage about those who were without sin casting the first stone?"

"So? What's your point?"

"Clint killed a murderer, but you…" Susan shook her head. "What you did is a hideous crime."

"What the hell are you talking about?"

"I'm talking about the murder of an innocent woman—your uncle's wife."

Doug's mouth dropped open. "I had nothing to do with her murder. That's ludicrous!"

"That's not how I see it." Susan tapped the picture of the knife. "We know for a fact this knife was planted in Duggart's garage. The only question—"

"Bullshit! How do you know that?"

Susan looked around the room and then back at Doug. "What do you think we've been doing over the last few days? Screwing off? We've been working the hell out of this case and we're fixing to break it wide open." Susan shoved her finger toward Doug. "You're a hypocrite if you think Clint should go to jail and you should go free for the crimes you've committed."

Doug pounded the desk and kicked his chair back, jumping to his feet. "I didn't commit any crimes and I won't stand to be falsely accused!"

Susan didn't even flinch. She calmly stood and met his gaze with her own. "You and I both know you didn't just stumble upon the murder weapon on your own. You were tipped off." Susan's eyes narrowed slightly when she saw Doug gulp. "Who was it? Did Bill tell you where to find it?"

Doug's eyes darted wildly about the room, as though looking for a place to hide.

"Come on, Doug." Susan's voice was soothing now. "It's over—time for you to be a man."

He stood tense, staring at Susan for a long moment.

"It's time to do the right thing," Susan said. "If Lance Duggart is innocent, you'd better hope he doesn't die in jail. That would be the same as murder and you would be worse than Clint."

Doug exhaled and dropped to his chair, his shoulders drooping. "Damn it, Susan, I didn't do anything wrong. I just followed up on a tip."

"What tip?"

"I was on my way to Duggart's house to help out with the search warrant when someone paged me." He wiped the sweat off his forehead and continued. "It was a number I didn't recognize. I stopped at a pay phone and called the number. The person who answered told me Duggart was the killer and—"

"Was it a man or woman?"

A scowl spread across Doug's face. "I couldn't tell. Whoever it was definitely disguised their voice and it confused me. I got the impression it was a woman trying to sound masculine, but I've never been sure."

"Okay, go on."

"They told me Duggart confided in them and told them he hid the knife in a rusty toolbox. They described it as the red toolbox with the gray lettering." He shrugged. "There was only one fitting that description, so it was easy to find."

Susan stared at her notes for a minute and wondered why he would keep something like that a secret. She finally posed the question to him and he hung his head.

"I know it sounds stupid, but when I found the knife, everyone started congratulating me and telling me I should've never been removed as the lead detective. The sheriff was at the scene and he pulled me aside to tell me he was proud of me. He told me I was like a bloodhound on a crime scene and he expected great things in my future." Doug sighed. "I didn't say anything when I first got the page because I knew Reginald would take my information and search the garage himself. Besides, I wasn't even sure it was good information. It could've been a prank."

"Why didn't you tell everyone after you found it? When you realized it wasn't a prank?"

"By the time I found the knife it was too late," Doug said. "I would've had to explain why I didn't immediately tell the lead detective, and I'd already taken enough shit over the case."

"Weren't you even a little curious to know who it was?"

Doug nodded his head vigorously. "I ran the telephone number and it came back to a payphone a mile from Duggart's house. I began to suspect it was Megyn Sanders and I was terrified she'd come forward someday to expose me. I kind of relaxed after the trial, because I figured she would've said something by then if she planned on it."

Susan studied Doug's face, searching it for any hint of guilt as she made a mental note of his last comment. Finally, she packed up the case file and told him she'd be in touch if she needed more.

When Doug was gone, Mallory entered the interview room. Susan asked if she'd heard everything.

"I did."

"Even his last comment?"

Mallory nodded. "What if he knew Megyn was going to tell Chloe about the tip?"

"What if the story about the tip is all bullshit and he planted the knife?" Susan suggested. "Clint said Duggart suspected Jolene of sleeping with another man, why couldn't it be her husband's nephew? Doug would have easy access to her. Maybe he found out about Duggart and killed Jolene out of jealousy? From there, it was an easy matter of planting the knife and then finding it."

"That's one theory," Mallory said, nodding her agreement. "We need to put a tail on him in case he does something incriminating."

CHAPTER 51

I looked at the clock on my dash. Almost noon. Isabel had promised to meet me across the street from the district attorney's office at twelve o'clock sharp. I had backed into a spot in the bank parking lot so I could watch the front door of the DA's office. I wanted to see Bill when he left for lunch. I couldn't have him catching me and Isabel together.

My eyes narrowed as I considered my meeting with Isabel. She had been such a good friend that I questioned my ability to be as objective as I'd need to be with her. Reginald had called earlier to say she located Chloe's phone in Bill's desk drawer.

"I swear," Reginald had said, "I searched every inch of his office. I don't know how she found it and I didn't."

"Are you sure it's Chloe's phone?" I'd asked.

"It looks like hers, but I'm not positive. Isabel put it in a plastic lunch bag and sealed it, so I didn't mess with it. We need to get it to the lab and have them process it for DNA and prints. I told her to give it directly to you and no one else. Bill leaves the office at quarter 'til, so if you can be here for noon that'd be great."

I'd agreed with him and drove to town to meet with Isabel. As I sat there waiting for her, I was unsure how to broach the subject of her infidelity. I needed information from her and, if she was guilty, I needed a confession. But how would I extract that information without her asking for a lawyer or refusing to talk? And could I be tough on her if it became necessary?

I was tempted to have Reginald with me when I questioned her, but I was afraid he'd beat a confession out of her—or worse, kill her—if she was responsible for Chloe's murder. I couldn't afford a suppressed confession. This would be my last murder case before I resigned and I needed it to stick. Chloe might've betrayed me, but she wasn't a bad person and no one deserved what happened to her.

I caught movement behind a parked truck and saw Isabel hurrying across the street toward the parking lot. She wore a form-fitting dress with thick black and white stripes. *How appropriate*, I thought, *a prison outfit.*

When she reached the passenger's side of my Tahoe, she quickly peeked over her shoulder before slipping inside. "I don't think anyone saw me," she said, a little breathless. She reached into her large brown purse and pulled out a plastic lunch bag. I sighed when I saw the phone inside. "Is this Chloe's?"

I nodded and took the bag from her. "Where'd you find it?"

"It was in Bill's bottom desk drawer, inside a cigar box." She pushed a lock of blonde hair out of her face. "I'm guessing this is it, then? Are you going to arrest him?"

"We need to talk first." I fired up my Tahoe and pulled out of the parking lot, heading west along the busy street. I drove out of town and headed south toward the sheriff's office.

Isabel looked behind us and then puckered her brow. "Where are we going? I need to get back to work."

"You'll see," was all I said as I continued driving south for twenty minutes. When we were about five miles from the sheriff's office, I turned east on a dirt road that cut between some cane fields. The road was bumpy and dust kicked up in our wake, making the highway behind us disappear from view.

"Good Heavens, Clint, where are you taking me?" There was a hint of panic in Isabel's voice.

I finally turned off on a side road and stopped beside a large canal. I shut off the engine and faced Isabel. "Have you ever been out here?"

Isabel shook her head, her face a deeper shade of pale.

"This is where Jolene Hedd used to meet her lover, Lance Duggart." I opened my door and stepped outside, waving for her to do the same. When Isabel was standing beside me in front of my Tahoe, I pointed to a patch of thick green grass. "That could be the very spot they made love for the last time."

Isabel stared blankly at the spot. "Clint," she began, her voice quivering, "why are we here?"

"I thought this would be an appropriate place to talk." I walked to the spot in the grass and then turned to face Isabel. Her dark eyes were wide.

"I still don't understand what's going on here." She rubbed her hands against her hips, smoothing out her dress. "Why did we come all the way out here?"

"So, as you might be aware, we recently learned that Bill was cheating on Jolene at the same time she was cheating on him."

"Um, I wasn't aware of that exactly," she said slowly.

"Yeah, as it turns out, he was cheating with a woman named Izzy Ridley." I squinted at her. "I remembered your husband calling you Izzy, and when my dispatcher ran your name, I found out your maiden name is Ridley."

Isabel reached out and grabbed the hood of my Tahoe to steady herself. "That…that has to be a mistake. That's not true."

"It's no mistake, Isabel. You were sleeping with Bill and you and he were the only two people who knew about Lance Duggart." I frowned. "It was either you or Bill—or both of you—who killed Jolene and planted the knife in Duggart's garage."

"That's ludicrous, Clint." Isabel grabbed at her throat with her hand and backed closer to my Tahoe. "I would never."

"Well, I received a call from Susan earlier. She had an interesting conversation with Doug Cagle. You know him, right? He's the detective who found the murder weapon in Duggart's garage. Turns out, he didn't just stumble upon it." I shook my head. "No, ma'am, someone tipped him off, and that someone was a woman who tried to make her voice sound husky. Do I need to remind you that the only two people who knew about Duggart and Jolene were you and Bill?"

"Clint, you have to believe me, I had nothing to do with Jolene's murder. For Christ's sake, I'm a mother, not a killer."

"I want to believe you, but you have to come clean about the affair before I can believe anything you say about the murder."

Isabel's chin trembled and tears welled up in her eyes. "Clint, please…it would destroy my husband."

"Your husband will be the least of your worries if I can prove you killed Chloe, Jolene, and Megyn."

"But I didn't kill anyone!"

"Prove it."

"How?"

"Start talking about your relationship with Bill, and don't leave anything out."

Isabel was bawling now. She dropped to her knees and buried her face in her hands. I remembered Susan's warning and didn't approach her. Instead, I kept my hand close to my pistol and watched her carefully.

"Go ahead," I said. "Spill it. I'm running out of time and patience."

Through breaks in her sobbing, Isabel described a sexual relationship that began when she was a single intern for Bill and continued until after she was married and working as an assistant district attorney. "He wouldn't let me break it off," she said, tears flowing down her pale face. "Every time I'd try, he'd threaten to tell my husband. I didn't want to lose my family. I was trapped, can't you see?"

Not feeling any sympathy for her, I asked if she knew anything about Jolene's murder.

"I always suspected he might know something, because of how it impacted him. He carried on like a person who was overcome with guilt, not someone who was grieving." Isabel had calmed down a little and wiped her nose on the sleeve of her dress. "I was really scared after that happened and I felt like he would kill me if I tried to break it off again, so I simply went along with whatever he demanded."

"Where were you the night Jolene was killed?"

"Home, I guess. I mean, I don't know exactly when she was killed. I just know I got a call from him one morning saying she had been found murdered at their house. I was home when I got the call."

"Where was he the night before that call?"

"He was at a conference. I would usually attend with him, but I couldn't go that time because I had to be in court all week, so I was home."

"Your husband...did he have any clue you were screwing around on him?"

Isabel started bawling again and could only shake her head.

"Did Bill ask you to page Doug and tell him about the knife?"

She shook her head again, saying something that was indiscernible.

I walked up to her and grabbed her by the arm, pulling her to her feet. "Get in the car. I'll take you back to your office."

"Are you going to tell my husband?"

"I don't know yet." When we were seated in my Tahoe and jostling along the cane field road, I noticed Chloe's phone on the center console. "Where were you Wednesday night?"

Isabel sniffed and shook her head. "I don't know. Work, maybe."

"You'd better hope you have an alibi," I said under my breath. I gripped the steering wheel as I drove, wondering if I'd used the right approach with Isabel. She'd come clean about her affair with Bill, but was she telling the truth about the murder? Up to this point, all we had were statements from our main suspects, Bill, Isabel, and Doug, and all of them denied doing it. What I needed now was physical evidence—something real to link one of them to the case. If I couldn't find that evidence, Duggart might end up spending his life in prison for nothing, and Chloe's murder would go unsolved. Both were unacceptable to me.

When I reached the district attorney's office I pulled right up to the front door. Isabel's eyes grew wide. "What are you doing?" she asked. "You can't drop me off here."

"Just get out of my truck," I said sternly. "I've got work to do."

"But what if Bill sees me?"

"That's your problem." I stared coldly into her bloodshot eyes. "I really don't care if he sees you or not."

CHAPTER 52

Chateau Parish Sheriff's Office

After getting Isabel out of my Tahoe, I drove back to the sheriff's office and reunited with Susan and Mallory in the large conference room. Melvin was also there and he greeted me with a huge grin.

"How's it going, Chief?"

I shrugged. "It's going okay, I guess. How're things in town?"

"Quiet, actually. It's almost as though people are scared to go outside." He rubbed his bare crown. "Claire is still trying to pressure me into quitting, but I told her this is what I want to do with my life. She's not happy with me at the moment."

I nodded my understanding, and then updated them on my conversation with Isabel. "I'm leaning more toward Bill being the killer," I said, "but we need some physical evidence linking him to the crimes."

"The only physical evidence from Jolene's murder points to Duggart," Susan said. "So, we need to try and link him to Chloe's murder and then work backward from there."

"All we have are projectiles," Mallory pointed out. "And we compared the projectiles from their murders with all the projectiles we recovered during the shootouts at the police department and Clint's house, but none of them match. We've got nothing."

"Wait a minute," Melvin said. "Did you get a look at Bill's shoes?"

I shook my head. "Why?"

"Remember? I recovered a dozen shoe prints from the bridge cabin. Most of them were from the floor and could be anyone's prints, but I recovered one beautiful print from the door. Whoever kicked the door open dumped Chloe's body in Bayou Tail, so all we have to do is match the print to a shoe, and we've got our killer."

"Where're the prints?" I asked, suddenly excited.

Mallory jumped to her feet. "They're in our evidence locker. I'll get them now."

When she was gone, Susan turned to me. "How are we going to get a look at Bill's shoes?"

I smiled. "If need be, you're going to kick him right in the face and I'm going to pull his shoe off."

We laughed and made small talk until Mallory returned carrying a stack of large evidence envelopes. She pulled a scissor from her desk drawer and began carefully cutting each of the envelopes open so we could examine the prints. Several of the shoe prints from the floor appeared to have been made by the same type of boots Amy wore, and one set matched Melvin's boots.

"I thought they were mine," Melvin said, "but it was hard to tell in the low light of the cabin, so I took all of them."

I nodded my approval and continued going through the prints. Mallory finally pulled one from an envelope and announced, "This is the one Melvin recovered from outside of the door." She placed it on the desk and we crowded around it.

As soon as I saw it my heart stopped beating for at least ten seconds.

Susan looked up at me and cocked her head to the side. "You look like you've seen a ghost. Do you recognize this print?"

I nodded slowly as the pieces started to come together inside my head. I pointed to Mallory. "How fast can you type up a search warrant?"

"As fast as you can spit the facts from your mouth."

"Good, fire up your computer so we can get to work." I turned to Melvin. "You're a genius. Get your gear together. I want you coming with us."

"Wait a minute," Susan said, grabbing Melvin's arm. "No one's going anywhere until you tell us what you know."

CHAPTER 53

3:00 a.m., Wednesday, November 4

Susan and I crept across the soft grass, careful not to make a single sound as we approached the house. Somewhere in the distance a neighborhood dog barked. I froze in place and squatted in the wet grass, gripping my pistol firmly in my fist. I could feel Susan's hand on the small of my back, waiting for me to move again. When the dog quit barking and I was sure there had been no movement from inside the house, I continued moving forward until I reached the front door of the residence.

Cupping my hand over my mouth, I spoke quietly into my radio mic. "Melvin, are you and Mallory in place?"

Melvin's voice was loud in my earpiece. "Ten-four. Waiting on your command."

I turned and made eye contact with Susan, nodding my head. The nearest street light was a block away, but there was enough ambient light to make her brown eyes sparkle. She grabbed my hand and leaned close to me, pressing her lips to my ear.

"Just in case something happens to one of us," she whispered, her warm breath tickling my ear, "I need you to know I have feelings for you."

My heart began to race inside my chest. I turned my head and stared into her moist eyes. "What are you talking about?"

I must've said it too loud, because she winced and pushed her finger against my lips to silence me. Pushing her lips back to my ear, she said, "We'll talk about it later. If something happens to me inside, I just didn't want to die without telling you. When I was shot with that arrow, my one regret was not letting you—"

"Chief, did you copy?" Melvin called into his radio. "We're

waiting on your command."

Susan's words had cut to my core and I lost my focus for a second. A million thoughts began running through my mind and Susan had to give me a shove to bring me back to the present. I shook my head to clear it and looked toward the opposite corner of the house, where a sheriff's office SWAT operator was waiting with a battering ram. I looked back at Susan and gave her a nod. She nodded back and I waved the operator forward.

The operator scurried forward and stopped directly in front of me. With my pistol pointed toward the door, I held up the five fingers of my left hand and counted down. When I dropped my last finger, the operator flung the ram violently into the door, blasting it open.

I rushed through the opening, hooking to the left and following the wall of the room toward the hallway. Susan had crisscrossed to the right and followed the opposite wall. I made it to the hallway a split second before she did and she followed me toward the second door to the left.

Just as we reached the master bedroom, I heard the back door crash open, and I knew Melvin and Mallory had made entry. Before they could start yelling out commands, I smashed my shoulder into the hollow-core door, busting through to the other side. Susan's flashlight lit up the room and I caught movement to my right. It was a half-naked woman and she was scrambling about the bed and screaming for her life.

On the other side of her, a man was just pushing himself to a seated position, staring about in confusion. Before he could register what was happening, I leapt across the woman and smashed my pistol into the side of his head, sending him sprawling to the floor. The woman thrashed about under me and I got tangled up in her legs and arms.

The man was pushing himself to his feet when Susan came around the other end of the bed and kicked him squarely in the chest. He crashed into the wall behind him, causing a large hole to form in the sheetrock.

I rolled off the end of the bed just as Mallory and Melvin came through the door and secured the woman. I hurried around the bed to help Susan, but the man was already on his face handcuffed and she was reading him his rights. When she turned him over and the light from Melvin's flashlight caught his face, I saw blood dripping down the side of his head.

"What's going on?" Reginald demanded. "And why the hell are you in my house?"

"Let's get him to the living room," I said, helping Susan lift him and drag him away.

Reginald's wife was already seated on the sofa and the lights were on when we pushed him onto the loveseat across from her. His eyes were slits and his face was purple. "Do y'all know who I am? I'll have Bill Hedd indict every last one of you bastards for home invasion! All of y'all are going to prison! Your careers are *over!*"

"Bill actually knows we're here," I said, shoving a search warrant into his lap and turning it so he could read it. "He agreed that we had probable cause to search your premises and to arrest your ass for murder."

"Murder? You can't even get me for jaywalking. There's not a shred of evidence..." The color slowly drained from his face as he read the allegations in the search warrant. "This is bullshit! You can't pin this on me!"

Melvin appeared from the back of the house carrying a clear plastic bag that contained a pair of large leather ankle boots—the same boots I'd seen when Reginald threw his feet up on the desk at the sheriff's office Saturday morning.

"They're a match," Melvin proclaimed.

"There're a million boots like that," Reginald said. "That's not evidence of anything!"

"If they were new, you might have a valid point." Melvin turned the sole of the boots around so Reginald could see them. "Do you see how the sole is worn on the outside of the right heel? And you see this missing chunk from the center of the heel? Those are like fingerprints—unique to this pair."

"I was not in that bridge cabin. I didn't touch Chloe—I loved her!"

"Like you loved Jolene?" I strode across the room and looked down at him. "You used Chloe, is what you did, so you could keep tabs on her investigation. And when she started getting too close to the truth, you killed her and Megyn to shut them up."

"You can't prove any of that."

"It'll be hard for you to explain away the fact that Chloe's earring was found in the back of your truck."

Reginald's mouth dropped open. "You know how that got there! We were having sex on our lunch break—long before she was killed."

"That's not the way the jury will see it. When we present the facts to the jury, they'll believe the earring came off when you were moving her body around."

"You're just pissed off because you came in second to me! That's what this is about, isn't it?"

Reginald's wife was bawling on the sofa, her hair a tangled mess and her nightgown hanging off of her. "Who's this Chloe person? And why were you having sex with her? Oh, my God, you're such an—"

"I've got it!" screamed Doug, as he burst through the back door holding a brown paper bag in his gloved hands. "I found this in an old rusty tool box under a bunch of shit in the garage." He shot a finger at Reginald. "It's that bastard's favorite hiding spot! I bet it's where he hid his porn as a kid."

"Men are definitely creatures of habit," Mallory said, laughing at Doug.

I laughed, too, pleased with myself for calling in a favor to Sheriff Turner, who agreed to reinstate Doug's detective status at my request.

I walked over to where Doug stood holding the bag under the living room light and glanced inside. There was a handgun and several spent shell casings at the bottom of the bag.

Reginald hung his head and began to cry when Doug pulled the firearm out of the bag and held it so we all could see. It was a cheap, silver nine millimeter pistol with obliterated serial numbers.

"Based on the way he's carrying on," I said, shooting my thumb toward Reginald, "I'm guessing you found the murder weapon."

"Yep, and I acted on the tip he called in twenty years ago…trying to make himself sound like a woman." Shaking his head, he returned the pistol to the bag and walked outside.

I followed Doug into the darkness and looked around for Susan. She wasn't in the back yard or in the garage, so I walked around to the front of the house. A white Escalade was parked in the driveway and a large man was talking to someone I couldn't see because of the shadows. I approached the vehicle and heard a booming voice that I recognized to be Bill Hedd.

As I rounded the corner and came up behind him on the driver's side, I heard him say, "I acted like an ignorant ass and I'm really sorry for all the pain and trouble I've caused you. Your dad was a good man, Sergeant, and I'm sorry for trying to say otherwise."

"I really appreciate that, sir," Susan said, her voice soft and sincere. "I harbor no ill feelings. As far as I'm concerned, it never happened."

Susan looked up when I approached and Bill turned around. He stuck out his hand and pumped my arm vigorously. "I can't thank you enough, young man. To think this evil bastard has been working for me all these years and I never had a clue he did all those horrible things and..." His voice cracked and he just shook his head, trying to hold himself together.

CHAPTER 54

Three hours later…

"How'd you figure it out?" Susan asked as we got in my Tahoe to drive back to her house.

"When I talked to Duggart I got the feeling he was telling the truth, but I wanted to give Reginald the benefit of the doubt." I turned the wipers on to wash away the dew that had formed on the windshield. "It was when I talked to Bill that I started doubting Reginald. I could tell Bill had no clue that his wife was sleeping with Duggart."

Susan nodded her head knowingly. "If Bill didn't know about Duggart, then the only way Reginald could know was if he was the one who followed Jolene and caught them together."

"Which meant he was the *number two* Duggart was talking about."

"And since he worked for Bill, he knew Bill was away at a conference and he'd have the opportunity to murder Jolene." Susan nodded. "Motive *and* opportunity. If you think about it, he was brilliant to kill Jolene right after she'd slept with Duggart and then stage the scene to look like a rape."

I rubbed my tired face and nodded in agreement. "He's a great manipulator, that one. I should've seen it from the beginning. He was the one person connected to everything—to Duggart, to Megyn, to Chloe—and he controlled the investigation into Jolene's murder. There were some holes in the reports, but he filled them with believable information that he figured I wouldn't second-guess, and I didn't at first. I think I wanted it to be Bill. I wanted him to pay dearly for what he did to you, and that clouded my judgment."

"You're not the only one who fantasized about Bill Hedd being locked away forever, but it turns out he's not a bad man." Susan was quiet for a long moment. When she spoke again, her voice was soft. "You know, had it not been for Chloe's investigative work, Duggart would have to spend the rest of his life in prison for a crime he didn't commit. Basically—but not knowing it—she traded her life for his."

I only nodded as we continued traveling south. The sun was rising to the east and it was shaping up to be another beautiful day in swamp country. Now that the case was closed, my mind was free to wander. I had lots to think about, but I had to do one thing before making any decisions.

"Are you okay?" Susan asked when we pulled into her driveway. "You haven't said much on the drive home."

"I'm just tired, I guess."

"Well, why don't you grab a shower and I'll scramble up some eggs." She stretched and I couldn't help but notice how the polyester uniform shirt pulled against her ample breasts. "After we eat, I plan on calling in sick, taking a long hot bath, and then dying in bed for a while."

I smiled and nodded. "If you plan on calling your chief, he won't be in today."

She winked at me and stepped out of the Tahoe. I followed her inside and hurried through a shower, my mind preoccupied on my tragic past, confusing present and uncertain future.

When I was dressed, I met Susan in the kitchen and we ate in silence. I wondered if she regretted telling me she had feelings for me earlier. She hadn't said another word about it, and I began to think it was just a spur of the moment comment uttered in a high-stress situation—one to be forgotten later.

I cleaned up the dishes while Susan went in to take a bath. When I was done, I gathered up all of my belongings and loaded them into my Tahoe. I took one last look around the living room that had been my home for the last few days and hesitated, listening by the bathroom door. I could hear the ripple of water and an occasional squeaking sound as her bare body slid against the porcelain tub. Should I knock on the door to tell her goodbye? What if she asked me to stay? What if she invited me in?

My heart began racing again and my hand trembled. I turned and walked away. "Come on, Achilles, let's go."

I drove to the town hall and walked inside. Several town employees did double-takes when they saw me wearing jeans and a button-down shirt. I just nodded and walked to Pauline's office. She looked up from her desk when I entered and then quickly stood to her feet.

"Clint, thank God you're okay. It's been one hell of a rollercoaster ride the last few days. I...I didn't know what was going on and who the murderer was and what to tell the townspeople or what to do with—"

"It's okay now," I said. "Everything will get back to normal soon."

She stood there wringing her hands, nodding. "Okay, so does this mean that being a mayor will get easier from here?"

I laughed and nodded.

She stopped fidgeting and pointed toward my hands. "What're those?"

I looked down at my badge and commission, contemplating my next move. Earlier, I was certain what I would do, but now I was as confused as ever. When I felt like I was taking too much time, I sighed and stepped forward.

"To hell with it," I said out loud and placed the badge and commission on Pauline's desk. "Ma'am, I'm turning in my badge. I'm resigning as chief of police."

Her mouth dropped open. "What in the hell are you talking about?"

"I can't be chief of police anymore."

"But...what am I supposed to do with the police department? I don't know how to run a law enforcement agency. What am I to do?"

"Susan Wilson will make an excellent chief—I can promise you that." I turned to walk away, calling over my shoulder, "I'll get the Tahoe back to you, but there's something I have to take care of first."

Pauline was calling after me as the door slammed, begging me to reconsider, but I hurried off before I changed my mind.

I drove out of town heading north and then east, making my way toward the city. A little over an hour later I reached my destination and brought the Tahoe to a stop in a small shell parking lot. I turned to Achilles, who had sat beside me on the drive, his head hanging out of the window and his long tongue flapping in the wind. "Come on, boy, there are some people I want you to meet."

Achilles jumped to his feet when I slipped out of my seat and he bounded after me, landing lightly on the ground. We walked through the rusted metal gate and strode down the long row of tombstones, enjoying the smell of fresh-cropped grass. I slowed my stride when we reached the large oak tree with the heart-shaped scar. The leaves were still green, but starting to turn brown on the edges. I hesitated for a moment and then turned right. The last hundred yards was a blur and it felt like I was walking in slow motion. If I thought I was scared earlier, I was terrified now.

After what seemed like forever, I finally reached the end of the grassy lane and stopped in front of the only two headstones there. One displayed Michele's name and the other displayed Abigail's, and the date of their death was inscribed beneath their names.

"It's time for you to meet the rest of your family," I said softly to Achilles. I turned to the tombstones and knelt in front of them. "Hey, y'all, I know it's been a while, and we have a lot of catching up to do..."

I hesitated, a million thoughts swirling through my mind. There was so much to say and I had so many questions, but I didn't know where to start. I was lonely and tired. As I knelt there staring at their tombs, my heart utterly destroyed from the pain of missing them so much, I broke down crying, unable to utter another word.

CHAPTER 55

"God, that felt amazing," Susan said as she walked out of the bathroom drying her hair with a long towel. "I almost fell asleep in there…" She stopped drying her hair and glanced around the living room. The place seemed unusually quiet and empty. "Clint? Where are you? Where's all your stuff?"

Her feet padded softly against the floor as she hurried through each room and then out onto the front porch. Panic gripped at her chest when she noticed his Tahoe was gone. Dropping the towel, she raced inside and grabbed her phone, fumbling with the screen. She called Clint first, but his phone went straight to voicemail. She called Melvin next.

"Susan, what the hell is going on?" Melvin was screaming into the phone. "The mayor just said Clint resigned! She said he told her to make you the next chief and he walked away. He left his badge and commission on her desk."

"Where is he?" Susan asked, her bottom lip trembling. "Where'd he go? Did he just run off without saying goodbye? Do you really think he'd do that to me?"

"I don't know," Melvin said. "I tried calling his phone a hundred times, but it goes straight to voicemail. Amy hasn't heard anything either. God, Susan, what are we supposed to do now? Do we try to find him? What do we do?"

Susan dropped her phone and sank to the floor in the kitchen, leaning against the wall. Tears flooded her eyes and blurred her vision. Was this her fault? Had she scared him off when she expressed her feelings earlier?

"Damn it!" she leaned forward and punched a hole in the nearest cabinet door. "Why couldn't you just keep your mouth shut?"

Blood poured from several cuts in her knuckles as she stood to her feet and stared wildly about her kitchen. How was she supposed to make this right? What if he was gone forever? What if she never saw him again? What if he was going out to do something destructive—?

"Holy shit!" Susan quickly wiped her eyes, remembering a conversation they'd had yesterday. She was almost too afraid to wish for it, but it was all she had at the moment. "Holy shit! I think I know where you're going!"

Wearing nothing but a thin T-shirt and skintight shorts, she snatched up her keys and ran to her old pickup truck. The engine hesitated when she turned the key, almost refusing to turn over. "Come on!" she screamed, turning the key again. Finally, it roared to life and she smashed the accelerator, racing down her street and then turning north, heading for the city. As she drove with one hand, she used the thumb of her other hand to call Melvin. He sounded bummed out when he answered.

"Melvin, are you near a computer?" Susan's wet hair whipped across her face from the cool November wind blowing through the window and it was difficult to hear Melvin's voice. "Say it again, but louder."

"I can be…why?"

"Get on it and find the funeral arrangements for Michele and Abigail Wolf—I think Clint's going out to their gravesite. Send me the address to the cemetery as soon as you get it." Without waiting for Melvin to answer, she tossed her phone into the console and sped up to pass a car traveling the posted speed limit.

A million thoughts raced through her mind as she drove, and her feelings vacillated between sheer panic and a slim chance of hope. She clutched at her chest often, complaining that her heart couldn't take much more abuse.

Susan was still twenty minutes away from the city when a text message came through her phone. She stomped the brake pedal and pulled the truck to the shoulder of the highway, kicking up rocks as she skid to a stop. She read the message with trembling hands. Melvin had located the cemetery and sent her the address. She quickly punched it into her GPS and waited impatiently for the information to load. She let out an involuntary screech when she realized it was only ten minutes away. Shoving the gearshift back in *drive*, she merged into traffic and drove even faster, panic beating her insides like a jackhammer. What if Clint had left already? What if she was completely wrong about his destination?

Afraid to consider the negative possibilities, she tried to

concentrate on something else as she drove, but it was no use.

Finally, mentally drained and physically exhausted, she turned into the cemetery parking lot. Her eyes misted over and she sighed when she caught a glimpse of Clint's Tahoe on the far end of the lot. Not really sure of what to do next, she parked beside his vehicle and just sat there, sparsely dressed, her hair a mess, and her emotions in turmoil. While she waited, she sent a quick text message to Melvin that she'd located his vehicle at the cemetery.

She received an immediate reply from Melvin. Her heart pounded as she read it, *You don't suppose he's decided to check out so he can be with his family again, do you? He might've been living to get revenge and now that it's over...*

"Clint! Oh, God! *Clint!*" Susan shoved her door open and dropped to the shells, ignoring the pain to her feet. She sprinted across the parking lot and smashed into a metal gate, nearly knocking it off of its flimsy hinges. She raced toward the back of the cemetery, her head on a swivel as she searched between the tombstones on either side. She screamed Clint's name as she ran, tears flowing down her cheeks.

When she reached an oak tree at the end of the aisle, she fell against it and gasped for air. She hollered his name, but it was barely a hoarse whisper as she tried to catch her breath. Tears blurred her vision and she wiped her eyes, trying to scan her surroundings, hoping for a glimpse of movement. She screamed his name again and then stopped suddenly. *What was that noise?*

She heard the sound a second time before it registered. Pushing herself off of the tree, she looked toward the right. Off in the distance, against the blinding sun, she saw a black figure running toward her. It was low to the ground and it was barking as it ran.

"Achilles!" her heart immediately sank. Where was Clint? Why was Achilles alone? What if Clint had taken his own life? She started running toward Achilles when another shadow emerged from the shimmering waves of light. As she grew closer, she recognized the walk and the shape of the man she loved. She rubbed her eyes with her hands and he slowly began to come into view.

"What are you doing here?" Clint asked when they were within speaking distance.

Susan didn't say a word until he had stopped right in front of her and stared down into her eyes. She fought back the tears that threatened to fall once again. "I...I thought you had left me. I thought you had just run off and...and you were never coming back again."

Clint smiled as Achilles ran circles around them, showing off his speed and athletic prowess. "No," he said. "I did it right this time...I got permission from Michele to move on."

"But, where are you going? Melvin said you resigned from the police department."

He smiled and his eyes sparkled. "I did resign, but I'm not going anywhere. I resigned so we can be together."

Without saying another word, he stepped forward and wrapped his strong arms around her and pressed his lips firmly to hers.

CHAPTER 56

One year later…

Sunday, September 25

Susan was already talking to the couple when I arrived at the boat launch and exited my pickup. The couple looked young—early twenties, maybe—and it was obvious they'd been enjoying a day on the water. The girl wore a skimpy bikini and her boyfriend had on a pair of boardshorts, and they were both bright red from too much sun.

"I swear to God," the man was saying when I walked up. "It's a dinosaur and it lives in the water!" He wiped his face and nodded. His eyes were wide. "We were fishing and it just floated on by like it didn't even care that we were there."

"Could it have been an alligator?" Susan asked.

"No way!" said the woman next to him. "It was too big."

"How big was it?" I asked, shoving a hand in the back pocket of my jeans. I'd responded to dozens of such reports over the past year, but none had panned out. While this one seemed different because the people were terrified, I wasn't going to get my hopes up.

"It was longer than our boat." The woman was chewing her nails and drumming her bare foot in the shells. "I thought it was going to flip our boat and eat us."

The man nodded. "She's right—it was bigger than my boat, and my boat is fourteen feet long."

I glanced at Susan, who was standing there in her polyester uniform, an air of authority surrounding her. She had taken to the chief job as naturally as a fish to water. She'd hired two more officers, purchased updated radio equipment, and they were set to move into their new hurricane-proof building by the end of the year.

"Where was it when y'all last saw it?" she asked.

The man described the area and shook his head. "We're never going back there again, that's for sure!"

Susan waved for me to follow her and we walked to the far end of the pier, out of earshot of the troubled couple. She hitched her gun belt up on her waist and studied my face. "Do you think it's Godzator?"

I allowed my eyes to rove over her tan uniform shirt and whispered, "I can't wait to rip that thing off of you tonight."

"Clint, stop it!" She looked over her shoulder to make sure the couple hadn't followed us. "Seriously, do you think it's him?"

I chuckled and shrugged. "Whatever it was, it scared the shit out of them. I'll go check it out."

A smile played at the corners of her mouth and she leaned close to me. "And I can't wait to rip those jeans off of you."

As she walked back to the couple and cut them loose, I got in my truck and backed my boat into the water. She came back to the wharf just as I was getting ready to push off.

"You know you don't have to keep doing this, right?" Susan said. "Someone will eventually get him—it doesn't have to be you."

"I let him take Dexter's arm and then I let him get away." I frowned. "I'm responsible for everything he does now."

"But he hasn't done anything in two years. In fact, he hasn't hurt anyone since Dexter."

She was right, but it was something I had to do. When I said that, she just smiled her understanding.

"Just be careful." She leaned to kiss me goodbye and squeezed my biceps. "The wedding is in two months and I want you carrying me across the threshold with these arms."

"Don't worry, love, I'm coming back in one piece, and we'll have lots of alligator sauce piquant for the reception." I pushed off and turned the key to start the engine. Once it roared to life, I waved to Susan and headed west toward Lake Berg, revving the engine and smiling as the front of the boat rose gently into the air and the wind began to blow through my hair. I'd spent the last year running swamp tours and I'd grown to love being on the water. Aside from being a great gig, my new job increased the likelihood that I'd locate Godzator and put an end to his reign of terror.

Once I reached the southern tip of Lake Berg, I turned down a small stream that cut its way through the swamps to the west. Giant cypress trees shot up from the water and thick clumps of Spanish moss hung from their branches. I surveyed the water all around me, but the surface was completely covered by duckweed. If this was the spot the man had described, there should be a trail through the greenery where his boat had traveled.

I puttered along for several more minutes scanning the surrounding swampland. I was about to turn away when I saw what looked like the beginning of a black path amidst the light green background up ahead.

I immediately shut off the engine and reached for my push pole. Careful not to cause too much of a ripple, I gently eased the pole into the water and strained against it, burying the duck web foot in the soft mud until it met some resistance and moved me forward. One push at a time, I drew nearer and nearer until I was about thirty feet from the black path.

I looked up from one of my pushes and cocked my head sideways. The path through the duckweed seemed to stop about fifteen feet from where it started, as though the boat that made it had been lifted into the air after making contact with the water.

Confused, I drifted closer. I was almost upon it when I realized it wasn't a path at all, but an actual black object jutting up out of the water. I gasped when the object shifted in the water, lining itself up with my boat. It looked like a giant torpedo waiting to be launched in my direction. That was when I realized I was looking at the enormous body of an alligator—and the head was facing my boat.

I gently placed my push pole down and snatched up my sniper rifle, bringing it smoothly to my shoulder and peering through the scope. I flipped the safety off with my thumb and allowed my crosshairs to come to rest on the spot between the alligator's eyes. I glanced at the side of the alligator and saw a number of scars from where I'd shot Godzator sixteen times two years earlier. My heart pounded in my chest. I'd finally found him!

"This is it, Godzator," I said aloud. "Time to meet your maker."

Godzator didn't move. He just hovered there in the water staring at me. I gently placed my finger against the trigger and took a deep breath, exhaling it slowly. When I'd reached my respiratory pause, I began to apply slow, steady pressure on the trigger, focusing on my crosshairs. I felt the trigger start to slowly creak rearward—

"He did what came natural…that don't rate a death sentence."

The voice was so real in my head that I jerked around looking for Dexter, knowing he was nowhere around.

"He did what came natural," I repeated. "That don't rate a death sentence." As I turned his words over in my head—words that had been spoken two years earlier—it finally occurred to me what he meant. We'd tried to harpoon Godzator after he ate Mrs. DuPont's German shepherd, which was no different than someone shooting a spear through my chest after I'd grabbed a hamburger for lunch.

The sun was slowly setting behind me and it painted the beautiful swamps in a golden hue, setting a magnificent stage for what would happen next. As we faced each other down—two battle-scarred warriors doing what came natural to us—I realized we were a lot alike.

"I'd be pissed off, too," I said, "if someone shot me with a spear." Knowing what Dexter would want me to do, I slowly lowered my rifle and stood there staring into Godzator's eyes. There was a brief moment of uncertainty when I thought he might attack, but with a subtle swish of his tail he turned away from me. As though bidding me farewell, he closed both eyes and slowly faded into the depths of the murky water, the duckweed swallowing up the hole left behind by his absence.

I sank to my seat and stared for a long moment at the spot I'd last seen him, thoroughly pleased with my decision. I sat there until the shadows began growing long and darkness started to fall across the swamps. Realizing I'd better leave before he changed his mind and came back to eat me, I started my engine and began the return ride home.

CHAPTER 57

"Did you get him?" Susan asked when I walked through the door of the old plantation home and entered the living area. She was standing on a ladder and held a paint roller in her hands. The last time I'd been in that room the walls were bare, but now most of it was coated in a fresh coat of white paint. There were blotches of paint on her arms and even a few droplets in her hair, but she didn't seem to care.

"You're getting more paint on you than on the wall," I joked, picking up a brush to help her finish the room.

We'd been working on the building for months trying to get it ready for the secret opening in October. At first, I'd felt weird about keeping the place since it had been illegally purchased in Michele's name for nefarious reasons, but Susan had made an offer I couldn't resist.

"I've always wanted to run a battered women's shelter," she'd said, "but I've never had the opportunity. This is the perfect location, we're the perfect people to run it, and we have the time to make it work."

We had driven out to the property and I'd stood beaming as Susan bustled about, relaying her dreams to me. She pointed out which rooms could serve as private living quarters, described where she would be putting the gym to teach the women self-defense, and even suggested a shooting range in the back yard where we could teach them how to safely handle firearms. "They'll feel safe here because it's in the middle of nowhere," she'd said, "and they'll fall in love with the view."

We'd gone to work immediately and had begun spending all of our extra time remodeling the place. "We'll be able to launch just in time for Domestic Violence Awareness Month," Susan had explained one evening as we looked over a calendar, "but we won't be able to make any announcements because it has to be kept secret."

With brush in hand, I moved to a corner of the room that needed attention and went to work. As we painted, I told her about my encounter with Godzator and how I'd decided to let him live.

"Wait a minute," Susan twisted around on the ladder to look at me. "After all the time you spent trying to find and kill him, you just let him live?"

I nodded, explaining my reasons. She smiled warmly, agreeing it had been the right thing to do.

When Susan had finished her side of the room, she dropped from the ladder and began cleaning up. "I'm ready for a hot shower and some personal time with you."

She didn't have to draw me a picture. I helped her clean up and we were soon on our way home. Once we arrived, we raced to the bathroom and began ripping each other's clothes off. Even after all of our time together, I still had a hard time containing myself when we were alone.

We hurried through a shower and I snatched her up when we were done—both of us still dripping wet—and carried her over the threshold of the bathroom door. She began giggling, but stopped when I bent to kiss her. Her lips were soft and moist and I moaned as our tongues came together. I kept walking and kissing her until my foot bumped against the bed. I then pulled my face away and lowered her onto the soft mattress. Looking into her dark eyes, I could see how much she wanted me. I felt the firmness of her breasts against my chest as I pressed my body to hers, and it turned me on even more.

We made love deep into the night, ignoring Achilles' whining and scratching at the bedroom door. When we were finished, we lay beside each other, breathless and fulfilled. As she played with my hair, I ran my hand over her breasts and down her stomach, enjoying how smooth her skin felt against my fingers.

"God, you're so beautiful," I said.

Her face turned red and she buried her face in my chest. I wrapped my arms around her, loving the way she still got embarrassed when I complimented her.

After a while, she pulled her head back and stared up at me, chewing on her bottom lip.

"What is it?" I asked.

"I'm thinking about taking a break from the police department after we get married."

"Well," I said slowly. "I was kind of hoping you'd take some time off for the honeymoon."

She chuckled. "Of course, I am—Pauline already approved it—but I'm thinking beyond the honeymoon."

I scowled. "Really? Why?"

"I want to have your child, Clint," she said softly. "I'm ready to start a family with you."

BJ Bourg

BJ Bourg is an award-winning mystery writer and former professional boxer who hails from the swamps of Louisiana. Dubbed the "real deal" by other mystery writers, he has spent his entire adult life solving crimes as a patrol cop, detective sergeant, and chief investigator for a district attorney's office. Not only does he know his way around crime scenes, interrogations, and courtrooms, but he also served as a police sniper commander (earning the title of "Top Shooter" at an FBI sniper school) and a police academy instructor.

BJ is a four-time traditionally-published novelist (his debut novel, JAMES 516, won the 2016 EPIC eBook Award for Best Mystery) and dozens of his articles and stories have been published in national magazines such as Woman's World, Boys' Life, and Writer's Digest. He is a regular contributor to two of the nation's leading law enforcement magazines, Law and Order and Tactical Response, and he has taught at conferences for law enforcement officers, tactical police officers, and writers. Above all else, he is a father and husband, and the highlight of his life is spending time with his beautiful wife and wonderful children.

http://www.bjbourg.com

Made in the USA
Columbia, SC
21 December 2024

50193891R00148